THE SMILING TIGER

THE SMILING TIGER

THE SMILING
TIGER

Lenore Glen Offord

FELONY & MAYHEM PRESS • NEW YORK

All the characters and events portrayed in this work are fictitious.

THE SMILING TIGER

A Felony & Mayhem mystery

PRINTING HISTORY
First edition (Duell, Sloan and Pearce): 1949
Felony & Mayhem edition: 2016

Copyright © 1949 by Lenore Glen Offord

ISBN: 978-1-63194-098-9

Manufactured in the United States of America

Library of Congress Cataloging-in-Publication Data

Names: Offord, Lenore Glen, 1905-1991 author.
Title: The smiling tiger / Lenore Glen Offord.
Description: Felony & Mayhem edition. | New York : Felony & Mayhem Press,
  2016.
Identifiers: LCCN 2016030235 | ISBN 9781631940989
Subjects: | GSAFD: Mystery fiction.
Classification: LCC PS3529.F42 S65 2016 | DDC 813/.54--dc23
LC record available at https://lccn.loc.gov/2016030235

To our mother
Laura Dell Offord

The icon above says you're holding a copy of a book in the Felony & Mayhem "Vintage" category. These books were originally published prior to about 1965, and feature the kind of twisty, ingenious puzzles beloved by fans of Agatha Christie and John Dickson Carr. If you enjoy this book, you may well like other "Vintage" titles from Felony & Mayhem Press.

———◆◆◆◆———

For more about these books, and other Felony & Mayhem titles, or to place an order, please visit our website at:

www.FelonyAndMayhem.com

THE SMILING TIGER

CHAPTER ONE

THEY WERE NOT CAREFUL enough about closing their Venetian blinds. From the sidewalk of Cragmont Avenue one could not, it is true, see into the windows of the house high above, but the lights in the Todd McKinnons' living-room were so arranged that the shadow of a moving person was projected onto a white wall, betraying the fact that someone was at home.

The young man who had been standing irresolutely on the walk, peering with lifted head at those lighted windows, began to climb the irregular flight of stone steps which led to the front door. Halfway up he paused for breath, turning his back to the buffeting of a northeast wind and looking out over the descending streets of Berkeley toward San Francisco Bay. There was not much to be seen tonight; the storm of the past two days was just beginning to dissipate itself before that strong drying wind, and the sky was masked with cloud, but below it the town lights shone new-washed in a sort of angry clarity. The wind came down again with a scream, and the young man shivered and sneezed and went on his upward way.

He paused once more, midway on the cement steps of the porch, and stretched himself to look cautiously through the adjoining window. All of the white-walled living-room was visible from this point. It had an air of comfort, although the furniture was sparse, mismated, and far from distinguished in design, and the fireplace gave forth an occasional puff of smoke. The two persons in the room, however, did not look comfortable.

The male householder was visible in profile, seated in a large shabby chair near the fireplace and gazing moodily into the flames. The profile was sharply cut and lean, with that hard texture that one instinctively classifies as Scottish, and the man's coloring was inconspicuously sandy. He got up once to give an irritable poke to the fire, revealing medium height and a slight build. When he returned, slumping down dispiritedly into his chair, the watcher outside rose from the crouch into which he had instinctively dropped—not so much in furtiveness but once more in palpable indecision—and again peered through the window.

The other occupant, a woman, was visible only from the shoulders up. She was sitting across the room, perhaps working at a desk, for her head of short brown curls was bent thoughtfully and her shoulders seemed tense. Her back was to the room, and she and the man appeared oblivious of each other's presence. It looked almost as if they had been quarreling.

The young man on the steps wavered once more. He mounted two steps slowly; his eyes located the doorbell but his hand did not move to touch it. He stood there with the wind whipping at his overcoat and tousling his uncovered hair.

Todd and Georgine McKinnon had not been having a quarrel. They had, in fact, seldom been closer together in spirit, which was saying a good deal for a couple who had been married and deeply in love for nearly five years. Tonight the bond between them had been forged to double strength by shared anxiety, and over money at that.

"We can make it, Todd," said Georgine slowly. She kept her eyes fixed on the column of figures before her. "Barby doesn't have to stay at boarding school; that's a luxury. You know she wouldn't mind much."— Not too much, she thought sorrowfully; but her daughter loved the Valley Ranch School, and, in the warmer climate behind the foothills, had been in better health than ever in her life.

"It seems a shame to penalize our cricket for this slump I'm in," said Barby's stepfather mildly, "and it's your income, from her father's insurance, that pays for her."

"Todd, if you think that both Barby and I wouldn't rather—" Georgine left her sentence unfinished and turned to face him, her eyes flashing blue with affectionate concern. "Oh, you know that. Let's not talk about it any more tonight. Something's sure to turn up—and we're lucky if we never have to worry about anything worse than a little shortage of money."

Todd did not answer. He took a small notebook from his pocket and leafed through it, frowning at what he read on the last page. Georgine looked around the room with invincible content: the harmonious dull colors of the draperies, the blue chair and the plum-colored sofa that she'd covered herself, no matter how amateurishly—her house, safe and quiet, and her husband in it.

"You look dog-tired," she said gently, considering him.

"How tired can a dog get?" Todd replied. "I am a li'le bushed, I'll admit, but as for—"

The wind, which had been thrashing in the garden shrubbery, had just died abruptly; and outside the McKinnons' front door there sounded a shattering sneeze.

"Someone's out there," said Georgine obviously, recovering from a start. "I didn't hear the bell ring!"

She and Todd exchanged a glance as the doorbell did ring, with a belated and guilty effect. "It's after nine," she murmured. "Who on earth—"

She wondered with a little sinking sensation how long the person had been there. Those blinds—but when you were so far above the street you didn't always remember. Georgine was wont to describe herself as the queen of the scaredy-cats, and on her list of terrors the Peeping Tom ranked not far from burglars.

Draughts billowed in from the open door, and she stood still, listening. The visitor's utterance was impeded by a hand-kerchief which he was using vigorously before announcing himself, and Georgine thought wildly of hold-up men. But what a household to choose, she told herself; he wouldn't get more than two dollars.

"Mr. McKinnon?" said the young man, putting away his handkerchief and speaking in a plangent, confident voice. "My name's Hugh Hartlein, and I'm an acquaintance of Frederic Devlin. Do you remember him?"

"I do. Won't you come in?"

Hugh Hartlein walked into the living-room, acknowledged his introduction to Georgine, and sat down in Todd's chair. He disposed crisply of the news about Ricky Devlin, whom the McKinnons had not seen since 1942; and indeed, even with the link of a murder investigation in which they and Ricky had been involved, they could not at this date think of much to ask about him except "Well, how is he?" and "What's he doing now?" It also transpired that Mr. Hartlein had known Ricky only casually, during a brief sojourn of both at the University of Washington, and had now completely lost track of him.

The conversation, however, did not die. It was evident that no conversation could do that while Hugh Hartlein chose to keep it alive.

"I came to see you because of something he told me," the young man announced. "You write mystery fiction based on true cases, don't you, McKinnon?"

Todd suppressed a sigh of fatigue. He knew what was coming and wanted to get to bed. "That's correct. My wife and I were about to have a drink; will you join us?"

"Thank you," said Hugh Hartlein. "I'll have a hot toddy, please, it might help this ghastly cold of mine."

Georgine, who had risen hospitably, almost sat down again. Todd's presence of mind did not fail him; he said smoothly, and mendaciously, "Sorry, we have none of the makings. It will have to be beer, I'm afraid."

"Beer will do."

They sat in silence until Georgine came back with the beer, Hartlein employing the time by looking around him with an air of ease. He was a thin and somewhat romantic-looking young man, hollow-checked and beak-nosed, with dark hair in windblown disorder. There was no telling whether the drooping lock of hair over his brow had been disarranged by the northeaster, or whether he kept it that way. His hatlessness was probably a student affectation, for otherwise he was thoroughly wrapped in a scarf, sports jacket and overcoat. He accepted a glass with an absent nod of thanks, drank at once and set it down.

"I have a story for you," he announced kindly.

Todd's eyelids drooped slightly. "Would you mind not telling it?" he said. "I'm sure you are acting in good faith, but I've known more than one colleague who was accused of plagiarism because he used a story someone had 'given' him."

"But I want to sell it," said Hartlein.

"I never buy them, either. Sorry."

"You don't—" Hartlein set down his glass with a thud. "But I was sure—Devlin said—"

"Devlin probably told you that I make a living writing for the pulp magazines, and that I use actual cases as material. But," said Todd wearily, "the cases have to be authentic, either from my own personal knowledge of 'em or from documents. And—"

"But that's all right. This is completely authentic, you could meet some of the people right here in Berkeley. There are no documents, I'll admit, but that's because—" Hartlein paused impressively "—no one has ever suspected that a crime was committed."

"And I can't afford to buy material, for more than one reason."

"But, McKinnon, no one knows about it, so you couldn't get involved in plagiarism." Hartlein glanced sideways, and a faint shine appeared on his brow. "As to affording, I—I can't afford not to sell this. I was so sure—I'd counted on it. Look, let me tell you about my situation." He moistened his lips. "I'm here on an instructorship; Romance languages. It's not a GI loan, I was not in the armed services, but I'm like plenty of the others, I have a wife and childr—a child. They're not here with me, I couldn't afford that, but naturally I must, uh, send them something. They're with my wife's mother in Grass Valley. If you happen to have children of your own, you'll remember that Christmas will be next month; you know how one wants to do something not to disappoint a child. I'd hoped for something from this story idea of mine—twenty dollars, ten, almost anything."

Georgine, silent at the far side of the room, thought grimly that if there was one thing she knew it was the value of twenty dollars. For charity to a complete unknown like this—who might well turn out to be a swindler—it was far too much.

Hartlein watched the slow negative movement of Todd's head, which managed to convey regret and a refusal to be taken in, in equal proportions. "You think I'm working a racket," he burst out in real indignation, "but I'm offering you something of value! Look here, McKinnon," he said more quietly, but with an urgent tone that somehow carried conviction, "will you do this? Will you listen to the story, and then if you use it, pay me whatever you think it's worth? I'll write out an agreement, I'll say that if there should be any trouble—which there could never be—I'd assume complete responsibility, I'll take out an affidavit if you like that it's true from my personal knowledge. I'll do that before you pay me a cent—trusting you, you see; can't you trust me enough just to listen?" The supercilious ease had gone from his manner; he was twisting his hands together almost in supplication. "You couldn't fail with this story, Mr. McKinnon. Look, I'll write that out now."

He felt in his overcoat pocket and dug out a used envelope, flicking out in the process a loose cough drop and a metal menthol inhaler. He scribbled four or five lines on the back of the envelope and signed them with a flourish.

Todd took the envelope and turned it over; it was addressed to Hugh Hartlein, at an address far down on Grove Street in Berkeley. Behind his impassive manner Georgine could discern a sign of weakening, a sort of forlorn-hope interest. "You're taking a big risk," he said without inflection.

Hartlein relaxed. His small sigh was so expressive of relief that Georgine looked at him keenly. She wondered if, now that he'd gained his point, he would again omit the "Mr." from Todd's name. And why was he so very much relieved?

"You've heard of the Beyond-Truth, I presume?" he said briskly.

"I haven't."

Hartlein looked at him incredulously. "You don't know old Mrs. Majendie, or anything about Cuckoo Canyon? Why, it's not a mile from here."

"You'll have to tell me, I'm afraid." Todd's eyes looked tired, but he settled back patiently in his chair.

"I should have thought you—" Hartlein began, and was caught by a crashing sneeze before his hand could reach his pocket. He gave an unfriendly look at the empty beer glass, which had so obviously failed to comfort him. Todd moved his chair back out of range, and said, "I'm an ignorant sort. You might start at the beginning."

"Cuckoo Canyon isn't called that on the map, of course," said Hartlein loftily. "Possibly that misled you. It's had that nickname since anyone can remember, because of the eccentric people who used to live there. The place has been sold off bit by bit, and the new residents are normal enough, but— there's still one of the old ones left." He looked away from Todd, and a small bulge of muscle showed at the side of his jaw. "She sits there—she sits up there in that rich house on the top of the cliff, and grows flowers, and listens to music as if she'd never done anything else. People look at her white hair and her dowdy clothes, and are fooled; but there must be a few, here and there, who suspect what she is. They never could prove anything, but they'll have that suspicion in their minds for a lifetime—wondering just how their wives and sisters died."

He paused, perhaps for effect, looking straight before him. Todd said flatly, "Well, how did they?"

Young Mr. Hartlein gave him a peevish look. "I'm coming to it! It's all a part of the Beyond-Truth, and old Nikko Majendie's prophecies. Those deaths looked natural, but to the other believers it would seem that—those women didn't dare to live any more."

He leaned forward in his chair. His material was well in hand now, and he was talking rapidly and rather well, even including Georgine from time to time in a compelling glance. "The Beyond-Truth is one of those vague philosophy-religions that sounds almost plausible when someone spouts it at you from a platform, especially if the professor's one of those magnetic characters with burning eyes. One gathers that old Nikko Majendie was the type.

"He was on the faculty at a screwball college out there near Mount Diablo, teaching comparative philosophy and religion, and it got to him. He began to work out a religion of his own, and foisted it on the students. Fairly soon he had other converts, and the Beyond-Truth was a going concern by the time the college folded. I can't remember its name, but one could check. This all began back in the Twenties; of course," added Hartlein loftily, "I was scarcely born at the time, so this is all hearsay."

Todd, who remembered the 1920s vividly, gave a faint shudder but said nothing.

"The old man, you see, set himself up as a prophet. The Beyond-Truthers are after the sort of thing that their name implies, a cosmic interpretation of what the uninitiated believe to be truth. They have a few bizarre rules, no religion's much good without those: they're not vegetarians or teetotalers, but they're forbidden hard liquor and shellfish and one or two other things, and they have a day of complete fast each week—Tuesday, just to be different. Toward evening, one gathers, they get light-headed from hunger and begin to see visions, and that's when they think themselves into the Beyond-Truth, and come back from these trances with a next-sphere vibration that interprets worldly events. Old Majendie never came back without something startling. It was his racket, after all.

"At the very beginning he'd made a strong prophecy, that within twenty-five or thirty years there'd be some kind of scourge that would strike the human race. It would be ghastly, he left the disciples in no doubt about that. He made it plain, too, that people now alive couldn't escape; but in order to spare the future generations, he arranged the rules of Beyond-Truth—note this, please, it's the crux of the matter—so that there shouldn't *be* any future generations."

Hartlein's emphasis, and the pause which he made to let this sink in, caused Georgine to suppress a smile. She had known a few instructors like this, youngish and arrogant and seldom bothering to conceal their contempt for the students' intelligence. Todd was looking polite but unimpressed.

"They were pledged to do their part toward race suicide, do you see?" Hartlein added sharply. "They could go through a form of marriage; one even gathers that the Beyond-Truth didn't actually forbid sex relations. If husband or wife happened to be sterile they'd be within the laws, but the unforgivable sin was having children. And except for a few cases, which I'll take up in a minute, the ruling was obeyed. The disciples were mostly of the born-spinster type, male and female, who would take up a cult of that kind.

"But—" he drew in his breath "—they got some converts among children, their own who were born before they joined the cult, or orphans that they took care of. They're good to all children, in a pitying way. One gathers that they feel the young might as well have their paths smoothed until the scourge actually comes. The Colony has gone on until this day, you see, living peacefully enough on a big tract of land in Contra Costa County—old Nikko made some sharp real-estate deals in his early days, and his widow owns a lot of ranch property over there. They might have died out gradually, except for the Majendie prophecy's seeming to come true. Many of them must have thought that he meant the late war, but after all a good many survived that. But *now*—"

"The atom bomb," Todd supplied drowsily, since the pause was drawn out almost beyond bearing.

"Yes. It recharged their beliefs. They're working twice as hard as before to get converts and to enforce their own rules. There was a time when a backslider could have drifted quietly away from the cult, when some of the older ones were dying off and the thing might have broken up naturally. Not now; you can see that? Old Nikko himself died in the early Thirties, and the widow—she was one of his most ardent disciples—carried on the work. Now there's this new impetus; the prophecy makes sense—more than anyone had ever dreamed—and nobody can be allowed to depart from the Beyond-Truth's principles, no one who has ever been a convert." He glanced at them both. "She'll see to that," he added in a queer dull voice. "She has seen to it before."

This time Hartlein's effect was genuine. Georgine, who had been strangling yawns over a desultory piece of sewing, raised her head in startled interest. She looked at her husband, who had not moved or raised his eyelids, and yet seemed to have shot up an invisible antenna of attention.

"She has seen to it before," the younger man repeated. His hollow cheeks appeared to have drawn in farther; he kept his head rigid, darting significant glances from one to another of his auditors with intensely flashing eyeballs. "She kept watch over the Colony—the mantle of old Nikko fell straight onto her shoulders—and pretended to care for their welfare. Actually, she was on the alert for any signs of faithlessness. There were a few backsliders. They died, or disappeared, and no one ever questioned the fact. If any Beyond-Truther had noticed the coincidence—it wouldn't have been Chloe Majendie that caused it, but the Hand of God."

"You mean they let God into this religion?" Todd inquired.

"Certainly. A Beyond-Truther, if he chooses, may also be a member of an established church."

Where all else had failed, this actually roused Mr. McKinnon. His eyelids flew up. "He may *what?*"

Hartlein nodded impatiently, and opened his mouth to continue. "Well, I'm damned," Todd forestalled him with a flow of speech. "That's a new one. Another established church? How d'you suppose they reconciled—and yet, come to think of it, there aren't many churches that would object to continence, or charity or temperance. Nor yet to an occasional day of fasting, for that matter. But how did they treat the business of leaving money to your church?"

"They were above it," said Hartlein briefly.

"Did the Beyond-Truthers have to live in poverty too?"

"No, no indeed. Most of them have done very well, and there's no rule against their making as much money as possible." For the first time a gleam of humor appeared on the cadaverous young face, giving it the attraction of irony if not of gaiety. "The richer they are, the better things vibrate in that next sphere; you can figure it, the disciples' minds are free from mundane worries."

"Now you begin to make it sound attractive."

Hartlein regained the thread of his story. "There's no question of leaving money to the cult, it's not required. Some of the Beyond-Truthers do, of course, for lack of anything else to do with it. As a matter of fact, very few of them do belong to other churches, they're after something screwier, and they've got it and are satisfied. None of them, obviously, has considered the danger. And there is danger, the worse because it hasn't been expressed in the rules. That Hand of God is only implied, but so far as they know it's always hovering.

"And," he added with a sudden odd break in his voice, "I'm cursed if I know how she's managed it. She had only to make sure that one of the disciples was disobeying, and then—it looked so natural—"

"You're implying that this is sort of a ritual murder?" Todd inquired.

"Yes. That's it."

"But then, surely, the deaths should all have some unusual feature in common; there should be a ritual tinge about the method."

"There isn't," said Hartlein stubbornly, "except for the Hand of God touch. One dies in childbirth, one of pneumonia, one in an automobile accident—"

"I see. Well—" Todd's voice was brisk, "I'm afraid this is nothing I can use, Hartlein; I'm sorry."

For almost a minute no one spoke. The last embers of the fire collapsed with a soft ticking sound; a gust of wind thrashed the bare fronds of the willow beside the house, and then died down, so that in the silence the rasp of a match seemed very loud as Georgine lit a cigarette. Hartlein looked stupefied for a moment, and then visibly marshaled his forces.

"You think it isn't interesting?"

"The background is, in a mild way, but it's no good for my purposes. On the strength of two or three natural-seeming deaths, over a period of twenty-five years, I can't work up much of a mystery."

"Two or three—" Hartlein gulped, and coughed. "If you began to look into it, the list would be staggering. I could give you names, you could ask—ask what became of Hildegarde Latham, and Stella Dubois, and Sibyl Grant, and Harriet Withers, and Frances Sagers, and Grace Vane, and—and—"

"Yes, I see you've given it a remarkable amount of study." Todd's face was at its most wooden. "It scarcely seems worth it, if I may say so."

"It would, if you knew how it had touched me. You think these deaths are all in the remote past? They're not; one of them occurred only last year. It was one of her own nieces, old Chloe's; the girl married an outsider, and everyone knew she meant to make it a normal marriage, and—she and the man both went over a cliff two hours after they'd driven off for their wedding trip. And her sisters—" Hartlein hesitated, and looked sullenly from Todd to Georgine. "Her sisters are living under the fear that the same thing will happen to them." He waited a moment, and seemed to detect a flicker of incredulity in Todd's eye. "I ought to know," he blurted out. "I married one of them!"

"That's the lady in Grass Valley?" Todd inquired.

"In what? Grass Val—no, no, that's not—" Hartlein thrust confusion away with a gesture. "Never mind that. This girl actually flew up to Reno with me; and then, after we were married and I started talking about the plans for our life together, things I'd taken for granted as any normal man would, she—she changed." An old bewilderment was in his voice and eyes. "All at once, in five minutes, she was terrified; it had all been a mistake, she'd never live with me, she would get an annulment. And why, if she wasn't afraid of that old woman? That Majendie witch—she seems never to lift a finger, she just sits there; maybe she goes into a trance, and calls down some vengeance from God, and then waits; but however she does it, she's evil. There's—there's another niece, too." He licked his lips. "She hasn't disobeyed openly yet, but the old woman may be able to read her mind, because she's given a warning—a warning in poison."

He stopped, drew in a hoarse breath, and had recourse to his handkerchief in an absurd anticlimax. More quietly he said, "And the spell's so strong that the victim won't believe it herself. *No one sees it.*"

"What do the police think?" Todd inquired wearily.

A dull flush stained Hartlein's forehead, under the hanging lock of hair. He hesitated again. "Can you imagine?" he demanded at last with a faint sneer. "'Give us chapter and verse, two witnesses, proof of intent and proof of method—' then they say there's nothing in it, and brush you off as a crank."

"Has anyone actually consulted them?"

"No," said Hartlein sulkily. He gave Todd a resentful look, compressing his lips almost into a pout; then suddenly he got to his feet. "Never mind, I get it. I've wasted an evening. I'll be going now. Don't bother to let me out."

He snatched scarf and overcoat together over his chest, made for the front door and wrenched it open. It closed behind him with a crash; his very footsteps sounded angry, running down the porch steps and diminishing along the stone walk that led to the street.

The McKinnons looked at each other. "*He* wasted an evening!" said Georgine, when she could speak.

"That did seem a bit gratuitous, considering everything else." Todd, putting up the fire screen, gave a mirthless chuckle. "The man thought I looked like a fool, I've no doubt. He spent enough time outside the window, sizing us up."

"Oh, dear. Was he out there for a while before he rang?"

"I think so. There were two sneezes, some minutes apart. Maybe he wouldn't have rung if he hadn't given himself away with that second one, but then once he was in he had to deliver that nonsense."

"You think it was all nonsense? Do put out the lights and come on, Todd dear, you must be exhausted."

Todd paused by the switch near the staircase, and ran a hand over his smooth sandy hair. "I am, and puzzled too. What d'you suppose that was about, Georgine? There were some of the most palpable lies I've ever heard; the wife in Grass Valley, and that list—Hildegarde Withers and Grace Latham, good Lord! Too bad he didn't kill off Sherlock Brown and Father Holmes too."

They began to mount the stairs slowly. Georgine said, "Who were the other ladies on the list?"

"Characters out of soap operas, like as not. But why the devil was he so insistent on telling that story? The queer part of it is that though the whole story may have been nonsense, he believed some of it. The part about the old woman, for instance: he didn't invent the hatred he feels for her."

Georgine paused in her hasty preparations for bed. "Do you think you could use any of this?"

"Well—I'm a li'le curious about Mrs. Chloe Majendie, but that won't get me far."

A few minutes later his wife's voice came out of the darkness. "Todd, are you asleep? I just thought of something. If that man knew Ricky Devlin, and came to you because of it, he must have heard something about the business at Grettry Road. He must have known that you and I handed over evidence to the police."

"Yes," said Todd slowly, "that's possible. He comes here and loads that story—which no policeman would touch—onto me, in the hope that I'll start writing it up and find something that would interest the Law." He turned uneasily in bed. "You know, Hartlein must have felt fairly sure of himself. He was careful to leave us his address on that envelope."

"He wants to use you and then take a commission? That self-centered young squirt," said Georgine indignantly. "I hope you're not going to have any part of it."

She was caught unawares by a wave of sleep; but her indignation was not forgotten overnight. It became more pronounced the next morning when Todd came down with the young squirt's cold.

CHAPTER TWO

Todd MCKINNON WAS not the worst patient in the world. During his infrequent illnesses he was usually content with a radio, paper and pencil to work with if the mood struck him, and an occasional tray of food. This time, however, he was running a slight fever, and Georgine found his attitude almost more than she could bear. He was restless, he was morose, and he spoke frequently of the obscurity of the path ahead of him, all this combining to make her snap at him with increasing violence as two or three days went by.

The financial worries were real enough, but they took second place beside Todd's mental state. He was in that dread condition of the professional writer, a time in which no plot goes right, no word is apt, and the very will to work sinks lower each day from lack of stimulus. It was getting him down, and there was nothing that Georgine could do to help. If she took a job herself it might relieve the money pressure, but Todd would be left just where he was before—maybe worse off.

The impasse troubled her constantly, as she hurriedly pushed the vacuum cleaner around the living-room of a morning, or harvested the eternal crop of housekeepers' moss from under the beds. It was a pity that ideas didn't present themselves as freely as dust or dirty dishes. If only she could do something—short of committing a murder herself, for Todd to use as material—

She was ripe for the plucking, she admitted to herself, when on the third day of Todd's cold he asked for the telephone book and looked up a name in the M section. There was really a Mrs. Nicholas Majendie, living on one of the winding hill streets not more than a mile away.

"I could go up there tomorrow, for a look at her," Todd mused aloud.

"Tomorrow? With that cough? Not a chance, chum," said Georgine firmly. "You stay home and take your nice red vitamin capsules."

"Oh, I'm taking the damn things. I wish they worked on the brain."

Georgine saw the frustrated look that drew his brows together, so that the deep-set eyes retreated almost to invisibility. She said doubtfully, "Would it help any if I went?"

He turned his head, considering, and put out a hand to rest lightly on hers. "If you'd be willing, Georgine—"

She nodded, and watched his face relax. —I'm caught, she said to herself. I can't get out of it now; but why should I want so much to be let off?—

Her heart sank still farther on the next day when, early in the afternoon, she had to put on her wraps and back their ancient car out of the garage, and start. "Todd," she said, coming to stand beside his chair in the living-room, "there's one thing I'm going to do, no matter if you do laugh. I'm taking along some of my old identification cards, the ones I had before we were married. I'll have to introduce myself somehow, but those people might just as well think I'm Mrs. James Wyeth."

Todd didn't laugh. He looked up at her and said in his most casual tone, "Dear Georgine, consider the four years I've spent digging up old cases and following new ones, and never a minute's danger in any of 'em."

"All right," said Georgine, "but you'll look pretty silly when the Hand of God gets *me*." She laughed cheerfully and got out before her nerve failed her.

Cuckoo Canyon might at one time have harbored ladies in batik draperies and gentlemen in sandals, and nude children of both sexes. In this year it looked like any other newish street in Berkeley, sparsely built up with middle-class homes and well-kept gardens, and shaded with the omnipresent eucalyptus. It was a narrow street, and Georgine left her car around the corner at its foot, and began to walk up past the redwood cottages and the equally modest gray or white stucco ones. She came to the end of the settled portion, and still saw nothing that resembled a "rich house on a cliff" where a malevolent old lady might sit spider-like; but the road went on, and she climbed with it, listening to the clacking talk of quail in the underbrush, and smelling the new grass that had sprung up at the roadside after the first fall rains. "Maybe," she told herself half-aloud, "there's no such house after all; or maybe she's out, or they won't let me in."

The road swerved to the left, but on her right a graveled footpath continued upward. At the junction a one-car garage stood, its doors open so that a sleek convertible was visible within, and beside the garage a ramshackle car was parked in the grass. At some distance behind the garage was a small wooden house, painted a silvery gray with scarlet doors, and covered by a magnificent trumpet vine; and beside the footpath ran a low hedge with a gate in it.

Georgine, pausing for breath, looked over the gate as the sound of voices reached her, coming from the open door of the house. She was too far away to distinguish words, but the tenor of the sound was unmistakably quarrelsome. It rose to a shout; at once a dark-haired girl leaped out of the door, slammed it behind her, and came running down the path.

From under the drooping branches of a huge olive tree close to the gate, another voice spoke: a cool, languidly amused one.

"So soon?" it said. "He's only been here fifteen minutes."

The running girl saw Georgine, and slackened speed. "We have other company," she said, and added rapidly over her shoulder as she approached, "Yes, he started in right away. Lucky it isn't raining and I can get out of the house before he hits me!" She spoke to Georgine. "Were you looking for someone?"

She was a good-looking girl, her eyes large and gray under fine eyebrows, her dark hair drawn up into a little crown of curls on top of her head. She stood breathing fast and smiling widely and pleasantly, her hands in the pockets of a dull-blue wool dress with a round white collar.

"Yes, I am," Georgine said. "Is there a Mrs. Majendie who lives somewhere around here?"

"Right up the hill. The house is on this same road, around two or three long curves. You'll think you're never going to get there, but you will."

"Thank you." Georgine prepared to go on, but the girl stopped her. "It's really a lot quicker," she began, and paused. "You didn't want to—I don't suppose you're trying to—as a matter of fact, she never buys anything from—"

"I'm not selling anything. You don't happen to know if she objects to giving interviews?"

"We do happen to know," said the blue girl, considering, "she's our aunt, you see. You might have a try; and if you go up, it's twice as quick by this path, and hardly any steeper."

"You're awfully kind."

"Not at all." The girl turned her head and called, "Ryn! Do you know if Chloe's at home?"

The person who had been hidden by the olive leaves leaned forward, evidently from a reclining position in a deck chair. "She's home," said the cool, slow voice, "and the Godfrey, too. They both went up from the greenhouse a few minutes ago." She was addressing Georgine directly, now, saying something about finding them in the garden; her face was framed in gray-green foliage, and Georgine lost the rest of the sentence in her sudden admiration.

These two young women were sisters beyond doubt. Their coloring was almost the same, their heads were shaped alike and they had the same attractive mouth and chin; but the candid good looks of the girl in blue faded to nothing beside the real beauty of this one. There was not a jarring note in it, from the gloss on the shoulder-length black hair to the shape of the eyes that almost matched the color of the olive tree's leaves. There was a transparent pallor, a stillness and delicacy about Ryn's face, that reminded one almost irresistibly of the Queen Nefertiti; but she could smile, too, slowly and with closed lips. —Dear me, Georgine thought, that girl's a Helen of Troy. Maybe it's just as well I came instead of Todd!—

She nodded her final thanks and set off up the graveled path. Over the hedge floated the voice of Ryn's sister, saying cheerfully, "I'd better rescue your milk shake before it turns to butter. I guess it's safe to go in now!"

Georgine looked across at the house, and saw a large young man framed in one of the windows. His shoulders were drooping and his hands were jammed into his pockets. Even at that distance she could read penitence and dejection into his pose. The girl in blue skipped nimbly up the steps and disappeared into the house.

Georgine climbed on, her path zigzagging across the face of the steep hill. She looked down from one point of vantage and saw a foreshortened blue figure moving toward the olive tree, carrying something on a yellow saucer; something else moved, too, in the green of the garden: a leaping streak of fawn and white that made for the deck chair.

The path twisted back on itself, and she paused behind a clump of bushes to catch her breath and cool off for a moment. When she came into the open again, the scene below her was still visible, very clear in the mild, sunless air. The lively sister had gone in again, it seemed, but the cat was still leaping back and forth.

There was a stir among the leaves of the olive tree, and a white blur that might have been Ryn's face seemed to be tilted upward for a moment. Then a hand set down a yellow saucer on the ground, on the side of the chair that was away from the house. The hand began pouring something into the saucer, and the cat swooped toward it; it poured and poured, slowly, and the little patch of fawn and white crouched over the saucer, seeming to be lapping steadily. The hand with the glass in it stayed there. The glass was never raised to anyone's lips.

Georgine went round another hairpin turn, and the garden below was lost to view.

Some paces back she had gone past a small but professional-looking greenhouse, with a compost heap half hidden behind it. Now the last turn of the path brought her to the top of the cliff, and she stood breathing hard and looking about her.

This garden, and the low redwood house it sheltered, must have been here for a long, long time, and for all those years it had been carefully tended. There were trees and shrubbery, meticulously pruned and shaped; there were different levels of flower beds, dormant now except for a glorious bank of chrysanthemums at the end nearest the house, and there were patches of lawn bordered by succulently dark and rich strips of cultivated soil, where the green spears of narcissus were already appearing.

About fifty feet away knelt a small figure in a tweed skirt and a denim smock, working at a sloping patch of ground. Georgine walked toward the woman, making her footsteps as audible as she could, and once clearing her throat; but she received no greeting except for a half turn of a head bound up in a multicolored scarf. As she approached she could see tiny bulbs in a box, and watch the neat, rapid movement of a brown hand that set one after another into the soil and covered it.

"Oh, grape hyacinth!" said Georgine involuntarily; she had had a vision of that bank in the spring, blazing with violet-blue flowers. "How lovely—"

The woman turned now, displaying a little pointed face with darting eyes as bright and black as a sparrow's, and a wrinkled neck adorned with several chains of colored beads. "Yes," she said in a quick, pecking voice. "Had to take them all up and separate them. Anything you wanted?"

"I'd like to see Mrs. Majendie. Are you she?"

"No. Godfrey's my name. I'm her companion. Who are you?"

"Mrs., uh, Wyeth. I'm not selling anything," Georgine added quickly. "I'm interested in Mrs. Majendie as a leader of the Beyond-Truth."

"Oh. Oh, you are? The place to go," said Miss Godfrey with a suspicious fixing of the black eyes, "is to the Colony. They'll give you literature, you study it. Then you come back and make a formal profession of your interest."

"I'm afraid I'm not a convert."

"Then what's your business? I can't let every stranger that comes around see Mrs. Majendie. I'm here to save her time and energy. They're precious."

Georgine murmured, "It was for a personal interview."

"If it's about the Beyond-Truth," said Miss Godfrey, "I can tell you all you want to know. It was founded by our first great mental leader, Dr. Nicholas Majendie. He grasped the truth which has been self-evident for centuries but which the blindness of most minds has kept obscure, that all human facts are relative." Her sparrow eyes seemed to grow opaque, and her brittle voice took on a chanting tone. "They send out vibrations which on meeting in other dimensions form combinations and patterns vastly different from their original semblance in the fallible human mind." She paused for a gulp of air and

Georgine interjected, "It was Mrs. Majendie herself that I—"
"*Therefore*," said Miss Godfrey, drowning her out, "what
appears as a distortion or contradiction of mundane knowledge may, in the sphere just beyond us, be perfectly true, true
in perfection. The human mind may, by the exercise of self-
control in the simplest forms—"

"Joan!" said a deep voice from behind the bank of earth.

The sentence broke like a synthetic rubber band, the
brightness came back to Miss Godfrey's eyes, and she turned
on her heel. Over the top of the bank rose the head and shoulders of a tall, craggy-faced old woman, who must, Georgine
thought, have been squatting in hiding for some minutes.
"Joan," she said, "you should have learned by now to judge
voices. I'll talk to Mrs. Wyeth."

"Thank you," said Georgine faintly, and moved in answer
to a directing nod toward a wooden bench under an apple tree's
denuded branches. She sat down, watching Chloe Majendie
walk unhurriedly from behind the sloping bank, taking off
heavy gardening gloves as she came.

There is a type of elderly woman which may be indigenous
to other university towns, but which seems to reach its fullest
flower in Berkeley. Its exponents may be the daughters or wives
of professors, or may long ago have won their own doctorates,
or may simply have taken on color from their surroundings; but
almost without exception they have a look of being far above
fashion and beauty-culture, a touch of eccentricity worn as
proudly as Dowager-Queen Mary's toques. Without exception,
they look highly intelligent and sometimes they look formidable. Their eyes are young.

Georgine thought that in her years of residence in this
town she had never seen a more magnificent specimen of
the Berkeley Old Lady. Mrs. Majendie had probably been
a tall, rawboned and homely young woman; she had spread
conspicuously about the hips now, and was cheerfully uncon-
cerned about it. As she sat down she took off a man's ancient
felt hat, and crinkly gray hair sprang out in a wild bush above

a weathered and hawk-nosed face. She brushed a chunk of leaf mold from the knee of her jeans, turned a pair of piercing gray eyes on Georgine, and said, "Well, my dear? What can I do for you?" in that startlingly deep voice whose beautiful overtones seemed to linger humming in the ears after she had fallen silent.

Georgine began her prepared story, feeling more than glad that it was not too far from the truth. She and her husband were writers, rather obscure ones, and they were about to try a series of stories on noted personalities of the Bay Region. Mrs. Majendie was, of course, particularly interesting as a person who was carrying on her husband's work—unusual background—old estate—great help to them if Mrs. Majendie would consent, especially since the articles were to be in the nature of an experiment and might never see print—

She heard her own voice going on and on, sounding normal and earnest, for which she was thankful. There was something disconcerting about the steadiness of those gray eyes; they were not suspicious, only penetrating; but it was not unheard of that a Berkeley Old Lady might have a touch of the fanatic in her make-up, too, and Georgine wondered if the living brilliance of this gaze was not only alert but a bit screwball. Mrs. Majendie nodded when she had finished. "I'll be glad to help you," she said. "We have a saying at the Colony, to the effect that we never miss a chance for dignified publicity. Someone who sees it may be looking for the right path." She gave Georgine an unexpected smile, disclosing good and genuine teeth. "I must say, the undignified kind is just about as good."

Huh? said Georgine's mind, while she looked expectant and poised a pencil. —What does that mean? Is she poking a little fun at her own beliefs, or does she see through me? I feel rather mean as it is—

Mrs. Majendie was giving her an outline of the beginnings of Beyond-Truth, substantially the same as Hartlein's, but making it sound different indeed. —I could almost believe it made sense, thought Georgine, scribbling industriously on her pad. That voice, and all those long vague words; there's that bit about going into the Beyond-Truth after fasting, but she makes it sound as if she really could do it—

"And will the—the new generation carry on the work?" Georgine prompted.

Mrs. Majendie gave her a considering look. "We hope so. Of course, there are no children of the members."

"It's a celibate community?"

"In one way, yes," said the old lady smoothly. "There is no marriage in the world sense, though many couples are legally man and wife, and very dear companions. But—" She paused, and there was something in the silence that brought Georgine's eyes up to hers; her voice softened and deepened almost hypnotically. "But it wouldn't be consistent of us, would it, if we deliberately brought children into being to face the future that my husband saw so clearly?"

"Of course not," said Georgine, her eyes still held by the shrewd old ones. There was something in that idea, maybe; if you believed the visions, you couldn't—if you believed? It wasn't only the Beyond-Truthers who could imagine Hiroshima reenacted in America, and who wondered about their children. She'd thought of it herself plenty of times. And if the only way to push away that dread were the refusal to have children—

She forced herself to look back at her notebook. Her breath was coming rather fast. Why, this was the way converts were made: the grand old lady, making everything sound so reasonable, quietly playing on your own hidden fears, almost forced you into belief. The whole thing was based on fear; it couldn't be right.

But that, she thought with a sudden chill, was what Hartlein implied.

Joan Godfrey had gone back to her planting, but as Mrs. Majendie was dismissing her own stewardship of the cult in a brief final sentence, she got up and stood by the bench. "May

I interrupt, Chloe?" she said intensely. "You'll never say this yourself. Anyone hearing of the Beyond-Truth for the first time must be told. There were those who thought we could not go on after dear Dr. Nikko passed into the cosmos. We did. We believed. We are stronger than ever. And it is due to Chloe, the inspired mental leader, as inspired—yes, I will say it!—as great as Dr. Nikko. She has fanned the flame."

"The members themselves have kept it alive, Joan."

"No, no, it's you! And you, Mrs. What's-your-name, ask any of the members who have been with us since we began; go out to the Colony if you want the full story. Talk to Jennie Michaelson, Alvah Burke, Tina Cortelyou. They'll say the same."

"May I take down those names, please?" Georgine said. "They're, uh, charter members? It might be interesting to have a list, could you give me some other names? Joseph France, May Gordon—" She looked up, half laughing, choosing a name at random from Hartlein's absurd collection. "Was there one called Sybil Grant?"

There was an instant of silence, so filled with feeling that it seemed to stretch out endlessly. Georgine's heart began a slow and sickening descent toward her heels; she was conscious of the creaking bench under her, and of a strange far-off growling sound from some unidentified animal. Then Mrs. Majendie spoke with infinite regret in the depths of her voice.

"Sybil Grant is dead. She died last year."

Georgine was looking, not at her, but at Joan Godfrey. The scrawny neck had gone taut, the whole slight body quivered, and on the sparrow-face a light seemed to blaze for the fraction of a second: a light of triumph. Then it was gone.

"She passed into the cosmos," Joan Godfrey corrected gently. "Young, and lovely, and—*forgetting all that she*—"

"Joan," said Chloe Majendie without inflection.

The little woman turned away without another word, and walked toward the house.

"Does that give you enough material, Mrs. Wyeth?" Chloe inquired, obviously preparing to rise.

No guest ever took a hint faster. Georgine was on her feet before the question was finished. "Oh, yes. Yes, thank you very much. Good-bye, you've been very kind."

She was halfway down the twisting path before her heart stopped thundering. —Good heavens, what a moment that had been—like touching an innocent-looking button and finding that it set off a burglar-alarm. Everything was going perfectly well up to then—

She glanced down and saw the garden of the gray cottage. A man had emerged and was walking rapidly down the path toward the gate. She lost sight of him as the bushes obscured the last few yards of her descent, and when she came along beside the hedge he was nowhere to be seen. There were muttering and coughing sounds from the far side of the garage; someone was working at a car engine.

Georgine was within a few feet of the garage, just stepping onto the roadway, when the coughing suddenly swelled to a hoarse roar. The ramshackle car that had been parked beside the garage came shooting out in reverse, turning up the hill toward her. She saw a dusty rear window, a lopsided taillight. —Good Heavens, it wasn't stopping, it was aimed right at her! It swelled into a grayish-black mass and a cloud of fumes half an inch from her elbow—

She jumped backward, staggered for a moment on uneven footing and sat down hard on the graveled path. The car went past for half its length; confusedly she glimpsed broad shoulders hunched over the wheel, a face set blindly forward; then with a crash of gears it shot off forward down the hill and was lost to view at the turn. The roar died away. For a minute there was nothing but the angry chipping of birds disturbed in the hedge, the smell of crushed grass, and the waves of anguish going up Georgine's spine.

She tried to get up, uttered an involuntary grunt of pain, and stayed where she was, fighting back tears of shock and a rising fury. Feet sounded inside the gate, and the cool voice of the girl called Ryn inquired, "Oh, dear, did you fall and hurt yourself?" A pair of beautiful gray gabardine slacks appeared in Georgine's line of vision, and then a violet sweater and a white, concerned face. "My God, it wasn't David? Did his car hit you?"

Georgine, unable to unclench her teeth, shook her head. The girl called toward the house, "Cass! Come out here! An accident—" and the sister in blue appeared at headlong speed.

"I can get up by myself now, thanks," said Georgine crossly, resisting the hands under her armpits. "How do I feel? Like something out of a s-slapstick comedy. I've never been so mad!" Her shock-released anger had the upper hand. "No, your friend's car didn't hit me, because I jumped, but it darned near wiped the plaid off my skirt. May I ask who that crashing idiot is, gunning a car up the hill backward without so much as looking around first?"

"How about the aromatic spirits, Cass?" Ryn said quietly from above her. Cass nodded and made another of her headlong rushes for the cottage. Her blue-clad behind gave a quaint little hitch like the flicker of a rabbit's tail, as she scampered up the low porch steps.

Ryn looked down at Georgine. "That was David Shere," she said, "and he's not always a crashing idiot, but sometimes he's—out of temper, and then he gets reckless. I can't apologize enough for him. If you'd been a few feet nearer, I suppose he might really have killed you, and then he'd have wanted to die himself of remorse."

Her sister returned, breathing fast; Georgine set her teeth against a fresh wave of pain and angrily accepted the small glass that was pressed into her hand. "A fat lot of good that would do me," she said. "I'd be just as dead. They'd have a hard time making *that* look like the Hand of God!" She held her breath and got the spirits of ammonia down with the inevitable moment of choking afterward. When she looked up it was to see the sisters exchanging a long gaze over her head, which broke hastily as her eyes met theirs. Cass stepped through the gate and came back with Georgine's bag, which had burst open and scattered cards, compact and writing pad over the grass. "Thank you," Georgine snapped, shakily grabbing out one of her own cigarettes and trying to light it.

"Suppose you relax for a few minutes," Cass said briskly. "Good Lord, I do hope you're going to be all right; somebody hurt at our own gate by our own guest—"

"I see you got your interview," said Ryn, glancing upward. "Aunt Chloe's quite a personage, isn't she? I can't remember her looking any different in twenty years, and I suppose she'll be the same when she's eighty-seven. She didn't frighten you, I hope?"

Georgine could manage no more than a shake of the head.

"That's good. She can be pretty terrifying when she's in the mood. She brought us up, you know, my two sisters and me. Our name's Johnson, by the way, Chloe's our father's sister."

"You're Mrs. Wyeth, aren't you?" Cass put in. "I couldn't help seeing the cards when I picked them up."

Georgine changed the subject after a faint smile which might have been taken for affirmation. "Are there three of you living here, then? You have a very attractive house."

"No, just Cass and me, or do I mean 'I'? When Bell was here it was something of a crowd, but we never minded." Ryn's lovely pale face seemed to grow a shade whiter. She turned suddenly and moved toward the house with a sort of controlled haste, her steps wavering a little. Cass, looking anxious, said, "Ryn hasn't been very well, really. D'you have a family? Well, are they all absolute sillies about taking care of themselves? Honestly, I don't know what to do sometimes! Being the practical one in the outfit isn't much fun; I hate to see Ryn going on these long fasts, but there's no stopping her."

"Long ones?" Georgine murmured.

"Oh, yes, not only the Tuesday but four or five days at a time, eating absolutely nothing. And then she has to work back gradually to regular eating—only liquids for a day or so and then very light foods. Of course she doesn't sleep properly, she needs drugs; *awful!* But that's not the worst of it, there's something she does that's actually dangerous, the doctors and all of us have warned her but she won't believe anyone. She poisons herself with paint."

"What? How?"

"You know she's a painter, maybe you've seen some of her things in Berkeley exhibits, and she has one or two in permanent collections in the City. They're queer and beautiful, gouache mostly. Well," Cass gave an exasperated little laugh, "it seems you can't be haunting without using lots of green; and it seems that painters can't get a good fine point on a brush without putting the tip between their lips; and green paint is jam full of arsenic and you can eat enough of it, that way, to keep yourself half sick all the time. I ask you, what can a body do with someone like that?" She flung out her pretty hands in an appealing gesture.

"It would be a problem. And you, what do you do?"

"I'm Martha," said Cass, grinning. "I was just a good ordinary English major at Cal, and now I cook and give two or three days a week to a day nursery, and—just exist."

She added wistfully, "Bell was the one of us who could really have done things. She sang and she acted and she wrote. There was never anyone like her, so lovely—but she was always wanting to break free. Maybe she wouldn't have gone far anyway, after she was married. Sidney Grant wasn't much for the arts."

Georgine's pulses stirred. "I wonder if I haven't seen her name or heard it, somewhere? Was her first name Isabel?"

"No. Sibella." Cass looked round and sprang to help Georgine to her feet. "You're sure you feel like moving?"

"Yes. I must get home."

"You must let me drive you."

"No, thank you, my car's at the foot of the street."

"Oh; well, if you're certain you can make it comfortably." She went on, walking protectively beside Georgine to the gate, "I suppose our parents thought they'd take the curse off Johnson for a last name, so they fixed us up with fancy first ones. Bell was Sibella, and Ryn's Dorinda—and mine, of all things, is Casilda. I've always expected to find myself married to two gondoliers at once."

Georgine laughed. "They're pretty names, though. Look here, you needn't get your car out; I'd rather walk this little way, I'm going to be stiff tomorrow anyway."

"Then I'll see you safely into your own car," said Cass with determination. "Is there any way we could find out how you are? Call up tomorrow, or something?" Her gray eyes were anxious.

"No, thank you, don't bother," said Georgine strongly. "You've worried too much over a stranger as it is."

❀ ❀ ❀

"And a stranger I mean to stay," she told Todd half an hour later.

Todd was hovering about her with penitent concern. "I wish to the Lord's sake you'd lie down."

"I'm standing by choice."

"Then I'm going to fix you another drink."

"All right. I haven't had so much hard liquor since New Year's eve, but for once I need it. Right here on the mantel-piece, thank you, dear." She sipped the drink and sighed. "Of course, next time you'll know better than to send me. I *would* see fit to bring up the Sibella Grant business, so that the old lady knew I was onto something. I'm sorry I made such a hash of it, Todd."

"You didn't. And I'm only sorry that you were hurt and frightened."

"Hash," said Georgine with a sigh. "It reminds me of dinner. I can cook standing up, anyway."

While she was stirring about beyond the swing-door, Todd sat down in his shabby blue armchair and looked unseeingly at the cold fireplace. Presently, with an automatic gesture, he brought a mouth-organ from his pocket and began tapping it gently on his palm. Georgine came into the adjoining dining-room to set the table, and he began thinking aloud through the clink of silver and glassware. "The annoying part of it is that I didn't believe a word of Hartlein's story when I let you go up to Cuckoo Canyon. Queer—he's a queer guy all the way round. Now that we know there was some truth in his story, it's hard not to look for... The old lady's house doesn't sound rich, from what you said of it... And there is a case of slow poisoning, but the girl's under a doctor's care and they know what's causing it... No, Hartlein's all off."

After a few minutes Georgine heard him at the telephone. "Is Inspector Nelsing still in his office?... Hello, Nelse, it's Mac. Not too good, how's yours? Uh, huh, I know, sitting around there doing nothing, getting fat on the taxpayers' money. Have you a minute to check something for me? Did your people investigate a fatal automobile accident some time last year, in which a couple were killed on their wedding night? Sidney Grant and Sibella Johnson Grant... Oh, you knew her personally, did you? All three of them; I see. Yes, I'll wait..."

There was a long silence. Georgine opened the door from the kitchen into the hall and eyed her husband. "Nelse says the Johnsons were on campus all together, when he was taking his graduate work. Everybody knew 'em. He remembers when Sibella was killed... Yes? All right, I'm listening.

"Thanks," he said finally, and hung up. "I guess that does it," he said, following Georgine into the dining-room. "The Grants had got pretty high at their wedding reception and they hadn't driven more than eight miles before they went off one of those turns on Grizzly Peak Boulevard in a summer night fog. Grant was killed instantly, Sibella was thrown clear and lived about half an hour; the insurance people made a routine investigation and nothing more came of it. Nelse says there's nothing in it for me and I must be hard up for material. How truly he spoke," concluded Todd, applying himself to pot roast and savory vegetables.

Georgine glanced at him. His agate eyes were intent on something beyond her.

"I'm sorry you can't find anything to work on," she said, "but I'm just as pleased that we're out of it."

They had barely finished doing the dishes after dinner when the doorbell rang, long and peremptorily; and a vigorous male voice said, "Todd McKinnon? Was it your wife that nearly got knocked down by my car this afternoon? I'm David Shere."

CHAPTER THREE

"**B**UT I'VE GOT to see her," Shere was insisting frantically. "Good God, I nearly killed her, and I didn't know a thing about it, not until the Johnsons got hold of me. I have to see how badly she's hurt. For the Lord's sake, man, don't you know what this means to *me?*"

Todd seemed to be standing his ground at the front door. David Shere's voice dropped lower. "Arrange for a doctor's care if it's necessary, and apologize...do that if nothing else..."

"Oh, let him in, Todd," said Georgine, wearily accepting the inevitable and coming into the hall. Shere stepped through the door and looked her over with an anxious flash of light-brown eyes. He stood still, but Georgine found herself catching her breath as if he had rushed at her.

He was a squarely built young man in his late twenties, light-haired, good-looking enough in an irregular way. It would be hard for a woman to notice his looks closely at a first meeting, or to analyze them for some time after, for he was possessed of the kind of vitality that surrounds its owner with a zone of almost palpable electricity. It crackled in his voice and in the intensity of his look; if you were in a state to fall in love, it might make him irresistible, and even if you disliked him you could not be unaware of him.

"Mrs. McKinnon," he said hoarsely, "—you are Mrs. McKinnon, aren't you? The girls got your name from the steering-post in your car, and we saw the same car in your garage—Mrs. McKinnon, I'm abject. There's no excuse for me, except that I'd just been turned down on a proposal and I was simply in no state to know what I was doing. I want to find out if you're hurt."

"Oh, that's all right," said Georgine, still wearily.

He glanced from Georgine to Todd. "You don't look like the kind of people who'd be planning to bring suit for huge damages, and break me. I guess Mrs. McKinnon would be lying down groaning, if you had anything like that in mind."

Todd said neutrally, "My wife will see a physician if it's necessary."

"And you'll let me pay for it, I hope—or do anything I can to make it up to you." He took another step forward, looking earnest and young and worried. "I haven't a job; I'm taking graduate work in metallurgy, and right now I haven't got anything to my name except an old house in San Francisco that my grandfather left me. The rent's my only income. If you were really seriously injured, Mrs. McKinnon, of course you could have that and welcome, but I couldn't scrape up another cent."

Todd laughed involuntarily. One could not help being touched by such candid indiscretion.

"Well, come in and sit down for a minute," he said.

"Is there someone else with you?" said Georgine. "You said 'we' noticed the car in the garage." —So much for my careful disguise, she added to herself.

"Yes, Cass and Ryn Johnson are down in the car."

Todd neither moved nor changed expression, but his wife felt a quickening of attention which could be read only in one way. "But do ask them in, too," she said. "They were very good to me this afternoon."

Shere nodded and plunged off down the steps. As he returned more slowly, with a young woman on either side, his extremely carrying voice could be heard floating upward: "Damn' decent. I hope it'll last!" One of the Johnsons presumably hushed him.

Ryn Johnson paused on the threshold of the living-room as introductions were being completed. She looked it over with a comprehensive sweep of the gray-green eyes, and nodded decisively. "She likes your color scheme," said Cass, coming up beside her with a twinkling glance at Georgine. "See how I can read minds?"

Standing together, dressed in loose casual coats and plain wool dresses, the Johnsons looked more alike than at a first impression. One thought of Cass as shorter and plumper, because of her healthy coloring and roundness of cheek, but she was of much the same height as her sister. Ryn, although she looked better than she had in the afternoon, was still moving slowly and dreamily. She wandered toward a chair and sat down abstractedly. It was not necessary for her to talk much, she gave pleasure merely by letting you look at her, but now and then the perfect carmine lips opened for a murmur in her cool voice. She said now, "Cass said she felt like an under-cover man."

Cass giggled. "Of course, it was possible that you'd borrowed the car, but I couldn't help seeing your driver's license too, when I was putting things back into your bag. And we couldn't just let you walk away, and leave it at that!"

"My wife uses her professional name for interviews," said Todd smoothly. Georgine prayed that nobody would ask what profession, and nobody did. "Besides," Cass went on, "we wanted to see you again; we liked you, for one thing."

"Thank you," said Georgine. —You ought to see me when I haven't just cracked my coccyx, she added to herself.

"Ryn thought you people might be on the faculty," said Cass. "No? You're not even connected with the University?"

"My husband's a writer," said Georgine guardedly. Cass gave a cheerful nod of comprehension. "That's one way of getting around, certainly. We couldn't help wondering how you'd met Hugh Hartlein."

There was a minute's pause. Across the room David Shere was telling Todd something surpassingly dull about a new temperature control to be used in assay work on gold, and seemingly holding his audience; but Todd's ears were remarkably selective and his attention all-embracing. The Johnson girls both looked at Georgine, with a hint of strain under their easy manner.

"I have just met him—once," she said at last. "Why, is that so remarkable?"

"He's always saying he has no social life, aside from us." Cass smiled at Georgine. "Now I know better! We were sure you knew him, from the way you used one of his pet phrases this afternoon. Do tell me, what kind of impression did he make on you?"

"It wasn't a long meeting. He seemed rather intense and moody."

The Johnsons looked at each other and laughed. Ryn said, "An understatement if I ever heard one. Hugh's neurotic."

There was an odd, almost indefinable ring in her voice. What was it? Relief, eagerness, satisfaction at having said what she had come to say? Georgine could not decide, but she was aware that Todd's mind had been alerted. Though there was no eagerness in his voice or look, from clear across the room she could feel his attention.

He entered the conversation now. "That's one of those words that has almost lost its meaning, isn't it?"

"Oh, I'm not using it lightly," Ryn returned. "We know him rather well. He was—" she smiled slightly, "—nominally in the family."

"Which one of you *did* he marry?" said Todd, also smiling.

"Me," said Cass Johnson in a mournful voice, her eyes twinkling. "The things I let myself be talked into! You know— Hugh can be awfully interesting and even charming when he works at it, but he stopped work about five minutes after the

knot was tied. Quite a honeymoon we had." She chuckled reminiscently. "Four hours at the Reno airport and in the plane,
fighting all the time."

"You started earlier than most," Todd murmured.

It was Ryn who replied. "It was good luck that it happened
that way. Hugh couldn't wait a minute to go back on everything
he'd said earlier. That awful mother of his, for one thing—he
announced that she was to come down and live with him and
Cass. It isn't even as if he liked her himself! And—there was
plenty besides that," she went on hurriedly. "But what you can't
get into Hugh's head is the fact that he could ever be to blame
for anything that goes wrong, or that anyone can dislike him
for himself alone."

It had been a long speech, for Ryn. She subsided,
breathing fast as if her vehemence had tired her. Cass had been
sitting with lowered eyelids; now she flashed a brilliant glance
at David Shere, and observed, "And as long as he thinks of my
Aunt Chloe as a witch, he needn't come mooching round trying
to get me to marry him again!"

"Don't look at me," said Mr. Shere with some heat. "I don't
mind your aunt. And why are you bringing this up, as though
it was the only impediment?" He began to scowl; he leaned
forward and added seriously, "I'm an impediment, damn it!"

Cass laughed. "Maybe you are and maybe not," she said
lightly. "And how *did* we get onto the subject? Isn't it silly, the
way you start talking about one thing and end up miles from
where you began? We ought to be leaving, you know. We only
came so that you could ask after Mrs. McKinnon's health." She
got up briskly and Georgine also rose, but in a slower and more
painful manner.

"Of course," said Shere, "but that was all settled long ago."

Todd had been helping Georgine up. At the complacent
sound of this remark, his eyebrows rose. "Was it?" he said. "I
don't remember our settling anything."

"Well, I'm damned," said Shere with sudden violence. "I
told you where I stood; what d'you want me to do, crawl on my

belly?" He swung to face Georgine. "Don't try to make out that it was all my fault. If you hear a car—"

"David, hush!" Cass cried out. She grasped his arm and began urging him toward the door, but he literally brushed her off and went on, "—a car starting up out of sight, why don't you get into a safe place and wait till it's gone? These damn' pedestrians, walking right into the path of—"

"You'd better get out, Shere," said Todd in a metallic voice. The young man paused in mid-speech to give him a startled look, and before anything more could be said the Johnsons swept forward as one woman and hustled their friend to the front door. "He would have to spoil it," Cass threw over her shoulder in an anguished tone, and the door closed.

Georgine took a long breath. "Quite a salon we're running here," she observed acidly. "The flower of America's young manhood, a new flower each night. How *do* we attract them? Is there something wrong with us?"

"Only with me. I'm not quick enough to the punch."

"Thank heaven for that. That's all my salon needs, a good brawl. *What* was this all about?"

"I'm not sure," said Todd deliberately. He had got hold of himself, and was moving toward the desk. "I've been pumped before, and I've had information forced on me, but never quite so obviously! Where did I put that—"

"What are you looking for?"

"The envelope with Hartlein's address." He rooted in the desk drawer. "The checkbook, too."

"Todd, did those people make you think there was something in his story—after all?"

"Not exactly," Todd said. Under Georgine's dubious gaze he dated the check Nov. 3, and began to fill it out. "This may be a dirty trick, though Hartlein did lay himself open to it—but I'm going to use *him* in some kind of a yarn."

"H'm. If you're going to play a dirty trick on anyone, why don't you have a go at our Mr. Shere?"

"He's too simple, I'm afraid," said Todd regretfully. "He blew up right after Cass started teasing him."

"You mean just a frustrated love could cause all that?"

"There may be a li'le more to it, but as a psychiatrist of long standing, I'd say that he'd feel lots better if he were married to some lusty wench."

"If you slap me there I'll kill you," said Georgine ominously.

Todd addressed his envelope and laid it on the hall table to be mailed in the morning. "That non-existent wife and child in Grass Valley are going to have a Christmas after all," he said. "Young Hartlein's a clumsy liar; and that's the most interesting thing about him."

On the evening of November 10, the driver of a Number 7 bus stopped on his way down Euclid to wait for a young man who was running down the last half-block of Cedar, signaling to him. The young man got on, breathing fast and coughing as he asked for a transfer; he wore no hat; there was a shine of perspiration on his cadaverous face; he sat huddled into his overcoat, gazing at the floor of the bus. There were not many passengers, but several of them got off at Shattuck and University, where the young man also disembarked. They stood waiting for their various buses and cars on the corner, paying little attention to each other.

It was noticeable, however, that the hatless young man was suffering from a cold. He sneezed and made an abortive attempt to blow his nose, and then took something from his pocket and held one nostril after the other while he inhaled deeply and quickly. A student standing nearby happened to be looking at him idly while this went on. She then transferred her attention to the street, but for a few seconds only.

The young man appeared to be strangling, he grasped his throat, stumbled a step or two and fell full-length on the sidewalk. For seconds more his companions in waiting stood stunned, and then there was a concerted rush toward him.

Whatever had been in his hand fell unnoticed and rolled or was kicked toward the street. He was still making convulsive movements. Somebody took off a raincoat, rolled it and thrust it under his head; somebody else raced across to the Low-Cost Drugstore to telephone; out of the street which had seemed almost deserted a minute before, dozens of people appeared to crowd around the prostrate figure.

The ambulance came, and a police officer who interrogated the original members of the group on the corner and found that no two of them could agree as to just what had happened. The young man died on the way to Herrick Hospital, to the great disgust of the ambulance interne. The doctor on Emergency began a routine check, frowned, bent close, and sniffed the dead man's nostrils and upper lip.

A few hours later, under the chill bright lights of a deserted street intersection, two uniformed policemen went methodically along the curb, peering down into the gutter and turning over scraps of newspaper and crumpled cigarette packages. They found part of what they were looking for in a spot where it might have been crushed, a dozen times over, by feet or the wheels of cars, and yet had by chance remained intact. Its other part lay in the doorway of a hardware store, half-flattened but with its mechanism still recognizable.

The laboratory expert worked on it when the first light of a November dawn was just graying the windows. He said, "For cripes' sake, I never saw anything like this one before. Take a look, Slater, but don't sniff it too hard."

The object was a small metal inhaler with a screw top. Its under portion, which had contained a volatile substance to shrink the nasal mucosa, had been cut off at the base and neatly resoldered, after another substance had been introduced. The replacement was crystalline cyanide, and a tiny ampule of acid had been set among the crystals. Against the ampule had rested a long and minutely narrow tongue of metal, passed through the hole in the top of the inhaler and fastened at the upper end to the inside of the screw cover.

"Give that top a twist," said the expert, "which you have to do to unfasten it, and that tongue breaks the ampule of acid. It's a portable gas chamber. The guy must have taken two good whiffs and got his bronchial passages full of it before he knew what smelled funny."

"He'd get enough of it, the doc says," contributed Slater in a deep voice that set the laboratory glass humming. "He died without regaining consciousness." He stood up and exchanged glances with the expert. "Looks like a job for us, all right."

At seven a.m. Inspector Nelsing began to issue instructions. The dead man had carried full identification, so that was no problem. His department at the University was notified, a carefully edited story was released to radio and newspapers, and at ten-thirty Nelsing was looking over a collection of personal papers, one of which gave him a considerable start.

He reached for the telephone.

Todd McKinnon opened a glass-topped door on the second floor of the Hall of Justice, and looked down a short corridor of offices. "Inspector Nelsing in?" he asked a tweed-clad member of the force.

"He's busy at the moment. Will you wait?" said the young inspector, with the monumental courtesy of a Berkeley policeman.

"I'll be out in the rotunda. Tell him it's McKinnon, about the Hartlein business." Todd turned away, glancing at a small woman hung with bead necklaces, who had been hovering at this end of the main hall and darting sparrow-bright glances at the door he had just closed. He recalled his wife's vivid description of the Majendie household, and his mind sprang to attention.

The little woman was pattering after him. "Excuse me," she said breathlessly, "but did I hear you say Hartlein? And what's the name of the officer to talk to about him? Nelsing? I want to see him too."

"Then let's sit down here." Todd indicated a bench at the head of the broad staircase. The woman nodded jerkily and came to rest on the bench, her beads rattling as she arranged her coat. She was breathing fast, and the muscles around her eyes were taut. "Tragic thing about his death, wasn't it?" said Todd conventionally.

"Tragic? Oh, no; in the spheres where vibrations meet there is no tragedy, but an unalterable rightness," said Joan Godfrey with solemnity. "Truth has enfolded him now, although only last night he was struggling against it, he was speaking in negation of the Words. That terrible laughter, I have heard it before, when a Warning is given and denied." She darted a glance at Todd. "Our Mental Leader is not given Long Prophecy, as the first one was, but so often, so often!—the simple mundane words she speaks are Truth in Perfection. She warned him about his heart, you know."

Miss Godfrey's voice came out of its holy hush and turned into the chirp of an impassioned gossip. "Dear Mrs. Majendie, so motherly, she saw him panting and coughing after that trip up our hill, which he took *much* too fast, it's almost a mile straight up hill from the bus line. And then he grew so intense, he was suffering a dreadful distortion of Truth; you know, that in itself would be enough to set up warring vibrations within him. No, I was not surprised when I heard on the radio that he had been touched by a ray from the cosmos, but it seemed that the police—I suppose they are the only ones to handle such cases?—the police wondered where he had been just before his passing in, and so of course it was my task in Truth to give them the story."

Todd sat still and let it pour over him. He was rather adept at evoking confidences, but never before had a few casual words brought forth such a flood of talk. Miss Godfrey swept on.

"At the time I wondered how Mrs. Majendie could sit there so quietly, with such dignity, and listen to the dreadful things he said about her and about the Beyond-Truth—blaming her, Mr., Mr.—?"

"McKinnon."

"Mr. McKinnon, for the failure of his marriage, and in the next breath admitting that he had meant it to be marriage in the world sense, and that he had told Cass what he intended! The dear girl was strong then, but he would not accept her dismissal, and he has come back over and over in this past year, trying to make her forget what she knows of the Truth—oh, *I* know how many times, it is my task in Truth to watch. I've been afraid for her," Miss Godfrey confided with a glittering look at Todd. "Only last week she went out quietly at night, and it was given to me to know where she went: to his rooms, and of course it was my task to follow, sometimes it is laid upon us to remind one who is in temptation, but I could not go in or stay as long as she did; Cass and Ryn do not understand about these tasks, and they—if they complain to—" For the first time her voice wavered, and a brown hand moved nervously among the chains of beads. Then she took on new confidence. "I was reassured that time, because the voices were not loving at all. Not sharp like a quarrel, but low and heavy and hoarse, so I knew. She was safe for that night. And then the poor blind young man accused Chloe Majendie, as if it were a fault on *her* part! I shouldn't have been surprised if the Ray had touched him then and there. The things he said were terrible. Terrible, Mr. McKinnon. I called it blasphemy, yes indeed I did; I stood up and leveled my finger at Hugh Hartlein—" She leveled it at the long desk across the rotunda, and the sergeant behind it gave her a startled look "—and I said it was blasphemy. And dear Chloe would not let me go on, she only smiled and told him that he would injure his nasal tissues if he used his inhaler so often, and that she had never interfered in his affairs but that she disliked seeing him impair his health. And that was when he laughed, Mr. McKinnon, like the crackling of thorns, and went away, along the cliff path in the dark. But the Ray did not touch him until there were witnesses to see how the scoffer is punished."

Miss Godfrey sat breathing fast and nodding to herself. Slater, Nelsing's assistant, had just come down the corridor from the Homicide Division; he caught Todd's eye and flashed a quizzical look from him to his companion. The police, Todd reflected, were used to loony witnesses.

"Is Inspector Nelsing free now?" he asked Slater gravely. "I think this lady was here before me, with some information that he'll want."

Slater inquired the lady's name in a bass voice that struck booming echoes from the stairwell, sketched a bow and led her away. As they went, the free flow of Miss Godfrey's voice continued. "He came to me from Beyond, at dawn," she was saying, "defeated and submissive. Truth had enfolded—"

Todd shook his head as if emerging from a dive, and lit a cigarette. He'd been flattering himself when he imagined that his manner had evoked Miss Godfrey's confidences; if he hadn't been there she would have seized upon the desk sergeant or the first person who came in to pay a traffic fine. Now Nelsing was getting it. He'd give a good deal, he told himself, to see Nelse being enfolded by Truth.

"How'd you like your Marvelous Female Witness?" he asked the Inspector maliciously, half an hour later.

"Oh God," said Howard Nelsing simply. "We've had plenty of 'em before, but never as insane as this one. Have a chair, Mac." He sat down himself, a ruggedly handsome man in his late thirties, and fixed his friend with a keen blue gaze. "She may have let a few bits of the truth show through, here and there—"

"World-truth, you mean."

"Yes, that's the only kind that interests me just now. I guess Hartlein did go to see old Mrs. Majendie last night. I'll pay her a call myself, but I hope to heaven this screwball dame will stay in the next room." He leaned forward to offer Todd a cigarette. "That reminds me, Mac, I called up Georgine a few minutes after you'd left the house. She said she wouldn't mind if I did some interviewing there." Todd blinked. "The Johnson girls were down here this morning, pretty much upset about

Hartlein's death. One of them was married to him, you know, and they were both in a state of incoherence. I didn't want to send 'em home, their street is thick with reporters already."

"Good Lord, Nelse, are you softening up?" Nelsing had always held a poor opinion of womankind, considering them unreliable, cowardly, and without conscience in law-breaking.

Inspector Nelsing shook his head. "Not I. I told you, though, I'd known them on campus, and I can stretch a point for personal friends. They suggested you, themselves. Nobody can get at them, and I can talk to them later when they've calmed down. Neither of them had seen Hartlein for some time, so there couldn't have been any funny business."

"H'm," Todd said. "You think there *was* funny business?"

"You tell me. What was the check for?"

Todd told him. Beyond the glass walls of the cubicle men moved quietly and busily; across from the window rose the cream-colored bulk of the City Hall, with pigeons now and then swooping down from its roof to strut in the open court between. The fantastic story that Hugh Hartlein had unfolded on that windy night ten days ago seemed doubly incredible in these surroundings; yet as Nelsing heard it he began to frown, and his forefinger executed a rhythmic and quite unconscious tapping on his desk.

"They came around on purpose to tell you that Hartlein was neurotic?" he said when Todd had finished.

"Looked that way. I'd guess that they knew Hartlein had that bee in his bonnet about the Hand of God murders, that he'd discussed it with them and that they'd threatened him with dire things if he so much as mentioned it to the police. Hartlein quibbled, and brought me the story; I think he'd heard that I lay all my humble offerings in your lap." Nelsing snorted, but Todd went on imperturbably, "Then Georgine let slip that remark about the Hand of God, and the Johnsons knew that Hartlein had told somebody. So—prove that he's an unstable character, and the yarn doesn't get repeated. I'd never have wasted your time with it, if he hadn't died."

"Would you have come round with it if I hadn't called you?"

"Probably not. You haven't given out the details about the inhaler, have you?"

Nelsing shook his head. "Did the Johnson girls intimate that Hartlein was the suicide type?"

"Not in my hearing."

"What do you think yourself?"

"From my one passage with him, I'd say it was possible."

"Would he leave a note?"

"A suicide note? Pages of it." Todd's hard gray eyes kindled. "You didn't find one?"

"Not so far," Nelsing admitted grudgingly. "There wasn't one on him, nor in his room. He's got a mother up in Yreka, I gather; he might have mailed it to her, they do that sometimes." He stood up, and opened the door. "Slater; anyone else to see me? Okay, I'm leaving for a while. Call me at Mac's if anything turns up." He picked up his hat. "Got your car, Mac?"

"No. I'll take a lift home, if you're not driving the wagon." Todd, following Nelsing down the stairs, hesitated. "Look here, Nelse, how about letting me have a look at Hartlein's room? It can't be far from here, it's down Grove."

Nelsing gave him a sidelong look. "My God, you writers," he said in resignation. "Come on, then. We've been over it pretty thoroughly." He added, as his car engine purred into life, "I wish to heaven I knew whether this case really comes into our department."

Todd grinned. He told himself that that remark, from Nelsing, was the equivalent of a fictional detective ominously muttering, "I don't like this, there is some hidden evil that we haven't uncovered yet." That, in fact, was what he would have liked to say himself. There were vague pricklings of discomfort...

"The fellow was living on the cheap, wasn't he?" he observed, as the car drew up before a scabrous old frame house which many years before had probably been painted yellow. "I thought the University had a list of decent living quarters for faculty."

"That's up to the members themselves," said Nelsing dryly. "Hartlein was a thrifty soul. Come on, Mac, there's just time for a quick look." He led the way down a walk that led beside a half-basement floor, and the dried stalks of thick-growing bulb plants rustled against his legs as he strode. "Here," he said in the same tone, as they rounded the corner, "is where our Miss Godfrey insists she stood and heard voices, in one of those all-seeing visions of hers." Todd digested this in silence. Joan Godfrey had not included this detail in the information she poured over him. Nelsing opened a ground-level door which gave on a dank passageway, and turned the handle of an inner door on the left.

CHAPTER FOUR

THE ROOM WAS cheerless enough in all conscience. There were limp, drab curtains of the kind which a landlady hangs as a gesture and a bachelor does not notice, and a carpet faded to colorless lozenges. "Not much to steal, he never kept it locked, or the outside door either," said Nelsing. The men stood in the doorway, both looking about them with attention, but the looks were different: Nelsing observed minutely, although he had already examined the room that morning; Todd absorbed, and thought irrelevantly that the bindings of textbooks lent less color to a room than any other type of book, and that the frame which enclosed the photograph of a middle-aged woman was at once expensive and surpassingly ugly. It was the room's only ornament, if you could call it that.

"That's Mrs. Hartlein of Yreka, I suppose," he murmured, and remembered a snatch of conversation from the Johnson girls' visit: something about that awful mother of his; he doesn't like her himself. That picture frame was arresting, somehow, like a grand gesture made sullenly. Or was that a contradiction in terms? The woman in the picture looked at once avid and imperious. She would exact tribute, and this son wouldn't refuse it.

"Nelse," he said, "where did you find that check of mine?"

Nelsing gave him a brief glance charged with intelligence. "In a desk drawer with a couple of insurance policies, a bank book, and a marriage certificate. Nothing else."

"It doesn't seem that valuable, unless—he meant to call attention... He'd made me, in a way, a repository of his suspicions."

"I thought of that while you were telling me the story. We were meant to ask you, in case of his death, what the check was for." Nelsing turned decisively. "Seen enough?"

"Just a minute more." Todd stood motionless, with that look of attention which his wife likened to the raising of a radio aerial. What was the feeling of this room? Not convivial bachelordom, not the concentration on study that would ignore physical untidiness; the place was neat, too neat and barren. The only impression he could gather was a curious and indefinable one of despair.

He shook his head and said abruptly, "All right, I'm through." They turned to the door, Nelsing swung it open and they stepped out into the dingy hall.

It was no longer untenanted. David Shere was standing by the entrance door as if he had just come in. He looked startled and angry and suspicious in almost equal parts. "Who the hell are you? What are you doing in there?" he said.

"I'm from the Berkeley Police Department," said Nelsing crisply.

"Well, *you're* not, McKinnon!"

"—Doing a routine check-up after the sudden death of Hugh Hartlein," Nelsing went on as if he had not spoken. "Were you coming to see him?"

"No. I live here." Shere gestured at the door across the hall. Nelsing nodded; it was obvious that he had checked on the other occupants of the rooming-house.

"But you were friends?" he added.

"Well—call it that." He stood still in the dim passageway, his eyes intent, his strongly built body emanating his usual vitality. "We were neighbors, but sometimes days 'ud go by without our seeing each other."

"How many days has it been this time?"

"Two or three." He eyed Nelsing again, narrowly. "You said a routine check-up? —I just heard about his death, I've been out since seven this morning, and I didn't see a paper until half an hour ago. It said he'd dropped dead..."

Nelsing waited a moment. Todd, motionless and silent in the shadows of the hall, heard the wind rustling the dry plant-spears outside the house; and heard also a nearer sound of quick and shallow breathing from the blond young man who faced them.

"There was more to it than that, Mr. Shere," Nelsing said. "Since you knew Hartlein, perhaps you could help us. His death wasn't natural."

"Suicide," Shere said very quickly, and with no questioning inflection.

"You sound almost as if you'd expected it, Mr. Shere. When you last saw Hartlein did he seem in a suicidal frame of mind?"

David Shere retreated farther into wariness. "I don't know. I wouldn't know what that was."

"Had he suffered any recent shock or great disappointment, would you happen to know?"

"No," Shere almost shouted. "Why should I know? We weren't on those terms."

Nelsing nodded again. "I think I'd like to talk this over with you further, if you can spare an hour. Perhaps you'd come up to my office; I have the car outside."

"I'll go on home, Nelse," Todd said in an undertone, and as unobtrusively as possible slipped through the door, followed by Nelsing's significant "See you later, then."

There was a streetcar coming, but Todd did not run for it. He strolled unhurriedly to the corner and stood at ease, waiting for another. There, presently, he was rewarded by the sight of Shere going by in Nelsing's car, his ruddy young face a very mask of stubbornness.

Todd's eyes followed the car. He reflected on Shere's overtures to Cass Johnson, and their rebuff; on the presence of cyanides in a metallurgical laboratory; and on the palpable fact that whether or not Shere had been surprised at the unnatural aspects of his neighbor's death, he was a troubled and frightened young man who was rapidly becoming more so.

The past week had been a placid one in the McKinnon household, except for struggles with literary creation. Georgine didn't mind the typewriter, but she did mind the mouth-organ playing which was Todd's device for releasing a plot from his mind. He was practising part of Beethoven's First Symphony, and doing badly at it.

—If only I could help, if I could just help him somehow, she told herself over and over during the week. There wasn't much chance for that, though; her daughter Barby was coming home for the Armistice Day week-end, and domestic details went on inexorably and soothingly. They were still going on when, on the morning of the 11th, the call from Nelsing summoned Todd to the Hall of Justice.

Georgine heard his brief account of what had happened, saw him off, and returned in a kind of daze to the kitchen where she and Barby were making cookies. She moved irresolutely about, picking up things and forgetting to put them down, listening with only a fragment of attention to Barby's unceasing chatter: the school play, the hope of a swimming pool some day if the money could be raised—

Hugh Hartlein was dead, ten days after he had thrust himself into the McKinnons' lives and talked about the Hand of God. Nobody had yet told her how he died, but it was obvious that something was very wrong about it.

—And we're in it, Georgine thought with a sinking heart. —We were in it from the moment when Hartlein looked in our window. Todd didn't ask for it, and I've been reluctant at every step. It's been laid on us. Well, then—I wonder if there's any use fighting? Maybe that just makes it worse, as if we were a conquered people and invaders had been billeted in this house...

"And maybe that's what I can do to help Todd," she said half-aloud. "Relax, and let 'em all come."

"Let who come, Mamma?" Barby inquired without much interest, preparing to leave.

"Oh, anybody," said Georgine vaguely. "Be back in time for lunch, won't you, darling?"

Half an hour later, talking on the telephone to Nelsing, she was still in this queer passive mood. Have the Johnsons up for the day? Nelsing wouldn't ask her that if the girls were suspects in—anything. Perhaps this wasn't even a murder; and Nelsing did Todd so many professional favors—

"Let 'em all come," she said almost blithely into the telephone, startling the Inspector into a moment of silence.

Even if one relaxed, she thought as she waited for the guests, there was a social problem involved. With what degree of sympathy should one treat the widow of a young man whose marriage had never been consummated and was about to be dissolved—if indeed it hadn't been already? The Victorians would have known, adepts that they were in exact shades of mourning; Georgine did not, and doubted that Emily Post herself had ever covered the situation, including as it did an interrogation by the police. She had also some difficulty in explaining it to Barby, who came plunging in after making plans for the afternoon with a friend.

"I guess it's one of Toddy's murders," said Barby with great sang-froid.

"No, no, I don't think so—and for heaven's sake don't mention the word! *Could* you tuck that shirt inside your jeans, darling? I see them coming—"

Her first sight of the Johnson girls, however, confirmed her judgment about Hartlein's death. Cass was red-eyed and obviously tense under a matter-of-fact manner, all of which seemed fairly natural; but Ryn wore a curious expression, with-drawn and inward-looking, like someone trying to evaluate the first faint twinges of an ominous pain. *They're scared,* Georgine told herself. But why should Ryn be scared?

Georgine found herself taking on the brisk and bustling air of a good nurse. The girls would want to freshen up, perhaps; Barby could show them the bathroom, and take them—(*"Is your bed made?"* in an urgent whisper) take them into her room where there was a good mirror. There would be coffee when they came down, and Georgine would get lunch started. Oh, yes, they must plan on it, there was no telling when Nelse would arrive.

She hastily put noodles on to boil, listening to the murmur of voices from Barby's room above. Her child had improved socially, too, at school; she'd lost some of her polite reserve and was more out-going... There was a can of shrimp somewhere in the emergency cupboard. There ought to be asparagus, yes, there it was, and where on earth had she put the mousetrap cheese? If Todd and Barby had eaten it all—!

Presently the voices ceased, and the two young women came downstairs, followed by Barby. There was something odd about Barby's gait, and she kept her eyes fixed on the elegant back of Ryn Johnson; evidently she was trying on that gliding walk in view of future theatrical performances. Georgine glanced at her daughter's face with some curiosity; it was cheerful enough but showed no signs of the inner radiance that appeared in the presence of someone she liked very much.

Cass stopped by the telephone at the foot of the stairs. "May I?" she said, and put in a call. She talked in a low voice for a few minutes, and on rejoining the others said to her sister, "Nelsing is going to call on Chloe before he comes here. They're waiting for him now." Ryn made no response. She kept her eyes fixed on her coffee-cup. Cass added, with a faint smile, "I'd be willing to bet he won't get much change out of her." She looked at Barby, and the smile became one of fondness. "Tell us some more about your school, honey. It must be such fun!"

Barby talked. She talked all through lunch. It had been a long time since she had had three such grateful listeners. Nobody mentioned the name of Hugh Hartlein.

Inspector Nelsing arrived a little after two o'clock, and Georgine withdrew to the kitchen. For a short time he talked to Cass and Ryn together in the living-room; then the swing-door flashed and Ryn appeared alone, to sink without ceremony into one of the kitchen chairs. She laid her hand flat upon the table-top and massaged its enamel with a slow nervous sweep of her palm. "It's just awful," she said just above a whisper, her green-gray eyes focused on a point beyond Georgine. "Poor Cass, my poor darling, if only it needn't have happened to *her!* She can't bear to think it's suicide because she's afraid that might somehow have been her fault; and she said—before she took time to think—that someone must have murdered him."

"It couldn't have been an accident?"

Ryn looked full at her, with an odd shine in her eyes. "You don't know about the inhaler?"

When she had finished, Georgine sat silent and appalled. "But," she said finally, "it's so *elaborate*—who could—I mean, anyone who wants to kill himself usually takes sleeping tablets, or jumps off the Golden Gate Bridge. This isn't—"

Ryn nodded. "That's it. But you think of—the other things, and you can't imagine who—"

From the living-room came the sound of Cass's voice crying out, "No, no! That can't be right—" and then Nelsing's, firm and quiet but unintelligible.

"What's he doing to her?" said Ryn in a sort of wail.

"Was he tough?"

"Oh, no, no. Just horribly polite, you know, but—frightening. I know he thinks we're lying."

"That's Nelse for you. He'd suspect his own mother of evading, just because she was a woman."

"But with us—it seems the Godfrey got at him and told some absurd story about having seen Cass go down to Hugh's rooming-house stealthily, at night, and quarreling—it's one of her crazy dreams, of course Cass did nothing of the kind, but Nelse doesn't seem sure at all. If he believes anything the Godfrey tells him he's sunk from the start!"

"Dear me! But even if Miss Godfrey were right, surely—"

"Well, she's not. I'd swear it. Nelse said she couldn't be certain it was Cass, and he looked at me as if it might have been *I* who—"

"Even then," said Georgine, "what would that have to do with his death last night?"

Ryn sighed, pressed her palms together hard, and said in a low voice, "Don't you see? That inhaler thing could have been planted on him any time. —Good Lord, what am I talking about? As if Cass of all people—"

A familiar head moved past the kitchen window, and in a moment Todd came in the back door. He greeted Ryn, laid a hand lightly on Georgine's shoulder, and glanced toward the swing-door. "Nelse still at it?" he asked.

"Yes. Did you have lunch, Todd?"

"I did, thank you, but I'll have a few of those cookies." The plate from luncheon was still on the table, and he helped himself.

"May I, too?" said Ryn. "They're awfully good, and this affair seems to be affecting me disgracefully—I'm hungry still, even after I ate two helps of everything at lunch. So greedy of me." She smiled suddenly and beautifully.

"I'm afraid your poor sister is really upset, though," said Georgine. "She didn't touch a thing but coffee and fruit. I began to wonder if I had you mixed up, because she said something about *your* having, uh, digestive trouble."

Ryn's green eyes went at once brilliant and blank. "Cass does exaggerate so; she worries about me as if she were my mother. Once in a while I do have an upset, but not today— and your food tasted especially—oh, listen; I think they must be through in there."

"*Ryn,*" said Cass Johnson, arriving unceremoniously through the door, "come in here, there's something terribly awkward that I hadn't known a thing about." Her round pretty face looked almost haggard under the smoothly upswept hair. She glanced around at Georgine and Todd. "It's terrible to keep you out of your own living-room. Nelse won't mind, he'll explain."

Nelsing looked up with a sardonic gleam as the party filed in. "Can't keep you out of it, can I, Mac?" he murmured. "Well, it's up to Cass... It seems she's the beneficiary of some of Hartlein's insurance."

"But what's wrong with that?" Ryn said in soft bewilderment. "I don't see—when was it taken out?"

"Just before the, uh, trip to Reno," Nelsing said. "Probably as soon as she'd agreed to marry him. Of course the fact that she let him down immediately after the ceremony didn't affect the policy's validity, he'd paid a year's premiums in advance. He could have had the beneficiary changed, but I take it he hoped to make Cass change her mind again."

"He did, Nelse," Ryn put in. "He was always at her, but she never gave him any hope, we told you that! Still I don't see— that policy can't still be good? He hadn't paid on it again, had he? Because that was—let's see, over thirteen months ago."

Nelsing stretched his handsome length in the blue chair and nodded. "In the ordinary course of events, it would be valid for a while more; that is, if Cass wanted to pay up a few back premiums, she could get the five thousand dollars. That's in a clause in fine print, the sort of thing most people don't read on their policies. There's a nice question here, though; if Hartlein died by his own hand, the policy's automatically canceled by the usual two-year clause."

"And I kept insisting," Cass broke out, "that Hugh couldn't have! I swear I didn't know about the policy's still being good, I didn't even know it was still made out to me—but I talk and talk, and now it sounds as if I wanted the money, and were just trying to make out that he didn't kill himself so that I'd be sure to get it."

"But why shouldn't you take it, dear? That is, if it's coming to you at all. We both accepted our share of poor Bell's estate, she wanted us to have it. Why is this different?" Ryn looked around appealingly at the silent McKinnons. "It wouldn't count as defrauding an insurance company, would it? —Or look, Cass, if you feel truly uncomfortable about it, you could pay up the back premiums and then not take the money, give it away."

"Then who'd get it?"

"Mrs. Hartlein, I suppose," Ryn said, suddenly doubtful. "But isn't she provided for somehow?"

Nelsing cleared his throat. "Hartlein's mother benefits from a much larger policy, taken out eighteen months ago. He seems to have been a most dutiful son, because he stinted himself on clothes and lodgings to pay for that. It still raises that nice question, though." He got to his feet. "Was his death suicide or murder? You both knew him well, you can't seem to make up your minds about it." He stood looking down at the two Johnsons, unsmiling. "If it was suicide, one or the other of you might be able to figure out the reason. If it was murder, there may be a few things you're not telling; but until we know if it was, naturally I can't put any pressure on you. Thanks for as much as you've been willing to tell."

Cass gave a sudden and forlorn little laugh. "I wish this were ten years ago, Howard Nelsing, and it were Friday night at the house, and you calling up to ask for a date! Well—I suppose you've tried to be nice."

Nelsing, about to leave, turned. "I can't ever be what you call nice, in the face of lies. Can't you see that, Cass? And if there's nothing on your mind, why have both you girls been lying off and on? Good-bye, Georgine and Mac. Thanks a lot for taking us in."

A moment after he had disappeared, the Johnsons also left. Cass remarked wearily that if the reporters were still haunting their street they might as well run the gauntlet now. Todd saw them to their car, returned and repaired straight to the kitchen where he found some beer.

"And do you know what struck me as a li'le odder than anything?" he said half an hour later, at the end of their fruitless if fascinated discussion. "There was one way to dispose of that insurance money that didn't occur to either of the Johnsons."

"Yes," said Georgine. "Not to pay up the premiums—and not to get the money at all."

❀ ❀ ❀

The inquiry into the death of Hugh Hartlein sank quietly beneath the surface of published news, and went on without causing so much as a ripple to show its direction. It had never been Nelsing's habit to confide the progress of his work to anyone outside his office, but on other occasions Todd McKinnon had been able at least to chart his general progress through news releases. This time there was nothing. Todd tortured the memory of Beethoven, and worked grimly at a story whose real basis had "gone out from under him," as he told his wife. He'd have to finish it now, but it didn't have the true ring.

Georgine asked how he'd worked it out. "I had Hartlein as the Policeman's Li'le Helper before the fact," Todd said, "going to the law with suspicions that couldn't be proved or disproved, laying the groundwork for a crime of his own. It's been used before, but it's not a bad gimmick. And now, damn it, he goes and gets himself bumped off—just to spite me, no doubt. I have to switch him from murderer to victim, and the whole yarn was slanted the other way."

"You have some suspects, all set up," said Georgine thoughtfully. "A next-door neighbor who regards the victim as an obstacle in his love-life, and who could easily have fixed up that horrible gadget and left it on his desk—I suppose it couldn't have been sent by mail, Todd, as a sample or something?"

"Could be," Todd ruminated aloud, "but I doubt it. What's to keep the victim from taking a good sniff of it as soon as the package is opened, and dying on the spot, leaving the wrappings for the police? Seems a lot more likely that somebody just put the inhaler in his pocket. Well, you're right—we have the Damn Fool, who acts nervous and guilty and loses his temper when he's interrogated, and who works in a laboratory where there's cyanide to burn. There's a Repeater for Ritual Reasons—"

"An old lady, I suppose, who's the head of a mysterious cult?"

"No, no, Georgine—this Repeater is impenetrably disguised, I'd make him a middle-aged man in the story. The mysterious cult, of course, stays in."

"I'm sure nobody could connect the fiction with the reality," said Georgine dryly. "But sticking to reality for a minute, you've also got a Maniac-Sane-on-the-Surface, only she isn't—she's as goofy as they come—and two mutually adoring sisters one of whom is being pestered by the victim."

"And," said Todd, "the remotest set of motives anyone ever heard of." He whacked his mouth-organ viciously against the palm of his hand. "I don't believe any of 'em myself, and how am I going to get a reader to swallow 'em? Hartlein wasn't a real obstacle or danger to anyone, so far as I can see. He wasn't actually a backslider from the Beyond-Truth himself, and there didn't seem much danger of his actually corrupting any of the true believers. He'd already told his suspicions about the other deaths, and murder couldn't be proved in any of those cases. *Why did he have to die?*"

"The Board of Health eliminated him," said Georgine, getting up to terminate the discussion, "as a carrier of the common cold. There were a couple of days there when I could have bumped him off myself!"

It was on Saturday of that week that she received what amounted to a Royal Command. The very voice over the telephone struck terror to her heart, although it was as beautiful as she remembered it and held no more than a faint tone of amusement.

"Mrs. McKinnon," said Chloe Majendie, "I believe you are the Mrs. Wyeth who called on me for an interview?"

"Yes, I am," said Georgine in a subdued tone. "I hope you'll let me apologize for that, Mrs. Majendie, I—my husband really is a writer, you know, and there were, uh, various reasons why it seemed best at the time not to give my own name."

"Yes. It's about those reasons that I wanted to talk to you. Could you find it convenient to come and see me, perhaps this afternoon?"

"Today—Saturday? We—we had promised my young daughter we'd take her to the City, and—"

"Possibly you could come early, bringing her, and go on from here," said Mrs. Majendie inexorably. "You see, Mrs. McKinnon, I have had some conversation with the police, but I am not sure about the basis of their suspicions. I think you know, and I think perhaps you owe it to me to pass it on."

"I—I think perhaps we do."

"You see," the lovely voice continued, "I understand about your husband's profession. He might find it useful to have some first-hand impressions."

Georgine hung up somewhat dazed, after making arrangements for the afternoon. She had not contemplated refusing, but if she had, there was that offer of a deal—of course, one didn't know quite what kind of a deal it was, Beyond-Truth or the McCoy.

"But maybe," she said hopefully to Todd that afternoon, "the cosmic kind will make you just as good a plot."

Todd said it was possible. He had expressed a preference for leaving their car outside the Johnsons' garage and climbing the zigzag path along the cliff. He now paused beside the Majendie greenhouse, as he had paused at nearly every turn in the path, looking downward at the studio cottage, some new angle of whose surroundings became visible at each level. He said softly, "Miss Godfrey of the green fingers presumably spends much of her time in here, or working on those hand-some borders along the path. Makes a nice view for her."

"And the girls are well aware of that," Georgine murmured in return. "It would feel awful, to know that you couldn't move without—" She broke off as Barby came toiling up behind them, mute and resigned at the postponement of her excursion. "It won't take long, darling, truly it won't," said Barby's mother, in an uneasy state of feeling apologetic toward almost everyone. "And there isn't much more of the climb."

They were almost at the top when a faint growl sounded from the shrubbery above, and a streak of fawn and white described a curve through the air and landed on the path in front of them. She recognized the sound and the coloration: it was a Siamese cat, then, that she had heard and seen on her first visit to Cuckoo Canyon. It faced them for a moment with an expressionless gleam of blue eyes in a black face, and then bounded away toward the upper level. The McKinnons, following, arrived at the rear of the lovely garden.

At its far side was visible a strange grayish hill, which on second glance turned out to be the mistress of the house, clad in a long tweed skirt and bent double to inspect a rock plant. Todd's eyes crinkled, and in a tone audible to Georgine alone he muttered, "High-o the derriére, the farmer in the dell."

Georgine tried to stifle a laugh, which refused to die. In vain she bit her tongue, dug fingernails into her palm and rapidly envisioned Barby laid waste by incurable disease; she had to advance toward her hostess crimson-faced and with tears in her eyes. In one way, it was awkward; in another, fortu-nate, for she had lost her uncomfortable awe of the old lady.

Mrs. Majendie came erect at the sound of their approach. "It was good of you to come," she remarked, stripping the glove and extending a big hand. "This is Mr. McKinnon, who is *not* a detective."

"I'm glad to have that se'led early," Todd said.

"And this is our daughter Barby," said Georgine, at last in control of her voice.

Chloe Majendie stood looking down at the blonde head, the freckled nose and the City-going outfit; her youthful eyes were grave and considering. Then she smiled and offered her hand to Barby in turn. "So you're at the Valley Ranch School," she remarked, "and doing very well, I hear. I'm glad they brought you along, Barby."

Barby looked up at her seriously, and something happened to her plain little face that was like the turning on of an inner high-powered bulb. —Indeed! thought her mother, watching— she's taken one of her fancies to the old lady. That may make things easier, because I honestly don't see how anyone could resist Barby when she looks like that—

"We'll go into the house, if you don't mind," said Chloe, leading the way into the redwood porch. "It's windy in the garden. You look rather warm after that climb, Mrs. McKinnon, you don't want to catch cold." Georgine followed, aware that her state of confusion had not gone unnoticed. Chloe Majendie had the air of a Mother Superior of long experience, who missed nothing.

The door opened directly into the living-room, but the folds of a huge screen cut off draughts and the immediate view. The McKinnons rounded the screen and stopped, Todd impassive and courteous, Georgine involuntarily blinking.

She had never before seen a room which so unobtrusively, from its every bit of furnishing, its every fiber, exhaled the presence of money. There had been no attempt to coordinate style or period of decoration, but there was no object that was not beautiful, and not one inharmonious note. Georgine, moving forward across a huge and magnificent Persian rug, noted isolated objects as if in a dream: something that she thought must be a black-hawthorn vase, a massive radio-phonograph of a make that sold for a minimum of fifteen hundred dollars, and a silver bowl of such purity of line that it might have been made by Paul Revere. There was a great window across the west side of the room, which in clear weather would show a glorious sweep of view. Today there was little to see but clouds, but the window was framed in heavy folds of drapery, hand-woven and shot with faint threads of metal. —And I'll bet Dorothy Liebes made those with her own hands, said Georgine to herself.

Among these objects Chloe Majendie, in her broad tweed suit and the uncompromising hat which she did not remove, might have looked out of place and did not. She sat down in a petit-point armchair of beautifully muted colors, and the room became subordinate to her. She said, "Barby, in that little room to your left you'll find some books that I think you'll enjoy," and Barby, still radiant, melted away without a moment's hesitation.

CHAPTER FIVE

"**I SHOULD LIKE TO** tell you my side of the story first," said the old lady, going straight to the point. She looked from one to another of the McKinnons; Georgine saw that Todd was returning her look with even more than his usual concentration, almost as if he were trying to remember something.

"Young Mr. Hartlein," Mrs. Majendie resumed, "has had a peculiar idea of me throughout the past two years. He evidently believed that I had great influence over my nieces, so much so that they were afraid to cross my will or deny any of my principles. When there was that unfortunate affair with Cass, a year or so ago, he came storming up here to see me, convinced that if I'd only release her, as he put it, he could get her back. I told him, of course, that I had nothing to say about my niece's affairs of the heart, and of course he didn't believe me." She folded the big hands in her lap, and again her glance went from Georgine to Todd. "Cass and Ryn have had young men around them since they started high school—poor Bell, too. It didn't seem to matter sometimes—" she smiled slightly, "which of the girls had which men; young David Shere, for example, was in love with Bell first; she chose Sidney Grant and he transferred his attentions to Ryn; and now, from all I hear, he's courting Cass. Now, there's a man who might possibly have been good for any one of them, but as luck would have it, the ones they've chosen so far haven't—in my view—had much to recommend them. Sidney—" she shook her head, "in the eyes of the world was a rich young man with a good deal of personal charm. In truth, I think, he was nothing at all: a hollow man who had to fill himself with alcohol before he, himself, felt any semblance of being. When I mourned for Sibella," said Mrs. Majendie, her gaze traveling far past her listeners, "I could not be very sorry for her death at the beginning of the path she had chosen; I was sad because she had chosen that path. But I would not have forbidden her choice, I didn't forbid it, and I couldn't have influenced Cass if she'd asked me about her own marriage."

Her eyes came back to Todd. "If she had asked me, I should have had to say that I did not like Hugh Hartlein. He was the opposite of Bell's husband, there was too much of him as a person; there was no resilience, no compromise in his mind from his own ideas of what was due him or what he should do for others. Or did you gather that impression of him?" she inquired suddenly.

Todd took a deep breath and nodded. "Very much so, Mrs. Majendie."

There was a soft sound behind a door at the end of the room. "Come in if you like, Joan," said Mrs. Majendie without turning her head, and the door opened to admit Miss Godfrey, her black eyes startled and glittering as she recognized the McKinnons. She darted to a seat with a rattle of beads; following her in a pounce came the Siamese cat, which—as Georgine told herself—seemed constantly appearing and disappearing like the Cheshire one. The cat leaped to the top of a sofa and curled itself there, regarding the visitors unwinkingly.

"So," the old lady continued, "when he came here on the evening of his death, to ask me once more if I wouldn't 'release' Cass, there was no way to make an impression on him. He'd come in a peculiar frame of mind, too," she put in with a sudden chuckle, "rather defeatist—as if he were asking John L. Lewis to dissolve the miners' union."

The McKinnons, attempting to follow this story with grave attention, were surprised into laughter. "I can imagine him," Todd said, his agate eyes alive and interested.

"Well, this John L. said no, in the politest manner she could manage. He gave me a good scolding," said old Chloe, her lips still curved in a smile, "and took a few digs at my husband's philosophy, and I couldn't do much to comfort him. Poor young fellow, he was wretched with a cold, and he seemed so dependent on that inhaler, that I was quite concerned for him."

"Chloe—when you're through, there's something—" Joan Godfrey muttered.

"It can wait, Joan. He left me," Mrs. Majendie continued, "in rather a distraught state of mind. He actually forgot the inhaler, it was lying on the end table at his side and I had to call his attention to it."

Joan Godfrey gave a sharp squeak and clapped a hand over her mouth. Old Chloe turned a tolerant eye upon her. "Yes, Joan, I know; for some reason you omitted that detail when you talked to the police, and they were surprised when I mentioned it. Of course," she added to Todd, "every omission of the kind, or any sign of reluctance to have me tell it, makes the detail more important to the police. Isn't that so, Mr. McKinnon?"

Todd would not commit himself. "Inspector Nelsing is an experienced officer," he said smoothly. "I doubt that he—"

At this moment the Siamese cat took off through the air, without warning, and landed on Georgine's shoulder with a good heavy thump. "Ow!" said Georgine, in shock and pain.

"Dian, get down," the old lady commanded. Dian dug in for the winter, from the way it felt, and gave a baleful growl.

"Oh, she must *like* Mrs. McKinnon," said Joan Godfrey fondly.

"Get your animal down, Joan, if you please." Chloe's voice was crisp, and Miss Godfrey obeyed her with a nervous jump, but none too soon for the struggling victim.

"I hope she didn't hurt you, Mrs. McKinnon," said Chloe in a voice that would have charmed away more serious wounds than Georgine's slight scratches and dishevelment. Georgine said not at all, and reflected that every time she came to Cuckoo Canyon she set herself up as a kind of target. She brushed her shoulder and felt unobtrusively for her best hat, which had been nearly knocked from its moorings. "Please go on, Mrs. Majendie."

"There isn't much more," said the old lady, smiling at her. "I could understand why the police were interested in that last visit, though I couldn't define for them whether I thought Hartlein was in a suicidal frame of mind when he left. When I learned what killed him, I understood why they'd asked what we used to fumigate our greenhouse."

"May *I* ask what you use?" said Todd.

"Cyanide, Mr. McKinnon... I was also able to tell them that both Joan and I are fairly handy at jobs with small tools; Joan, indeed, is a good amateur electrician." Miss Godfrey's beads rattled; she stood by the door, through which she had just pushed the cat, and looked down at her tightly clasped hands.

"But I could not understand," concluded Mrs. Majendie, "what conceivable reason they thought I might have had for wishing that young man's death. I think you have a clue to that, Mr. McKinnon."

Todd drew a long breath. He had got out of his chair a few minutes before to rescue his beleaguered wife, but had been forestalled by Joan; he had gone back and at once sunk into the motionless listening posture with which he had received the rest of Chloe's story. Now he sat up, at once relaxed and alert, and measured glances with Mrs. Majendie.

"I think I know, from Hartlein's point of view if not from Nelsing's," he said. "Hugh Hartlein tried to convince himself—and us—that you could guide the Hand of God."

Joan Godfrey spoke from the dim end of the room. "It needs no guidance," she said in a sibilant whisper.

"Joan," said the old lady without inflection.

There was silence. Chloe continued to fix Todd with her penetrating glance; she said slowly, "And on what, do you know, did he base that remarkable idea?"

"On the history of your religious group. He felt that once a person had joined it, that person was—in for life, on pain of your displeasure. And to a person with that obsession, Mrs. Majendie, any incident could have been twisted to fit the theory. There was the death of Mr. and Mrs. Grant, for example—"

"Bell's death?" said Mrs. Majendie, still gazing intently. "How was I supposed to have had any part in that? By the Evil Eye, or by actual tampering with Sidney's car?"

"That I can't say," Todd replied. "But you can see how he blamed the failure of his marriage on you; not because you advised Cass against him, but because she was afraid she'd die if she went through with it."

The old lady's lips twitched. "That's utter nonsense, if I ever heard it. You'd see it too if you knew Cass. The child never mentions the Beyond-Truth, and as for being afraid of me—!" She thought for a moment. "But—yes, that explains it, his hatred of my husband's philosophy, his idea that it was cruel and barbaric, when as a matter of fact—h'm. Yes, I see."

Georgine, listening in fascination, thought—She talks about "my husband's philosophy" as if the man were more important than the belief. I wonder how much *she* believes in it, actually—

"Well. Did Hartlein think I planned to wreak vengeance on all my nieces, Mr. McKinnon?"

Todd smiled. "He did mention poison."

The light of battle began to appear in old Chloe's eyes. "Ryn, I suppose. The young fool! No wonder nobody dared to explain this to me before."

"Well," said Todd peaceably, "don't scare *me* out of explaining it."

Mrs. Majendie relaxed and grinned at him. They seemed, Georgine thought, to understand each other very well. "Then tell me the rest. Hmf! If I'm as formidable as all that, no wonder we keep our converts, eh, Joan?" Miss Godfrey made a small scandalized sound. "Any more?"

"Yes, indeed. There was a list of names, most of 'em obviously faked, though there were one or two I didn't recognize; obscure story characters, no doubt."

"So? Who were they?"

Todd shrugged. "Your niece Mrs. Grant—somebody called Stella Dubois—"

Georgine remembered almost automatically the last occasion on which a strange name had been introduced into a conversation with these Beyond-Truthers; her head turned to see how Miss Godfrey was affected by this one.

Miss Godfrey was gazing at Todd with her squirrel-bright eyes opened to their fullest extent, and her jaw dropping. Then her look darted to Mrs. Majendie.

"Stella Dubois," said Chloe after a moment's pause. The rich overtones of her voice hummed away into a silence that lasted until she chose to speak again. "Yes, Stella is dead. She died many years ago; her child had been stillborn two days before."

Once more the silence held. Georgine felt as if ants were walking up her spine, but she could not have moved or spoken.

"Now I wonder," said Chloe Majendie musingly at last, "how he got hold of that." She looked at Todd. "Well, no matter. That is the whole case, Mr. McKinnon?"

"That's the whole case. But there's one more thing I'd like to tell you, though it may be irrelevant. I've been wondering, since my first sight of you this afternoon, when we might have met before—or where I'd seen somebody like you."

"Yes?"

"In Hartlein's room there was a photograph of his mother. You and she look somewhat alike."

"God help the poor woman," said Mrs. Majendie, with a little twist of her lips. She nodded, her gaze going past him. "Yes, I understand a good deal now. I'm much indebted to you, Mrs. McKinnon, for letting me meet your husband. Would your daughter like to come in now?"

"Chloe," said Joan Godfrey, coming nearer, "if you're really through—there's someone who wants to see you at three o'clock."

"Oh? I'm disappointed; I'd hoped for a purely social visit with all the McKinnons, but in that case—"

She went to the door of the library and glanced in at the tow head, bent above some unidentified tome. "I have to say good-bye to you now, my dear," she told Barby gently, and turned again to Georgine. "Will you come into my room, and we'll see if we can repair some of the damage that wretched cat did to you?"

"I'd be glad to." Georgine followed the erect old figure across a hall and into another beautiful room. "And—you know, I've been wondering about your cat. I can't remember ever seeing a lone Siamese before, most people have a pair."

"Joan did too, once," said Mrs. Majendie, indicating the chaste dressing-table.

Georgine hesitated. She remembered, with an odd creeping sensation, the little scene she had observed on her first visit: the hand pouring milk into a saucer, and the cat lapping it. She was almost afraid to ask her question. It was like setting a light to the end of an innocent-looking string, and not knowing... "Did the cat die?" she said as casually as she could.

"Disappeared," said Mrs. Majendie inattentively, finding a whisk broom in her closet.

"Oh? How long ago?"

"Two or three years. If you'll turn a little, my dear, I'll get those hairs... Now and then I wish Dian would disappear, too. Where's the beast now?" She glanced across the hall. "Ah, yes.

Your child is making friends with her. That's a very engaging young girl you have, Mrs. McKinnon."

"Thank you," said Georgine, breaking against her will into a fatuous maternal smile.

"She has Mr. McKinnon's coloring, but nothing else."

Georgine laughed. "That's little wonder; she is my child by my first husband. He died before she was born."

The alert eyes met hers in the mirror. "Hard," said the old lady simply.

This was not exactly a powder-room, but it seemed to be almost as productive of confidences; Georgine had her mouth open to make some, and caught herself just in time. Mrs. Majendie couldn't be interested in those brief months of marriage with Jim Wyeth, in the unformed and undisciplined love that had never had time to take enduring shape, nor in the terror of the three weeks she had lived through alone until his body had been found far down a Colorado river-bed, in the wake of a flash flood. She had actually been on the verge of confiding that after Barby's birth she could have no more children...

Although she knew that no words had been spoken, she had a queer feeling that a great deal had passed between her and Mrs. Majendie; the eyes that met hers in the mirror were full of comprehension. She said, "Todd is just like her real father, she's never known any other."

The old lady nodded. "You have a good husband, too. I like him; and I think he sees a long way into things." She waited a moment; when she spoke again her voice was lowered to the softest of murmurs. "He may even see beyond the world's truth, and if he does—I sympathize with him. It is often unpleasant. Sometimes it is even—unsafe."

Georgine's lipstick slipped from her fingers and clattered on the table-top. She said, "I know, I never have been able to forget that since I've known him." She was breathing fast. "But he thinks of it all in terms of fiction, not of truth!"

"You've heard of jesting Pilate, my dear?" said old Chloe.

They went out. Barby and Todd were still in the little room, gazing together at a small portrait hung between windows; the picture of a bearded man, deep-eyed, memorably handsome. Mrs. Majendie answered their unexpressed question. "That is my husband," she said.

Joan Godfrey, fluttering on the edge of the group, reached to readjust a small flower arrangement that stood below the portrait. "Chloe," she said urgently, "it's almost three."

Barby glanced out the window. "Look, Mamma," she said with interest, "there's Mr. Nelsing and Mr. Slater. How did they know we were here?"

"Those two? No, they must be after me again," said Mrs. Majendie with an ineffable accent of scorn. Georgine thought, —Cass said they wouldn't get much change out of the old lady, and I'll bet she was right!— "Are they the visitors we're expecting, Joan? Did they tell you what it's about this time?"

Miss Godfrey looked at her, the black eyes rolling brightly sideways.

"They did, I can see. Well, out with it!"

"It's so absurd—" Joan Godfrey muttered.

"Then we can all laugh. What is it?"

"It's—about what they found in the compost heap."

Chloe Majendie fixed her with a sudden look. "In our compost heap? Do you mean where they were raking, yesterday afternoon?" Joan nodded. "Did the Inspector tell you he'd found anything?"

"No, Chloe. I went down after they had gone and looked about myself, and for a time I found nothing at all, but there was a vibration of something—it was in direct denial of Truth, so that the waves were very sharp, and I didn't dare to stop looking. And when I found it, I hoped that the police had overlooked it; but there must have been others."

"Joan, *what* did you find? That young Inspector is ringing the doorbell, and I prefer to be aware of what he's talking about."

Hastily, mutely, before she scuttled to the door, Joan Godfrey brought a hand out of her pocket and exhibited a few scraps of metal. They were twisted and bent, but one of them showed the threads of a screw top, and another the fragments of a label.

The scraps had once been part of a metal inhaler, and it looked very much as if someone had been experimenting at taking it apart.

There was a door from the library into the garden, and the McKinnons made their exit unobserved. Todd and Georgine murmured together as they went hastily down the hairpin curves of the path.

"She'll say they were planted."

"Certainly, and they could have been; but that's what one would say anyway."

"That Godfrey woman's scared to death that Chloe's guilty."

"Or maybe just that she'll be accused; or maybe she *wants* her to be! Those vibrations of evil worked amazingly well—do you suppose she planted the inhalers herself?"

"Or is the old lady above justice, and would she throw them away, with magnificent carelessness, and not worry about their being found?"

Georgine slackened her pace, to let Barby get a little ahead. "Todd, if Mrs. Majendie had by any chance bumped off Hartlein, isn't the only conceivable motive a ritual one?"

"The only one I could guess," said Todd, "but that might not be the real one."

"Don't confuse the issue. I've been wondering just how much she believes in it herself. D'you notice she says that people *die*, not that they 'pass into the cosmos' or whatever the Beyond-Truthers say? What if she kept the thing going more as a memorial to the old boy than as a conviction of her own?"

"Seems like a lot of trouble to go to," Todd objected mildly.

"Look, she wasn't just one of his disciples, she loved him. She loved him as a man."

"Lots of women keep flowers in front of a portrait of the dear departed."

"That's Joan's doing, I bet you," said Georgine scornfully. "But Chloe has another picture of him. It's on her bed-table, and it's a little old snapshot—and he's in a pair of overalls, and laughing, and not a bit Messiah-like. He must have been attractive as all-get-out, if you happen to care for beards. But you don't have to believe in what a man teaches, if you love him enough." They had reached the level now, and Barby was running ahead to the car. Georgine added, "I leave Jim's picture in Barby's room, I don't have a snapshot in a cloisonné frame by my bed."

"I should damn' well hope not," said Todd, feeling for his car keys. Georgine giggled. "That," she amended, "was by way of a figure of speech."

She stood still, and put a hand on his arm. "Remind me to tell you later about the cat clue; it fizzled out completely. And, Todd—are you going to point out that resemblance to Nelse— between the picture and Mrs. Majendie?"

"Point out to Nelse?" her husband repeated with fine scorn. "That guy doesn't need things pointed out to him, I'll bet he was onto that while I was still getting my eyes into focus in Hartlein's room. —Yes, cricket, we're coming as fast as our age will allow."

The McKinnons never asked Inspector Nelsing to dinner while he was working on a case in which Todd might be interested, a delicate shade of feeling which he had always seemed to appreciate; yet on this Sunday evening he had flabbergasted them by calling up and asking himself. "We'd love to have you," Georgine had replied, and then inquired candidly, "Why tonight, Nelse? Strictly from hunger?"

"Well, no, not strictly," Nelsing had said. Before and during the meal, however, he talked with great vigor about anything except the death of Hugh Hartlein. Georgine was puzzled. He acted oddly as if he were shying away from the subject and yet wished to mention it.

She went round the living-room windows after dinner, carefully closing the blinds. She was conscious of Nelsing's look, half-scornful and half-amused, and was not astonished to hear him remark, "Scared of your own shadow, even in a case like this?"

"Now look," she replied tartly, "don't you sit there, full to the collar-bone with our meatballs and spaghetti and two pieces of lemon pie, and poke fun at me."

"Man's got no manners," said Todd.

"Man's speaking the truth," Nelsing rejoined.

"All right, you ought to know by now that I behave with, uh, normal caution. We did neglect the blinds for a while, and Hartlein spied on us, that night he came. What's more, we have that empty house next door, the Manfreds won't be home for two weeks more. I go in now and then—they left me the key so I could use their ironer and air the place for them—and I fairly hold my breath every time I open the door."

"You've got Berkeley's best and finest patrolling the houses whose owners are away."

"Well, sure, they drive by every night and look up to see if there are any suspicious lights or movements; you couldn't expect 'em to do more. But what if somebody's just waiting there in the dark? And there's that hedge across from our house to the Manfreds', in front of the drying yard. There could be a regular witches' sabbath going on there, and your officer wouldn't be able to see from the street."

"Now, hold on, Georgine," Todd said. "I really think that would attract his attention—one way or another."

"Maybe you're right. The girls fly in, I understand."

"Dressed in a li'le ointment and nothing more."

Georgine laughed. She certainly was not going to express to Nelsing her queer feeling of the presence that waited outside, and that seemed to retreat a little when the house was enclosed from the night. It should not be troubling her now, in the presence of her husband and a police inspector; nevertheless she tilted the slats of the blind in a front window, and glanced down toward the street.

There was someone down there now, going past Nelsing's car. She had caught a brief flash of light from a torch. That, however, could easily be one of the neighbors walking his dog.

"All right," Nelsing was saying, "make your cracks now and get them over with; but I need to talk with you two."

"Ha ha, so the police are baffled," said Todd rapidly, "and have been forced to ask for help from the brilliant amateur at whose theories they had always sneered. There you are, Nelse—it didn't hurt much, did it?"

"I'm assuming you'll tell the truth," Nelsing went on imperturbably, "because you haven't a stake in the business."

"You do pay nice compliments," Georgine murmured.

"It's natural for the rest of them to lie. There's that question, was it suicide or murder? Either way it goes there's trouble for somebody, or loss of money. You should have heard Hartlein's mother on the subject." Nelsing shook his head with reminiscent pain. "She thought he'd killed himself, you could see it sticking out all over her, but she can't bear to lose out on that insurance; so she has to thunder out that Sonny wasn't the suicidal type. What does she suggest instead? Oh, it must have been murder, but she hasn't a shred of evidence to back that up. Battle-axe," he added thoughtfully.

Todd grinned. "What do the others think?"

"They're wavering back and forth—all except the insurance company."

"I take it they hold out for suicide."

"Naturally. I must say that Mrs. Majendie and the coroner's court agree," said Nelsing with irony. "They prefer not to judge by whose hand deceased came to his sad end."

"There's one person who hasn't a stake in the matter—young Shere."

"We don't *know* that he has a stake in the matter. He's the worst of the lot; worked so hard telling me about Hartlein's depression and nerves in the week before he died, that he might as well have yelled 'murder' in my ear. He did point out," said Nelsing thoughtfully, "that no matter which way he expressed himself, it seemed to be wrong. He was right about that. If this case ever came to trial, either counsel could tear him to pieces in five minutes. I can't crack down on him, of course—nor on any of 'em."

"H'm," Todd said. "So you're still on the fence yourself."

"Sure. Damn' near everything we've got points either way. Take that business of the series of ritual murders— it's the worst poppycock I ever heard—and yet, Hartlein landed it on you and then died. We can't afford to ignore it completely."

"I know," Todd said. "I laughed like a fool when I first heard about it. Then we began mentioning some of the names that came into that list, and—we got a reaction. I don't suppose, uh, there were any more that he didn't include?"

Nelsing shrugged. "We checked with the Contra Costa people. This is all unofficial, of course, no reasons given. Sure, there have been deaths in that community, plenty of 'em since it was started. Bound to be, when most of the disciples were forty or more when they joined. There'd be an appendix here, and a case of food poisoning there, and a cancer another time. All open and above board, physicians' certificates and no suspicion. The Beyond-Truthers don't do faith healing. There was old Nikko Majendie himself, for that matter; he died of what sounds like virus pneumonia, though they didn't have that diagnosis then. Carried him off in four or five days."

"So?" said Todd, looking at him. "You can't help wondering if he was a backslider, too; and if any of those other people might have been."

Nelsing stirred rather uneasily. "No way to find out unless you went out to the Colony and put some of the disciples through the mill. Fat chance we'd have of getting anything there, what with the fact that we've got no authority in that county, and the fact that they wouldn't tell us if there was anything screwy about those deaths, and if they did open up it'd likely be Cosmic Truth and not related to the common variety—and the most important fact, that we're not sure if this is a murder. I'm stymied," he added in an unusual burst of irritation, "and yet I can't leave the thing alone. What happened to that Bourbon I brought up with me?"

He was served; he took a drink and appeared to be calmed by it. Todd, sitting down with his own drink, remarked, "Just the same, for my own part I'd like to see that colony. It's only fifteen or twenty miles from Barby's school. When we took her back this afternoon, I was tempted to make a detour."

Nelsing appeared to be turning over something in his mind. "Wonder how much they'd tell us about personalities, if nobody brought up the subject of mysterious deaths? There's the Godfrey woman, for instance. I'd like to know if she's been loony from the start or got that way after she'd started traveling into the cosmos. Maybe they're all loony."

"Now there," said Georgine, laying down the dress she was lengthening for her daughter, "is somebody I can see committing a chain of ritual murders—Godfrey, I mean. Only if she did, she would never be able to resist pinning the sign of the Pointing Hand on each victim's chest, and maybe staying around to gloat."

"You have a point there," Todd said. "Question is, would she have the ability to kill off those people in so many ways? Your Maniac-Sane-on-the-Surface generally sticks to one *modus operandi*; that in itself becomes part of his mania. Isn't that so, Nelse?"

"Most criminals stick to the same *m. o.*," said Nelsing unencouragingly.

"No, if this is a case of Vengeance to Backsliders," Todd pursued, "it's a li'le too subtly done for Miss Godfrey's type. The old lady could manage it if anyone could."

"Barby *liked* Mrs. Majendie," said Georgine.

Nelsing gave her a withering look. "How about dogs, do they love her too?"

"Why, I don't know!" said Georgine brightly. "Couldn't we borrow a dog and take it up there—"

"Or better yet," Todd interrupted, "test Barby on a series of known murderers, and if she lit up for any of 'em we'd know she's not infallible, but if she didn't we could hire her out as a human litmus paper. About time the cricket began to make you some money, Georgine."

Nelsing relaxed into a grim smile. "Well, so far we haven't any better way of testing Mrs. Majendie. With that manner of hers she could be lying all around the clock, and you couldn't prove it. There's one thing, of course, it's not only Barby that likes her. The Johnson girls do, and she brought 'em up."

"But how do they like her? As a grand old aunt, or as a Leader?" Todd inquired.

"Oh, that Leader business—there may have been a touch of that when they were in their teens, but before long it wore off. Ryn got to Cal before the others did, and it didn't take her a week to get into the swing. I guess she passed it on to the others, because they were three of the most normal girls you ever saw." Nelsing smiled wryly again. "I mean normal, too; they were slippery and self-protecting and altogether feminine, but any lying they did was strictly in—what's the Godfrey been calling it?—in the world sense. The rest of the Beyond-Truth went overboard as soon as rushing started, and they all pledged a good house."

"There isn't a chance," said Todd slowly, "that it went underground instead?"

"They laugh at it," Nelsing said. "Cass has a sort of wink she gives when you mention it—"

Georgine could see her: the round, pretty face made yet more attractive by that laughing complicity. "And after all," she remarked, "what harm would it do anyone to fast one day a week in secret? As a matter of fact, I think Ryn does it openly. Cass said something about that."

Todd was still looking into space. "It's the planning to marry and have children that seems to be dangerous. Grant wasn't a Beyond-Truther, I suppose... I'll swear David Shere isn't."

"Not he," said Nelsing, "but he's a bit more cautious than Hartlein; he doesn't insult the memory of the dead Leader."

"Ah, yes. And while we're on that subject, what about those pieces of inhaler you found on the old lady's property?"

"I might have known you'd be in on that," said Nelsing with resignation, "when I saw you easing yourselves out the back door yesterday. No comment. —Look here, Mac, I wish you'd go over that story that Hartlein told you, once more."

Todd began on it. Georgine's attention wandered; she finished her sewing to the accompaniment of suppressed yawns, thinking about tomorrow morning, there'd hardly be time to get the wash out before her dentist appointment, she could do it in the afternoon—left-over spaghetti for lunch, though not very much of it—

"Sure you can make yourself sick, sucking arsenic off a paint brush," she heard Nelsing say. "The old lady made Ryn go to two or three doctors, a couple of months ago. They all said the same thing."

The old lady had made her go. Then there couldn't have been anything to Hartlein's suspicions about that. Probably all the other business about the girls' being afraid of her had been the same, the product of a neurotic imagination... But as neuroses went, there were all kinds. There was David Shere, powered all the time by that overwhelming vitality—how would he act if that power went into channels of jealousy? He had loved Sibella Johnson first, and then turned to Ryn, and after her to Cass— would he be as devious as all that, possibly tampering with the steering gear of a honeymoon car to kill off the rival and the lost loved one? And then rigging up that inhaler for Hartlein, planting it in such a way that nobody was sure if that death was suicide or murder? If he were being as clever as all that, why didn't he get Hartlein to write something which could be construed as a suicide note? But then the insurance wouldn't be paid...

"Nelse," she broke in suddenly, "how much money did Bell Johnson leave to her sisters?"

"Huh?" Nelsing said. "Bell? Oh—money. Why, quite a lot, as it happened. She and Grant had made wills in each other's favor, before the wedding, and Grant died first. The insurance people checked on that. There was his estate, which was considerable, and her own share of the Johnson parents' money. All that was divided between Ryn and Cass."

"I see," said Georgine, turning it over in her mind. Shere hadn't many resources of his own, except that old building he'd mentioned, and you couldn't live on your GI loan these days. He was courting Cass—

"I always get disgusted with myself," she added firmly, "for conjecturing at all. Skip it, Nelse."

Nelsing rose and stretched, regarding her dispassionately. "Okay, I'll skip that if you'll forget your nightmares. If this is a crime you don't come into it."

"That's what I keep telling myself, but all I'm sure of is that you don't believe we did it."

"That's something, isn't it?" said Nelsing. "Look, Mac—I can't go out there in an official car, or make it look as if I were on official business. If you, uh, felt like gathering some material, I believe that visitors are welcome enough at the Colony. It'd make kind of an excuse—"

"Todd!" Georgine said, coming to sudden awareness of what they'd been arranging. "You don't mean you're going to ask questions in the—the very lair of the Beyond-Truth?"

"Good God," said Nelsing disgustedly, before Todd could open his mouth, "we might have known better than to discuss it in front of a woman."

"Must you, Todd?" She ignored Nelsing.

Todd said no word. He cocked an eye at her and began to whistle a theme by Ludwig van Beethoven.

"Oh, *money*," said Georgine in despair. "I wish we all lived on a desert island."

"Dear Georgine," said her husband, "we'd just starve a li'le quicker there. Nelse is going along to protect me in the lair, and who's more discreet than Nelse? Tuesday afternoon, then," he said to their departing guest.

"That's right; it's my day off. Good dinner, Georgine. Thanks a lot, and good night."

They watched him go, into a clear night that stirred uneasily with the gusts of a chill, dry north wind. It was the kind of weather that made hair crackle with electricity and put an edge on nerves. "That's part of what's the matter with me," Georgine murmured half aloud.

"Talking to me, dear heart?"

"Not exactly—there, his car started all right. I was rather wondering—well, never mind. Look how clear it is, you can almost count the lights on the Gate Bridge."

"Does the scenery comfort you when you're gloomy? Because I can see you are, and I wish you weren't."

"Yes, I'm gloomy. I have to be at the dentist's in the morning, and I am a millstone around your neck."

Todd said nothing. He only looked at her, with a familiar softening of his eyes, and the hint of a smile.

Georgine grinned at him. "I feel better now."

CHAPTER SIX

BEFORE MORNING THE WIND gained strength, making the night hideous with the banging of doors and windows that one had not realized were unfastened, and thrashing trees about so that the stars winked evilly through their branches. The morning was no better. When the wind dropped for a moment one baked in unimpeded sunlight, and when it came up again it blew with piercing coldness. Georgine fought her way to the dentist's and back again, and relieved her feelings by fairly hurling her wash into the machine.

Todd, with incomparable tact, had gone out for lunch; at least it would be a good drying day.

The clothesline whirligig in the side yard was putting up a spirited battle, at about three that afternoon, when Georgine saw something that unaccountably startled her. It was only a pair of smart moccasins, visible through the roots of the hedge; but the feet in those shoes had come without sound up the front steps, they were standing motionless now on the far side of that screen of leaves, and the whole thing gave a curious effect of stealth.

Georgine released the whirligig, which promptly whizzed around and slapped her in the face with a wet T-shirt, and went across the grass to peer through a narrow opening in the hedge. The owner of the moccasins was Cass Johnson. She was standing gazing down at them, lost in thought; she might have been a statue, except that the long circular skirt of her gray wool sports dress whipped and bellied in the gale.

"Have you been ringing our doorbell?" said Georgine. Cass jumped perceptibly, turning a startled face toward her.

"No," she stammered. "No, I—I thought you were busy, I could just see your arms hanging up clothes, so I—I wanted to see you, and I thought I'd wait."

"Next time, how's about singing out? You scared me, I hadn't heard your car drive up or anything."

"Oh, I walked," Cass said, recovering her aplomb and following Georgine back into the drying yard. "It's almost easier than driving, if you know the short cuts—and I ought to, I've been walking these hills for most of my life!"

"Well, wait a minute," said Georgine, "until I finish this job, and then come in." She dived for the last handful of napkins, thinking regretfully of her sheets, which she had taken down at exactly the right degree of dampness and left in the Manfreds' basement for ironing this afternoon.

"I'm terribly sorry to disturb you, but I've been trying for two or three days, and you're hard to catch. Tomorrow's my full day at the Community Nursery, too."

Georgine muttered something noncommittal, snapped on the last of the clothespins and picked up her empty basket. "Just a minute, till I lock a couple of doors; do you want to go into the kitchen? It's easier." Her movements were perhaps unnecessarily brisk, but not quick enough; the whirligig got her again with a dishtowel as she scudded back across the yard. "I wish I hadn't given up swearing," she remarked aloud, entering her own kitchen and hanging the Manfreds' key on a nail inside the door. "Well, that's done. Now, do sit down, and we'll have a coke, or tea, or something."

Cass accepted the coke, but instead of sitting down she moved to the front window and stood looking down at the street. "How is Ryn feeling?" said Georgine, impatiently making conversation.

"Oh—about the same, I think. She won't talk about it, or act ill if she can help it, but I can't help seeing. If she'd just take a rest—go away somewhere."

"She keeps on working?"

"Oh, yes, for hours a day she shuts herself up in the basement. It has a big north window, you know," Cass said, still looking vaguely toward the street. "I guess she's painting, down there. She never shows things for four or five months after they're done, but she talks about them."

Another silence fell. Georgine put down her glass and stifled a sigh.

"Oh, I did come at the wrong time," Cass said, turning swiftly about. "You must have things you want to do—but I did try last—yesterday, and tomorrow's imposs—"

Georgine interrupted her in the middle of a word. "Why don't you come to the point, then?" she asked flatly. "What you want to find out is how much we know. Isn't that right?" A sudden conclusion had formed itself in her mind. "I suppose it was you, walking up and down in front of the house last night while Howard Nelsing was here."

Cass swallowed. "Yes. I know his car." Her eyes lifted appealingly. "And you're right, that's just why I came today, but it's awfully hard to get started!"

"I'll start, then. We don't know anything more than you."

"Yes, you do, Georgine. You know whether he's still investigating."

"The Berkeley police like to have their cases closed," Georgine said.

"Hugh was a suicide," said Cass urgently. "I'd be willing to swear to it, now. I wouldn't care if people said it was because

I'd treated him badly. I didn't, and I know it, and the ones who matter know it. But would that help?"

"I don't know."

"I can't be like the Godfrey, trying so hard to make the police think someone's innocent that they automatically suspect her. No matter what anyone says, it makes things worse, and they mustn't get worse. There's stuff that would come to light—some things that don't have anything to do with Hugh's death—and that just can't be allowed to happen."

Georgine looked at the floor. "There's not much you can do about it, I'm afraid."

Cass sat down suddenly beside Georgine, leaning forward to lay a hand on her wrist. It was hard to see her face, with the bright hard blaze of the afternoon filling the window behind her. Georgine looked down instead at the long hand with its nails like dark jewels, gripping her own. "If I told you what I think—and what I know—couldn't you show me how?"

"You should tell Nelsing what you know," said Georgine woodenly.

"Oh, heavens!" Cass made an impatient gesture. "You know why I can't! Look, you're a woman; there are people you love. What if someone who's believed in something wrong, all her life, and is near the—edge of the pit because of it, is blamed for something that couldn't have been her fault? Wouldn't you—" She stopped to search Georgine's face. "No. I see. You want names and dates, don't you? Then I'll have to give them, because I'm frightened for her. I love her, and if things go wrong she'll be utterly lost. There are other kinds of poison," said Cass slowly, with an odd, far-away look, "than Paris green."

"Cass," Georgine said, "I don't really want to know what you're talking about, but if you must tell me, couldn't you use plain language?"

"I'll try." The girl's voice still dragged. "It's my—"

There was a sound of thudding feet on the outside steps, someone's head was briefly visible in the lower pane of a window, and a second later the doorbell rang.

"It's David Shere," said Cass breathlessly. "He saw us... Please, Georgine, please don't tell him what we were talking about!"

"Honey," said Georgine, "I don't know myself."

Young Mr. Shere flashed his most appealing smile at her from across the door-sill. "Is Cass here? She said I might call for her, we thought you wouldn't mind."

Georgine asked him in with as much cordiality as she could manage, and led the way back to the living-room. Cass was in her same position on the sofa, but it was a new Cass; the intensity, the desperate worry of the past few minutes had vanished, and she leaned back at ease against the dull magenta cushions, her gray dress swirling around her ankles and her face at once serene and merry. "Well, my pet, you took your time!" she said.

"Now, don't give me that," Shere said good-humoredly. "I'm the one who's supposed to get in a stew waiting for you."

"Well, you didn't make it this time," said Cass with an impudent twinkle. "What happened, were you in the Bastille again?"

"Not today," said Shere, frowning suddenly. He took a seat, at Georgine's gesture. "Not since—Saturday, I guess it was."

"Really? Why are you being neglected all of a sudden?" Cass sat erect, her eyes still shining. "It wasn't because you broke down and Told All?"

Shere looked at her quickly. "Did Nelsing get after you again about that night?" Then he seemed to remember that they were not alone, glanced at Georgine and twisted his mouth sideways as if in annoyance.

Georgine, who had determined not to be shunted out of her own living-room by two uninvited guests, smiled at him and sat tight.

"O-ho-o," said Cass on a long-drawn note. "So you did reveal the guilty secret. No, Howard's neglecting us, too. What night, Dave?" He looked pointedly at Georgine again, and Cass added, "Never mind her, she's hand in glove with the cops anyway. I can't get a thing out of her, but *you'll* tell me what goes on. What night?"

The young man stirred uncomfortably. "Well, the—the fourth of November. About a week before Hartlein died."

"Oh, yes. That night I was supposed to have gone to see him, and didn't. Godfrey's wonderful story."

"Well—you did, didn't you? I'm sorry, Cass. I had to tell them. I saw your car parked around the corner, in a dark spot under a tree, and when I went in I heard Hartlein saying 'No! No, I won't believe it, there'd be nothing to live for!' And on that," said Shere rather bitterly, "I shut my door, not wanting to eavesdrop. But I had to tell that much."

Cass was looking at him consideringly, still half smiling. "We checked back on that night, before. I was in the Cal library, looking up some stuff, and Ryn was at a Little Theatre rehearsal in Wheeler Hall, making some sketches. So you saw our car. I wonder—if I confessed that it was I who went to see Hugh, and told him I'd never go back to him, do you think that would clinch the suicide verdict?"

"Would it be true?"

"What do you think, David?" She smiled at him again, and then looked obliquely at Georgine. "Damaging, isn't it? And why do you suppose Howard Nelsing hasn't been after me again? He's had the evidence for three days."

"Maybe," said Georgine politely, "he didn't believe Mr. Shere." He gave her a look of sudden angry bewilderment. "I don't know, of course. He didn't mention it to us."

"Well, would it make any difference if I did give up and say that it was I?" Cass said, and Georgine shrugged in answer. "It's interesting to think about, just the same. Would it make any difference to *you*, David?" She turned her laughing face toward him, leaning forward. "What would you think if it came out that I'd driven my poor husband-in-name-only to suicide—by telling him I wouldn't have him?"

"You'd lose his money," said Shere in a surly voice.

"Oh, of course. But that would be much better than—further trouble. I'd have done it before, if I'd known. *Would* it make you think differently of me?"

Shere got up with a powerful thrust of his body. "Hell, I don't know. What do you care what I think of you, anyway? I don't know why I keep dangling after you girls."

"Why, we're just irresistible, that's all," said Cass with a soft giggle. "But we're too plural, you know. Can't you really decide which of us you *can* resist?"

"Who've I been paying attention to, the past three months?"

"Oh, me, I admit. You've honored me with all your fights and scoldings, I know it must be love." She was playing him delicately, like a big angry trout, and Georgine felt a sudden pang of sympathy for him. It was abruptly dispelled in the next moment, when Shere gave her an unfriendly glare and said to Cass, "Must we discuss it so publicly?"

"No indeed. We can drop the discussion, or finish it now."

Georgine continued to smile, to sit tight, and to think, —Why don't you leave, then?—

"You're always dropping it. That's one of the ways you keep me dangling." Shere jammed his hands into his pockets, and went to stand in front of her. Again, from several feet away, Georgine could feel the physical emanation of vitality that came from the big frame; but as far as she could tell, Cass Johnson was either unaware of it or impervious to it, sitting relaxed as she was in the corner of the sofa. "All right, let's have it out. Seems as if it's the dangling itself you enjoy, not any emotion—any decent human emotion. Why won't you ever come out and say you'll marry me?"

The gay, pretty face twinkled up at him. "What did Ryn say when you asked her?"

"Leave her out of this! It's you I'm asking!" Shere's jaws clamped together for a moment before he added, "And don't try to tell me you resent my having singled her out first."

"Why, David, I don't care which of us you chose first. It's all for one, one for all in our family." Cass smiled at him again, and then abruptly her face grew sober, her eyes fell. "Don't be angry. I know you want me to be serious sometimes. You won't like it, though, because it does seem as if—neither of us should ever marry."

"Oh, for God's sake!" Shere groaned. "What kind of a life do you think you're going to have, a sort of nunnery existence like your Aunt Chloe's?"

"What's wrong with her existence?" Cass inquired cheerfully. "Looks pretty good from where I sit: pots of money, every beautiful thing she wants to keep around her, a devoted companion—" Cass interrupted herself, screwing up her face comically. "If I were choosing, of course, I wouldn't have the Godfrey! But aside from that, every detail is perfect."

"Including that damn-fool religion?"

"Oh, that!" said Cass lightly. "But aside from the Godfrey, *what's* wrong with it?"

"Everything," said Shere. "Ask her." He swung around and waved at Georgine.

"Who, me?" said Georgine, startled.

"Sure. You're happily married."

"Well, you needn't shout it like an epithet."

"David," said Cass patiently, "Aunt Chloe was married."

"You call that a marriage? Beyond-Truth style, fleshless and all in the mind—no children, nothing but an abnormal sort of prison-camp love where you wave at each other over barbed wire fences!"

Cass laughed again. Her eyes were fairly alight with teasing. "But you have companionship! Don't forget how important that is!"

"Before God," said Shere with a despairing gesture, "if I didn't think you were baiting me again, I'd take you over my knee."

"Why, I mean it," Cass told him demurely. "Now it's my turn to appeal to Georgine. Isn't companionship important?"

"It has its place."

"But that isn't all?" Shere fairly shouted at her. "Tell her! Maybe she'll listen to you. She can't get any sensible advice from the rest of her family, Lord knows. What kind of experience have they had? But you—"

"She hasn't any children by this marriage," Cass said, smiling.

"Are you two inquiring," said Georgine with deadly sweetness, "into the nature of my relations with my husband?"

Shere fell back a little. "No. Well, of course not. I—I'm sorry if it sounds like that."

"Or are you asking me for a sex lecture? Because if so, I'll be glad to recommend a couple of good books, and that's as far as I'll go. But of all the cast-iron, brass-bound, copper-plated nerve—" She stopped, remembered that she was talking to a metallurgist, and began to laugh.

Shere remained in deadly earnest. "Can't you answer one simple general question without getting upset?" he yelled at her. "Can you have a complete marriage without..."

"Certainly not," Georgine yelled back.

Cass got to her feet, shaking her head with mild maternal deprecation. "Come on, David, let's go somewhere and plunge your head into cold water. He always gets this way over something," she confided to her hostess with a sigh, "but I never know what, ahead of time."

"Think nothing of it," said Georgine, still quaking with laughter. "It isn't often we have such drama in the front parlor."

Shere paused at the door, and turned to look at her. It was a curious look, made of exasperation and pleading and something else she couldn't define. "You're a big help!" he said between his teeth, and most unfairly plunged through the door before she could select a retort. Cass went flying after him.

Georgine sat down and ran her hands through her hair. In a minute, however, she got up and went toward the kitchen. For some time she had been aware of a curious resonance through the dining-room, which did not occur when the door between the two was closed. It was propped open a few inches, she discovered, and behind its shelter sat Todd. On the table beside him were a much-depleted quart bottle of milk and the cookie jar.

Georgine looked with deep suspicion into the jar and saw only five cookies remaining. "Uh-huh," she said.

Todd had risen to his feet and was saluting her gravely. "Dear Georgine, may I compliment you on your defense of that grand old institution known as Sex?"

She sat down wearily. "How much of that preposterous conversation did you hear?"

"All except Cass's girlish confidences. I arrived a few minutes before Shere, but at the time she was murmuring too quietly for me to hear her. Anything interesting?"

"I don't quite know," said Georgine slowly. She ate one of the cookies while Todd's agate eyes absently followed her movements. When she had finished, "I'll tell you what she said, as nearly as I can remember..."

Todd listened. "Someone who's believed in something wrong," he repeated, "and is 'near the edge of the pit' because of it. It's a woman, and she'll be 'utterly lost' unless things go right. You know what it sounds like to me? Something the Beyond-Truthers clawed back out of cosmic space."

"Or just plain double-talk." Georgine stirred uneasily. "You know, Todd, I think I booted one there. I was so bored and cross, and feeling so martyred, that I wasn't receptive. But that little talk with Cass had a sort of delayed action, and I'm just getting the impression now. Even if she wasn't able to get it into clear words, she was talking about something terribly important to her, something that came up out of the—deepest part of her mind. It was pushing at her so that she said more or less than she meant. I still don't understand it, but I think that's what was happening."

"It was someone she loved," Todd said, "and a woman. That lets out the Godfrey, and leaves two contenders." He regarded her soberly, and as if unconsciously reached into a pocket for his mouth-organ and began to tap it against his palm. "But she didn't say whether that person was the victim or the aggressor, did she?"

"Well, no. Nor whether it was a crime or just a loss of reputation. Maybe she was just putting on an act, but somehow

I don't think so." Georgine paused and smiled reminiscently. "That really was a good act she put on for Shere, though. The little brat—she had him jumping through hoops."

"That's funny," Todd said slowly, "that you should get that impression. From just hearing it, I couldn't help feeling that he was the one who was directing that li'le scene, and not making such a bad job of it either. But then, I wasn't watching him."

"And if he was, what was it all about?"

"Now there, my dear," said Todd, "you have me."

Early on Tuesday afternoon, another day of sharp wind and blinding sun, Todd drove Inspector Nelsing toward the "lair of the Beyond-Truth." Sedately, for the sake of the McKinnons' elderly car, they trundled through Walnut Creek and on in an easterly direction between undulant hills where cattle huddled and even the stiff branches of live-oaks stirred jerkily in the dry gale. There were miles of orchards, more miles of brown hilly meadow; then they turned down a well-kept side road and came to the Colony.

It looked as far removed from the eccentric as anything one could imagine. Except that there were no well-defined streets, it might have been a prosperous small village. Pleasant smallish houses, built in different styles but each well-kept almost to the point of looking brand-new, were dotted at a fair distance from each other over an expanse of land that seemed to be one continuous garden. The lawns were velvet green, the shrubs were clipped to the perfection of a junior executive's haircut, and from one or two garages shone the paintwork of cars, modest enough in make, but also groomed to within an inch of their lives. There was a roughly circular expanse of grass just beyond the gate, around which ran the only paved road in the Colony, and on the far side of it stood a white building, larger than the rest and with wide doors and high windows, which looked like a community hall.

Todd drove around the green, and parked in front of this hall. For a moment after he shut off the engine, the two men sat still, looking about them. In spite of the surge of wind, this was a quiet place. Still and shining-clean and almost lifeless it lay under the hard blue of the sky.

"What does it remind you of, Nelse?" Todd said.

Nelsing glanced around. "Expensive sanitarium, I guess," he said. "Or, no—maybe it's a cemetery. Very high-class one."

McKinnon nodded. "One of those. 'You pay for peace in Patrician Park,' something like that."

"No kids," said the Inspector, evaluating the scene further. "Not a tricycle, or a sand-box, or a path across a handy corner. And no yelling."

"Me," Todd said, "I'll take a few yells." He got out of the car and turned to face a woman who had come walking along the grass verge toward the hall. She was a nice-looking elderly person, with white hair carefully arranged, and a simple, suitable and extremely good wool dress in a grayed powder-blue. As she came nearer, it was possible to see that she also wore a subdued and tasteful make-up, and that there was a singular innocent sweetness about the set of her eyes.

She asked if she might help them, and Todd introduced himself as a writer and Nelsing as nothing at all. The woman seemed to take visitors as an every-day occurrence. She seemed only faintly hesitant about finding someone to show them around; after thought she went into the community hall and telephoned, and presently a little spruce dried-up man who appeared to be about seventy years old appeared, stepping along briskly between rows of red-berried shrubs. He was Alvah Burke, it appeared. He looked at the visitors with the same sweet and hopeful eyes as the woman had, and at once undertook to escort them on a grand tour.

Throughout the subsequent half-hour Todd McKinnon was acutely aware of the sardonic observation of Inspector Nelsing, following along in complete silence about half a pace behind and doubtless comparing Todd's methods with those of the police—not favorably, either. The gentlemen were treated to another description of the Beyond-Truth, about one-third of which was intelligible and all of which they had heard before. They met other members, all well dressed and all above the age of fifty; except for that look about the eyes, which all of them possessed in varying degrees, they might have been any elderly middle-class citizens in any part of the country. Todd, who had vaguely expected a few monastic habits and expressions of burning fanaticism, was conscious of disappointment.

"Is it always as quiet as this?" he asked Mr. Burke, who gave a dry little chuckle and responded that this was Tuesday and something of a holiday. "Other days you'd see the ladies brisking around at their housework. They take pride, our ladies do. The men are like as not out somewheres, watching investments, talking to the farmers—we own lots of this land around here, rent it out for one thing and another, mostly nuts and fruit. But Tuesdays we kind of take time off and get dressed up; then about an hour before sundown, there's a testimony meeting in the hall. Mighty interesting; we'd like you to stay for that if you'd care to." Alvah Burke, who had announced himself earlier as one of the charter members of the Colony, turned peaceful eyes on his charges. "We've shown Truth to a lot of people at those meetings; yes sir, a lot of 'em."

"I'm afraid I am not a suitable subject," replied Todd gravely, "but this gentleman is much interested."

For a moment he saw a fanatical gleam, but it was in Nelsing's eyes and presaged no good for himself. The next moment both men were impassive as usual, and Nelsing was able to turn aside with great courtesy the efforts of Mr. Burke to fasten on him.

They saw gardens, the beginning rows of orchards, the immaculate interiors of some of the small houses. They heard more snatches of history, the life and works of Dr. Nikko Majendie, and the virtues of his relict. At one point Todd managed, with exactly the right degree of casualness, to mention the name of Stella Dubois, and found that seemingly it made not the slightest impression on Mr. Alvah Burke. "I do not know that name," the little old man said mildly.

There was nothing, there was no single thing that could be interpreted as murderous fanaticism. There was no trace of fear. The only departures from the normal were the quiet and the arid neatness, unless you counted the other-worldly look in the colonists' eyes; this last, innocent and pleasant as it might be at first glance, had begun to affect Todd with a curious chilly sensation.

They met one more serene elderly woman, a Miss Cortelyou, and stopped to talk with her. No, she said in answer to Todd's question (Nelsing preserving his sardonic silence), this colony didn't house the entire congregation of the Beyond-Truth, there were many of them out in the world. Sometimes they came back for visits, sometimes not, but the members here felt that no one ever really left them, not in Truth. Anyone who had ever embraced the principles was welcome to return at any time. There was a guest cottage, kept especially for these returning ones, would the gentlemen care to see it? She was sorry that no refreshment could be offered, but since this was Tuesday, they would understand. Here was the cottage; there were two guests staying at the moment, but they were at the hall, helping with the arrangements for the Fast-breaking Supper. Yes, welcome at any time...

"Have some of the charter members gone out into the world?" Todd asked. Miss Cortelyou said that one or two had done so, and others had passed beyond. She mentioned Dr. Nikko again, and sighed.

—Hell, Todd told himself, I've got to test it once more. I can't use good old Stella, I've tried her on the li'le guy already and he's listening. Well, here goes—

"There was Frances Sagers, too, wasn't there?" he said, mounting the porch steps of a honeysuckle-covered cottage in the wake of the two guides.

Miss Cortelyou said nothing, but turned to give him a smile of quite piercing sweetness. At the same moment, two women who had been sitting in porch chairs behind the heavy vines rose to their feet.

"Our Leader," exclaimed Mr. Alvah Burke in tones of pleased surprise. "Mrs. Majendie, are we disturbing your meditation? Then—might I present these two gentlemen who—"

"The gentlemen and I have already met," said Chloe Majendie in a voice like cool steel. She walked to the top of the steps and stood looking down at them with eyes to match her tone. Behind her, Joan Godfrey gazed at them, and made no sound although her lips moved. "I had thought," old Chloe added, "that the gentlemen were satisfied with *my* answers to their questions."

Todd McKinnon was accustomed to finding himself in odd or ludicrous situations, and could generally get out of them by the use of some well-calculated absurdity of his own. At this moment his thought processes went literally blank, although his senses took in the scent of greenery, the dazzling white paint of the frame cottage, the gravity of Mrs. Majendie's expression and some subdued murmurs and rustles behind him, terminating with a dry official cough from Inspector Howard Nelsing.

"I am here unofficially, Mrs. Majendie," said Nelsing in his most appallingly polite voice, "in the capacity of friend to Mr. McKinnon. We understood that your members were glad to give out information."

Old Chloe gave him one of her long, measuring looks. She transferred it to Todd, who afterward confessed that he would have given anything he owned to be able to drop his eyes and shuffle his feet. By an Herculean effort he resisted this. "We owe you an apology, Mrs. Majendie," he said in his usual light voice, "for forgetting that Tuesday was your fast-day, and that you might very well be visiting the Colony."

"I am sure you do regret it," replied the old lady in her driest tone. "Since you are here, however, I should like to entertain you gentlemen alone, in the guest cottage."

Like three wisps of ectoplasm, the others seemed to melt away into the surrounding air. Old Chloe turned and led the way into a little parlor, all fresh chintz and glittering mirrors. "Will you sit down?" she ordered rather than asked, and took her own seat in a stiff chair facing them.

—Here I am in the innermost lair, said Todd to himself. —And if it weren't for Nelse over there on that window-seat, damned if I couldn't get a bit scared—

Nelsing seemed to be suffering neither fears nor compunctions. "I think you'll see, Mrs. Majendie," he said, "what the chief difficulty has been throughout this investigation. The best and most virtuous witnesses have been answering our questions with what we'd call lies and you'd call Beyond-Truth. That does not satisfy the police." He looked sidewise at Todd. "McKinnon, a few minutes ago, mentioned a name to Mr. Burke, and Mr. Burke said he'd never heard of it. Since he was a charter member, and you yourself had given a complete history of Mrs. Dubois' death, it's completely absurd to suppose that he wouldn't know the name. He was speaking in the Beyond-Truth sense, wasn't he? Mrs. Dubois had proved herself unworthy, so he thought she'd never existed."

"That may have been in his mind," said Chloe, with no diminution of her dignity. "He was not under interrogation, however. I think it is his privilege to say what he believes."

"Quite. But I should—" Nelsing caught himself. "I imagine that Mr. McKinnon has been wondering why the mention of certain names always calls forth certain reactions, none of them strictly truthful—in the world sense."

"Gentlemen," said Mrs. Majendie, "I'll put an end to this right now. Ask me anything you like and I will answer it, in the world sense."

Her hawk-like old face looked craggier than ever, and her mouth was set in a formidable line. "Anything you like," she repeated.

"Mac," said Howard Nelsing with a faint smile, "it's all yours." And as Todd half rose in his seat and directed an anguished look toward him, he added softly, "I owe you something." The memory of that betrayal to Mr. Burke was evidently still with him.

"Oh, if you insist I'll ask the questions," said Todd, giving way suddenly to the demon of imprudence. "Mrs. Majendie—is this a racket?"

"A racket? The Beyond-Truth?" For two seconds her eyes blazed; then she leaned back still erect, in the straight chair. "It may have been, at the beginning. My husband was a clever man, as well as a magnetic one. He had no money of his own. I brought him some when we were married; it was my chief attraction, probably." There was no change in her expression, no bitterness in her tone. "I am glad that I had it, because I loved him deeply and no matter what happened, it was worth it to me. You must consider, too, that no one has ever lost anything through being a member of our group. Nikko took their money, it's true, he invested it, but when the investments paid—and the great proportion of them did— the group was enriched as much as he was. Or very nearly as much," she corrected herself with a slight smile. "Is that what you wanted to know?"

"Not quite all," said Todd. He had drawn into himself, in a sort of trance of concentration, and spoke softly as if not to mar it. "How much of what he taught did he believe?"

"Yes, that's a fair question," said old Chloe, and sighed. "Very little of it, I'm afraid. And yet—it is a philosophy that was made for these old innocents; a vow of celibacy would have been easy for any of them, and for the rest it teaches kindness, self-denial, a few bizarre rules that don't do anyone harm. It has never done anyone harm, gentlemen."

"Never?" said Todd, still softly.

"Look around you." Mrs. Majendie gestured, taking in all the wide sweep of the Colony. McKinnon nodded slowly, thinking of the placid, innocent faces he had seen; if they were empty, too, it was from their own inclination. "If the premises of Beyond-Truth were false to begin with, these people have made something fine of them. I am not the one, Mr. McKinnon, to tell them that it was made up out of whole cloth. They confuse the faith with the founder to some extent; now they look to me as their leader, and I am not going to shatter the foundation of decent and happy lives." She eyed Todd again. "Anything else?"

"Yes," he said, and drew himself together for the crucial question. "Dr. Majendie died just in time, didn't he?"

"Not from my standpoint, Mr. McKinnon,' said the old lady gently.

Todd willed himself to stay relaxed in appearance. He was not used to examining witnesses, only to listening sympathetically while they told him as much as they chose, and the necessity of thinking up questions in this case was going to be too much for him—unless Chloe Majendie would loosen up a little and give him some kind of a lead. He sat negligently in his wicker chair, his inner being a core of concentration that seemed almost to burn.

He was aware of Nelsing, absolutely silent but somehow conveying amusement, a few feet away; of the spotless chintzes and white woodwork of this small house, and of the square of sky enameled with green leaves, framed by the window behind the old lady's head. It was very quiet, the wind had dropped to a breeze that did not lash and howl but only scraped the vines lightly against the house and uttered small sounds like sighs, like breathing. Within these walls he could hear the ticking of his wrist-watch.

After a moment or two of silence, Mrs. Majendie added, "It was a true marriage." Her penetrating gaze did not move from Todd's eyes. "It was within the letter of the Beyond-Truth, because I had been rendered sterile when I was seventeen, by an accident. I've already told you that I loved my husband deeply, and nothing that happened could have made any difference in that feeling."

Todd said in a barely audible murmur, "Something—happened?"

The Queen Mary hat, the unruly shock of white hair below it, moved in affirmation. "If you have any doubt of my good faith, I shall try to dispel it now," said Chloe Majendie. Her voice rang louder for a moment. "Perhaps it will put an end to this nonsense of investigating! —There is only one person besides myself who knows the circumstances of my husband's death, and you could not possibly learn them from her. I'm going to tell you gentlemen, in confidence."

Nelsing stirred in his seat, and Mrs. Majendie flashed him a glance. "It has no bearing on the death of Hugh Hartlein, I can assure you. —My husband died of pneumonia, as you've heard. I did not nurse him myself, nor see him alone while he was ill. What no one else knows—except this woman—is how he caught the original cold."

She moistened her lips, and gave a one-sided smile, rueful and entirely worldly. "In the vulgar phrase of the joke, he got it by getting up out of a warm bed and going home."

Todd's eyelids contracted, but he made no other movement.

"I think," she added calmly, "that the woman was on the make from the beginning, when she came here and pretended to be converted to his philosophy. She was good-looking, and younger than I. No doubt she knew enough about men to see that my husband was susceptible, if the temptation were presented in just the right way; and no doubt she meant to blackmail him. He escaped that. In that way, he did die at the right time."

"*He* died—"

Mrs. Majendie smiled. "Did you think I'd put the Evil Eye on her, Mr. McKinnon? No, indeed. She had to be sent away from the community, of course, but she didn't die. I wonder if you can guess her name?"

"Frances Sagers," said Todd softly.

"Quite right," said Chloe Majendie. "I hope you realize how much I have told you."

"Yes, I think so," said Todd in his most casual voice. "If we wanted to think of it that way, we could say that you had the Beyond-Truth so much on your mind that you did condemn all backsliders to death, even your beloved husband. And if anyone chose, he might think that you'd been completely frank throughout, hoping to disarm investigators of your latest—"

The door to the hall was flung open, crashing back against the wall. "It's a lie!" a high voice shrieked. "It's all lies!"

CHAPTER SEVEN

"J OAN!" MRS. MAJENDIE almost shouted, her habitual aplomb momentarily shattered. The two men sprang to their feet, and Joan Godfrey half fell into the room. Her face was sheet-white, and twisted until it was barely recognizable as hers; only the beads still clacked and tinkled in a horrid travesty of gaiety.

"I heard, Chloe. Yes, yes, I heard everything, you didn't think I was going to leave you alone with *them*? You were denying Truth, weren't you, even world truth?"

"No," said Mrs. Majendie with infinite compassion.

"I won't have it!" Joan screamed. "You'll—you—" Her breath caught and choked her, as she waved an arm at the two men. "You put—you put your own head in a noose, and with lies! I tell you, you can't divert the Hand of God that way, it points to the guilty, to the Denier, it may be through the law that it comes—but you shan't take that ray from the Cosmos on yourself—"

"Hush, Joan my dear," said old Chloe, still gently. She remained seated and uncompromisingly erect, but she stretched out a hand. Miss Godfrey looked at it and seemed to shudder into herself, crossing her arms over the bead chains on her thin breast. "You're talking very wildly. I don't believe I have put my head in any noose. Mr. McKinnon had just begun to state a hypothetical case, to clarify matters for us all."

"A case," Todd interposed, "which I meant to break down in a minute."

Miss Godfrey evidently did not hear him. Her sparrow eyes were fixed with a terrible brightness on Mrs. Majendie. She gulped again. "Chloe, in—in the name of everything we believe in, say that you had some reason—that the Cosmos distorted the vibrations, that it was not Truth about—about—"

"About Dr. Nikko? Joan, I wouldn't have had you hear that for the world, if I could have helped it; but it was true in all the senses we know."

"He—he didn't believe? He was of the flesh and the world?"

"Very much so, my dear Joan," said the old lady with a little sigh.

Miss Godfrey's hands went up, shaking, to her mouth. "Then," she stammered, "what's—what's left to—"

"You can go on just as I did, Joan; as I've done all these years."

"No!" Joan Godfrey cried out. Her head jerked this way and that like a small trapped animal's. "I won't believe it, not of *him*. Men's names have been blackened in the world before this, by unbelievers—I won't be taken in by such wickedness, such—such—" She faltered and came to a dead stop with her eyes on Chloe's.

"My poor Joan," said the old lady, "if you must pin your faith on a person, you'd better choose me. I'm alive."

"But you said—you told—" Again Joan choked on an indrawn breath, and buried her face in her hands. When she uncovered it she was calmer. She looked around, her mouth sagging a little open in infinite desolation. "There's nothing left," she said in a tired voice. "I must—I can't stand it, you won't ask me to—to stay."

"We'll talk about it when we're home again," said Chloe gently.

"I'm going now," Joan cried out. "Not another minute—I can't—I can't—" She whirled about suddenly and scuttled out, down the porch steps, across the velvet lawn, into a screen of trees. Todd and Nelsing looked at each other, and then at Mrs. Majendie, who had risen and seemed deeply troubled.

"I should go after her, and I mustn't," she said, compressing her lips. Then she added, "There is the meeting at the hall, in twenty minutes. This is the one day I must be here until after sundown." She stepped to the window and looked out. A faint smile appeared on her weathered face as a car shot out from behind the trees. "She's taken my car. Well, one of the others will drive me home. If you gentlemen would be interested, you are welcome to attend the meeting."

"Thank you," said Nelsing, "but we must go—unless you intend to make any revelations to the members?"

"There will be no revelations," said the old lady, slowly turning. "None of any kind. There have been too many already." Her lids dropped, and as they hid the youthful alert eyes she looked really old, and very tired. "I should have looked behind that door. I should have looked—or said less."

"Will she be all right?" Todd inquired with concern.

"Oh, yes. It may take her a little time to get over it; on one or two other occasions she's—well, no matter."

"And—may I ask—will *you* be safe?"

"I shall be safe," said Mrs. Majendie with a look of benign amusement. "Poor Joan is the type one finds in every religious group, intense to the point of—eccentricity, let us say; but she has never been anything but harmless. And now, Mr. McKinnon and Inspector Nelsing, are you quite satisfied?"

Todd looked sideways at Nelsing. The Inspector said, "One or two more questions, if you will be so kind." The old lady nodded, meeting his eyes with undiminished good humor. He drew breath and rattled out his questions like a drill sergeant giving orders.

"Who attended your husband in his last illness?"

"Dr. John Barnes," old Chloe shot back at him.

"Practicing now?"

"Yes. In Martinez."

"You said you did not nurse him. Who did?"

For the first time Mrs. Majendie hesitated. "We can find out from someone else," Nelsing reminded her.

"Very well. Joan nursed him, until the last two days."

"This Frances Sagers. You say she's alive?"

"She is."

"Will you tell me where, Mrs. Majendie?"

"No, I will not," said the old lady.

"I take it you could produce her?"

"If necessary, I could. But I can't see that it's necessary unless I am to be accused of murdering her. Is that the case?"

"Not to my knowledge," said Nelsing politely. "Thank you, Mrs. Majendie."

"Good night—gentlemen," said Chloe with the hint of a smile, and walked off into the late-afternoon wind.

The two men followed more slowly, retrieved Todd's car from the circle, and drove away in silence. In silence they retraced the winding road to the west; they were within a few miles of Walnut Creek before either spoke, although for some time past Todd had been monotonously whistling a theme by Beethoven.

(Beautiful, he was thinking—beautiful; a Repeater who's clever about it, and changes the method each time; a Repeater who's caught by the circumstances of her first crime rather than the last; and the first crime not only the one that sets the motive for the rest of them, but is the one that drives the murderer insane. There's a nice combination, the Repeater and the Maniac-Sane-on-the-Surface; makes sense, too; but this maniac goes farther, she's mildly loony on the surface—so much so that she can tell any lies she likes and they're put down not to guilt but to eccentricity.)

"Well, Nelse," he said at last, "aren't you going to thank me for that nice li'le party I put on for you?"

"Hah," Nelsing said on a kind of snort.

Todd clicked his tongue sorrowfully. "No gratitude. You ought to be paying taxes to keep *me* in a job. I give you suspects on a platter—I won't say silver, the budget won't run to that just now, but I give 'em to you anyway—and what do I get?"

"You get some kind of a story, I presume," said Nelsing. "And the more I see of your sources, the less I think of detective fiction. Couldn't be farther removed from life."

"No?" Todd said with a faint chuckle. "You mean you've absolved everyone concerned of crime?"

"Oh, I've passed no judgment on what we heard today," said Nelsing, unruffled.

"Why not? No opinion one way or the other?"

"You see, it all happened in Contra Costa County. We've no authority over here."

"For God's sake," Todd murmured, awestricken. "They don't even give you freedom of thought in Contra Costa County?"

"We don't exercise it unless it has some bearing on a matter in hand."

"Nelse, old boy," said Todd almost tenderly, "don't ask me to swallow that."

"I know how your mind works, Mac. Lord knows I've listened to enough of your tall stories. Everything's got to fit in, if somebody's third cousin by marriage dies of stomach ulcers in 1920, it's a prelude to somebody's murder in 1948. Now, you know it doesn't really come out that way. All this stuff has nothing to do with Hugh Hartlein."

"Then why did he die?"

"Oh, I'll make a guess, if you want guesses. Old Mrs. Majendie reminds him of his dominating mother. He takes out on her all the subconscious hatred he's felt for the mother while he thought of himself as a loving and dutiful son. He wants to die, but he has to do it in the way that will spite Mrs. Majendie most."

"Nice going," said Todd. "I'd thought of that myself. But in that case why didn't he leave a suicide note?"

"Insurance, Mac, insurance," said Nelsing patiently. "He couldn't cheat his mother out of all that dough. And he spited the old lady plenty, planting those inhalers in her rubbish heap, taking care to die right after he'd been to her house... Mind you, that's theory; your sort of thing, but that ought to make it easy to take."

"What, no fingerprints, no chemical analysis, no moulage?"

"You're not convinced, are you? Still trying to fix up a link somewhere?"

"There's a link, all right," said Todd thoughtfully. He swung his car to the curb in front of the Walnut Creek Coffee Shop, cut the engine and sat for a moment pondering. "Hartlein told me a lot of lies, but the one true thing was that he believed there was murder somewhere; and I'll swear that belief led up, somehow, to his death... And since you're off duty today, how's about a li'le drink to Theory?"

Georgine McKinnon, slicing potatoes into a casserole dish in the soft light of late afternoon, seemed a picture of placid housewifery; but there was an absent look in her eyes, and her hands moved as if they were independent of her brain. She looked toward the kitchen door when she heard Todd's footsteps on the porch, but did not stop work.

Todd kissed her and sat down beside the kitchen table. She said, "Tough sledding?" and after a moment's thought he replied, "Well, yes and no. I'll tell you..."

She listened, still automatically slicing, scattering dabs of butter, measuring salt. "So that's what it was," she said when he had finished, and turned to face him, leaning back against the drainboard. "Joan Godfrey was here this afternoon, Todd."

"Here? What time?"

"She must have come straight from the Colony." Georgine drew a long breath. "You never saw anyone in a worse state. It scared me, but now I can understand it better."

Todd said that she'd better sit down, and she dropped into a chair. "I'd been over to the Manfreds', using their ironer. I unlocked our kitchen door and lugged the basket in and—I heard something clicking and rattling in the living-room—just that, no voice or movement or anything. So when I could get my knees to hold me up, I tottered in, and there she was standing in the middle of the floor. We've got to get that door fixed, Todd," Georgine interrupted herself to say vigorously. "It's warped or shrunk or something, in the dry weather. It locks—but the latch doesn't catch right and if you shake the door it comes undone. That's how she'd got in. —Really, I thought she'd gone clean batty. She had to talk to me, it seemed, because 'those men'—that's you and Nelse, I suppose?—wouldn't listen; you thought she was crazy."

The McKinnons exchanged a rueful look. "So we did," Todd murmured, and Georgine went on, "You were right enough. That interview must have pushed her clean over the edge, poor thing." She looked at the clock, rose hastily to pour the last bit of milk over her potatoes, slid the covered casserole into the oven and sat down again. "I tried to get some food or coffee into her, but she wouldn't take a thing because the fast day isn't over until sunset. She just sat there and babbled about trying to save Chloe, and denials of Truth, and Hugh Hartlein coming to her in a vision at dawn. She was going away, I gathered, and not taking anything that Chloe had given her. There was nothing left, she said. I was horribly sorry for her, but I was scared too. She held onto my skirt so I couldn't move—" Georgine paused and her blue eyes darkened at the memory.

"She didn't say where she was going?" Todd asked sympathetically.

"Back to the Canyon first, I think, to leave the car because it belongs to Mrs. Majendie. But before she left she went off into the wildest ravings of all, some vision of hers that she'd been afraid to pass on to the old lady—and I don't wonder. It had a sort of—of unholy poetry to it; I've been thinking about it ever since."

"Can you remember how it sounded?"

"Pretty well." Georgine gazed at the table. "She knew that evil was hovering. She looked in the window and—let's see; 'her back was turned,'—not Joan's, the person's she was watching; 'but the door of the painted cupboard was open. Her hand went up and there was the round silvery tin in it, and inside—buried in something—another, smaller tin. And she carried that away very softly.'" Georgine shivered. "Joan went to the tin later, she told me, and found that the smaller tin had been replaced, and took out some of the contents—a white powder, she said. And then—how did she put it? 'I caught a ground-squirrel and gave it some to eat. And it died, after a while. It flung itself about, dying.'"

Todd's eyebrows went up. "Sounds pretty circumstantial—but it doesn't sound like cyanide."

"Well, I know. Miss Godfrey actually said she'd thought of that, but the animal took too long to die, so it was different and she didn't mention it to anyone."

"What it does sound like is arsenic."

"Yes. And later on, the poor Godfrey said something about—'when that lesson had been learned with the white powder she remembered what she had been taught, she remembered Truth.' Todd, there couldn't really have been anything in Hartlein's story? Do you think Chloe *was* giving Ryn a course of slow poison to teach her the error of her ways?"

"Did the Godfrey say it was Chloe?"

"No, she never mentioned her name; it was just 'she' all the way through. Oh, it was all ravings. I've probably made it sound more lucid than she did, and that's not saying much."

"And was that all?"

"Yes, except that at the very end she came out with something about the flaming door—and the painted cupboard and the 'hands with evil in them.' I was one mass of goose-pimples," said Georgine, half laughing. "And then she seemed to come to herself, back out of the Beyond-Truth, you know, and squeaked out something about having to hurry, *she* would be back from the Fast-breaking Supper and Joan didn't want to see her again. And off she went, like—like a lizard. I stood here for three full minutes, goggling around and wondering if it had really happened." She sighed contentedly and sat back. "Now that I've talked it out, I see there was nothing to bother about at all. Along with everything else, the poor thing was light-headed from hunger."

There was a faint sizzle from the oven, and she added, "And how have *you* been?"

"All right," said Todd absently. "I had a big lunch." He sat looking into space, his eyes narrowed in thought, and Georgine rested for a moment and watched him. His hand went into the coat pocket where his mouth-organ habitually traveled and fondled the little instrument, turning it over and over but not bringing it out. For the moment he was lost to the world; she glanced through the window and saw long shadows on the hedge behind their house. The sun was almost down.

"Todd," she said presently, "do you suppose she got home all right? Ought we to go up and see, or will Mrs. Majendie be there?"

"From what I gathered," said Todd slowly, "the feasting and games after the fast-day go on until about ten o'clock. I expect the Leader stays till the bitter end."

"Games?" said Georgine, washing her hands. "Really, games?"

"Bridge," said her husband simply. "They have a duplicate tournament every Tuesday night."

"Todd McKinnon, you're making that up."

"I'm not. Comes right on top of the solemn fast and testimonial meeting. Out of the Cosmos and into Culbertson."

Georgine burst into helpless laughter. "Did you ever in your life hear of a funnier religion?"

"You know, Georgine, one minute I'm laughing at it and the next—I find it giving me a cauld grue. It feels almost dangerous to laugh at it."

"Todd, for heaven's sake!" Georgine turned round to look at him sharply; but he was smiling now, and getting briskly to his feet. "We might just run up there, if you feel like it," he said. "Or can't the dinner be left to stew in its own juice?"

"Literally, it can. And I don't suppose we ought to be too upset if we don't see the poor old Godfrey around, I got the impression that she meant to go off in a sort of cosmic huff."

They drove up the winding road, past the Johnson cottage—whose garage was empty, and on whose porch full milk-bottles could be descried, supporting the conclusion that both girls had been out all day—and to the very top of Cuckoo Canyon. The sleek car was parked in the driveway, and on the porch of this house Joan Godfrey herself was visible, plying a broom in a sort of frenzy that caused dead leaves to spray madly into the air.

"Do you want to stop and speak to her?" Todd inquired.

Georgine shuddered. "Oh dear, no! Let someone else worry about her now. The sun's gone down, and pretty soon maybe she'll have something to eat and get her wits back again."

"Just for the record," Todd concluded, "I'll tell Nelse about her visit. And then—"

"Then we're clear," said Georgine. The sun slipped down behind the Marin hills, and before they reached home its afterglow was gone.

Todd's typewriter clacked busily all that evening. After breakfast on Wednesday morning he spent another hour in his upstairs workroom and then came down, bearing a big envelope of typescript. "It's kind of a shoeshine job, but I'll get it off and take more time on the others," he said, kissing his wife good-bye. "Do you need the car, Georgine? There are a couple of things I want to check on before I mail this."

Georgine said she didn't need the car, she'd be home all day. After he was gone she went upstairs to look at the carbon copy, which had been left out for her to see. It was called "Slender Thread," and though Todd had made the protagonist a bewildered-seeming little man whose later crimes were solved only when it was learned that twenty years before he had successfully concealed his murder of an unfaithful wife, it was not hard to trace the connection to Miss Joan Godfrey. Georgine stood thinking about it, idly passing her duster again and again over the surface of Todd's desk. The little man in the story had been subtle in diverting suspicion from himself and casting it on someone else who could be proved innocent; yes, Joan might have done that about the death of Hugh Hartlein. But—there was that conversation of yesterday. Through all its incoherence, one thing had emerged. Joan was thinking about another poison besides cyanide, and that train of thought seemed to lead directly to Ryn Johnson. Surely, if she intended killing Ryn, she wouldn't talk about it ahead of time?

Georgine gave it up. The telephone shrilled downstairs and she answered the questions of a bored feminine voice asking for Mr. McKinnon on behalf of some firm called Haynes and Hunter. No, he wasn't in. No, she wasn't sure when he would be. Very well, let Mr. Haynes try again late in the afternoon.

It was while she was dusting the living-room that she found, under a pillow on the couch, a handsome flat alligator handbag. Inside it was a plump billfold, and the identification cards and licenses indicated that it was the property of Joan Godfrey, white, of the female sex and aged 54. Georgine frowned at it; the overwhelming possibility was that Joan had forgotten it in her frenzy, though she had made that remark about taking nothing that Chloe had given her—but in that case, the bag should have been taken home and, so to speak, flung in Mrs. Majendie's teeth. Well, it would have to be returned, of course, but she didn't feel like walking up to Cuckoo Canyon with it this morning. Maybe Joan had another hoard of cash to draw on, at home.

The telephone rang again, and she thought, Oh dear— this is going to be one of those mornings when everyone wants you to buy an encyclopaedia or have your picture taken. — The voice in the receiver this time was again feminine, but not bored. It said, "Is this Mrs. McKinnon, Mrs. Georgine McKinnon? —You the one who used to be a Mrs. Wyeth?"

Georgine said she was. And who was this? Mrs. Trumbull, in San Francisco? No, the name wasn't familiar—

"My husband's *there?*" she repeated a few seconds later. "But—what's the matter? Has he been hurt? He left home less than an hour ago..."

She found herself sitting half on, half off the small telephone chair, gazing stupidly at the black thing in her hand that was still emitting quacking noises. It had said something—something—she hadn't heard it, surely? And how long ago had it been said?

"Say, are you all right? Are you still there?" The voice was shouting now, so that she could hear it though the receiver was far from her ear. Dizzily she lifted it again, and said through a dry throat, "Yes, I'm all right. *What* did you say?"

"I said, it's your real husband who's here, the first one. He says his name's James Madison Wyeth, and you thought he was dead but he isn't."

"There's—there's someone who says he's Jim Wyeth?" Georgine stuttered. She put out a free hand as if to push back something tangible. "He can't be! Let—let me talk to him."

"I told you, dearie, you can't. He's sick, see? I keep this rooming-house, and he's been here four, five months, and he told me how he 'n' you were married young, living in Colorado, and it got too much for him, and he saw his chance and skipped out. He found a fella who'd died and put his own boots and belt and stuff on him and pushed him in the water so's he'd get carried off down stream and not be found for two-three weeks. And your husband struck off across country and disappeared, and everybody thought the dead fella was him."

"No," Georgine whispered. "*No.*" She pushed again at the black swirling mist that kept moving down on her. "I—I don't believe it—"

"Well, suit yourself about that," said Mrs. Trumbull cheerfully, "only, he's here and he's broke and pretty sick. And he says, he'd found out where you were and he'd never have bothered you except there was nobody else to turn to. And he wants you should come pretty soon, because—" her voice sank and became confidential, "they think he won't last more'n a day or two longer."

"I can't—" Georgine began; and then her words trailed off. Every bit of her was sick with revulsion. She tried to stiffen herself with disbelief, and could not; the story was too circumstantial, it might just possibly be true, and—who but Jim Wyeth would have known those details? *No one outside her own family.*

If it were he—if by ghastly mischance it were he—she could not refuse what might be a last request.

And if it were a request—but not a last one? —No, she'd deal with that if it arrived. She'd have to go. She'd have to see him at least.

"I—I don't know where you are," she said, fighting off nausea. Her fingers found a pencil unsteadily, and scrawled the directions on a pad. No, she wouldn't be driving—yes, take a number 21 bus and get off at Gough and walk—not so terribly far from the Civic Center—turn on this street, turn on that one...

"I'll come as soon as I can," she said, and hung up, and bent forward until her head rested on the table. It couldn't be. It couldn't be.

After a few minutes she jerked up and began looking for the San Francisco section of the telephone book. If this were some horrible joke— No, there was an entry there: Trumbull, Mrs. Amy—and the address that woman had given. She kept her finger on it and called the number. No hope there; it was the same voice, and she had to stammer out something about not understanding some part of the directions. You turned *left?* yes, that was correct...

If she were to move at all, this horror of resurrection must be pushed into the back of her mind. Just concentrate on the immediate details, she thought, and found herself in her bedroom without knowing how she'd climbed the stairs. Something to wear—not too good, not giving any hint of prosperity—heaven knew it wouldn't be untruthful, and none of her clothing was expensive. It was an ignoble move, but it was safer. Money enough to get there, and very little more...

There were some things she must have done; she remembered her painstaking locking of the house and turning off the sprinkler, and even taking an automatic look into the mailbox as she went down the steps.

There were other things that she knew she had done. Todd's small pistol was in her handbag, for safety.

And some of the things she had done, also for safety, she had herself undone. She was walking along Gough Street, with very little recollection of the trip across the Bay, and she stopped to check on those cross-streets up which she was supposed to turn. Yes, she had brought the directions, she had picked up the whole pad, though she couldn't remember doing that either. The whole pad—and on the second page of it was the note she had written to Todd, telling him where she was going although not why—oh, no, not why!—and where to look for her if—if anything went wrong.

Georgine stopped on a street corner and shut her eyes hopelessly. Well, it couldn't be helped. Todd might not have come home anyway, he hadn't said how long he'd be gone. She had to go on. In some one of these shabby houses, around one corner or another, lay a sick man who might be Jim Wyeth. He had found poverty and uncertainty too much for him, and had taken a way out—but he'd known she would be provided for. There was his insurance... Like Hugh Hartlein and his mother; but Hartlein was dead beyond doubt...

She had turned the wrong way. She faced about and doggedly retraced her steps, forcing herself to think about the

weather, the street, anything but what she was approaching...
This was an unreal sort of place, this narrow lane of old dingy
houses, only a few blocks from the green dome of the City
Hall and the clangor of Van Ness Avenue. It was one of several
mid-block streets that didn't "go through," and across them
decaying wooden houses looked, sometimes at other houses,
sometimes at mysterious blank walls.

It was so *quiet*. Here and there an old car waited with its
wheels up on a curb, but no one came out to it. Once a grayish
alley cat went shooting across the street; in one of the basement
windows a small face peered out, unmoving, and giving the
impression of a child locked in the house by itself. There was no
other sign of life except the papers and trash that swept fitfully
along in the wind, and swerved and came to rest in areas
already carpeted with litter. The hard sun was still shining
overhead, making her shadow into a moving blot around her
feet, but this street was as lonely as a gray Sunday.

Her shadow moved with her, but more and more slowly. A
sense of utter horror was slowing the connection from will to
muscles, and she walked as if through water that grew deeper
and deeper. She looked, with the same reluctant slowness, at a
house number dimly showing on a clouded transom. 820—and
the next was 824; there was another block to go.

—This won't *do*, said Georgine savagely within herself.
She wrenched her mind away from the address in the next
block, and fixed it on details of the houses she was passing.
This street was not quite a slum; here and there were freshly
painted houses, but next to them might be one with dreadful
outside stairs angling up to separate doors across the building's face. At some of these windows were torn green shades,
pulled down against the beat of the sun. At others there were
rayon glass curtains, whole but sunburned and dusty, hanging
in limp folds as if the very look of the street had taken the
heart out of them. The window of one basement flat was
open, and through it was visible the tangle of blankets on an
unmade bed.

If you wondered what sort of people lived here, the answer was plain. They were the Existers, the people who had jobs, but who made enough only to eat and sleep and go back to work again. There might be a little bit over, and that went for movies, three or four of them a week, and not for the washing of curtains. "You can hardly blame them," Georgine said half aloud, and found herself stepping down from a curb, crossing a street—the address was only a few houses away now.

A car passed the end of the cross-street, but she had set her gaze forward and would not look around. It was something moving at last, but it was a block away; this street she was on was tranced in stillness. Two houses more. One house more. This was the one.

The sunlight beat cruelly on the board steps, from which the paint had long ago flaked away. She mounted them, one by one in her mind, one by slow one to her weighted feet. The roof of the porch enclosed her, and the sense of dread shut down as if that decaying wood were physically emitting it.

Her finger was on the bell. She could hear it pealing, far off in the shadows of the hall, and after a long minute someone began to move through those shadows. The door had a glass top, curtained with more of the dusty rayon panels, and through it could be dimly seen a section of worn carpet and the beginning of a flight of stairs.

The person who was answering the bell came toward the door. Her footsteps hesitated a moment, just inside; Georgine could see that it was a woman, that she was turning, raising her head; then swerving away from the door and mounting the staircase.

And at that moment came a sound from the street, someone walking and whistling as he walked. The tune he whistled was The Farmer in the Dell.

Georgine wheeled around. Her startled eyes saw the whistler, and then her knees gave way and she was sitting on the top step, her head bowed on her clenched hands.

"The Marines have landed," remarked Todd McKinnon from the sidewalk. He mounted to the porch and helped her to her feet. "Even a li'le bit early, it'd seem. Dear Georgine, what's the matter?"

She could only shake her head, grasping the wiry solidity of his arm. "Later," she managed to whisper, turning her head toward the door. It was opening, and a highly colored face was peering through the crack.

"Mrs.—Mrs. Trumbull?" Georgine managed to stammer.

"Yeah," the woman said, pulling the door wide. "That's me."

She was not the slattern that one might have expected in these surroundings. She was plump, but unmercifully corseted and zippered into a new-look dress of wine-colored rayon, with only a few spots visible on its front. This made a lively color-scheme with her hair, which was a dark orange-red with streaks of lighter pink. Surprised arcs of black were drawn above her eyes, her skin was a lovely peach-glow shade down to just below her chin, and in a laudable attempt to tie the scheme together she had put on dark red lipstick and light flame-colored nail polish. The effect shone out against the drab background of the house like a basket of Easter eggs.

"Sure, I'm Mrs. Trumbull," she repeated. "You the lady I called a while back?"

"Yes. Is he—could we see—"

"Oh, the gentleman. Now, I'll tell you, dear, it was bad luck—but just about half an hour ago they came for him in an ambulance and he went off to the hospital."

"They? Who came for him?"

Mrs. Trumbull shrugged. "I guess it was that doctor he had to see him once or twice. Now, I feel real bad about having you come all the way over here, but I didn't know they were taking him, and I wouldn't of wanted to stop them, anyway, he was pretty sick."

"But what hospital?" Georgine said painfully.

The woman's mouth sagged half open. "Why—" she said after a moment, "I guess—the Good Samaritan."

"Don't you know? Didn't you ask?"

"Now, to tell you the truth, I didn't. I thought I heard 'em say something about the Good Samaritan, but now I come to think, I couldn't be sure. I was on the 'phone, and I just let 'em in. No need to worry, he was paid up on his room rent, I'll say that for him."

Todd, who had been looking narrowly at Georgine throughout this interchange, now remarked in a suave tone, "But we can go up to his room, of course? He must have left some sort of message for us."

"No," the woman said quickly. "No, he didn't. I—I packed up all his things for them to take along, there's nothing left there at all."

"Oh? Then the room's vacant? Do you know, my dear," said Todd, turning a pleased glance toward Georgine, "this may be providential. It's just the place for my nephew. He's been looking and looking," he explained kindly to Mrs. Trumbull, "for a single room, not too expensive, but near to the center of things in San Francisco. This would just suit him."

He moved toward the door, and the woman stepped hastily into his path. "No, no, it's not for rent. I—I've got to clean it up, and then I've got a long waiting list, there's no room for somebody just coming in—"

"But we could see it anyway, just to give him an idea of accommodations and prices? Perhaps you could put him on the waiting list. I don't need to tell you how hard it is to get anything reasonable these days—"

"You can't see it," said Mrs. Trumbull harshly. "It wouldn't do you the least bit of good. This is my house, ain't it? I pay the rent, and I can keep out anybody I want to. That's all!"

She took a step backward and slammed the door in their faces.

"Come on, let's go," Todd said in a defeated tone. As they went down the steps he added more softly, "At least let's look as if we were going. Georgine, what is all this?"

Instead of answering, she said, "Todd, how did you know I'd come here?"

He gave one of his deep, almost inaudible chuckles. They were on the sidewalk now, going briskly along toward the corner around which the nose of the McKinnon car was just visible. "I tell people I'm no detective," he said modestly, "but of course that's far from the truth. Just li'le indications of flight in perturbation: your melba toast smoking up the whole kitchen—"

"Oh! It burned—I forgot it—"

"Yes, that's what I mean. Also your best suit in a heap on the bedroom floor, most of your folding money left on the dresser, and the face-powder box upside down on the floor. Open, I may add." He was talking freely along in his usual light tone, and although Georgine did not let go of his arm, her grip slackened. "Of course, you might have run away with your lover, but not, I figured, in your oldest suit. No note, either. I'd like you to remember that if you ever do leave me the least you can do is to write a note."

"I—I did write one," said Georgine shakily, "and then picked it up and brought it along without knowing what I was doing. But how did you know *where* to come?"

"I telephoned Barby's school," Todd admitted, "to find out if you'd had a hurry call from there. You hadn't. Then I saw the San Francisco telephone book lying open at the T's, with the mark of a fingernail under this address, indicating a queer part of town. And it seemed a safe bet. I thought at least," he added with a sidelong look, "that you might like a ride home."

He helped her into the car, and got behind the wheel, but did not start it. Instead, he let it roll a foot or two forward and adjusted the driving mirror so that it showed the street and Mrs. Trumbull's front steps. "And now, dear heart," he said in a low voice, "can you tell me?"

"I thought Jim Wyeth was there," Georgine blurted out.

"*What?*" Todd said after a moment's pause.

She nodded painfully. Her head had begun to ache with almost unbearable violence.

There was another pause. "Good God," he said slowly. "And I was joking about—"

"No, wait. It's—there's something horribly wrong about it, but I didn't dare to ignore it—and yet it felt like a trap even though I couldn't see how it could be!" She pulled herself up wearily. "There was this telephone call," she began...

And when she finished, Todd's hand was on her wrist in a close steadying pressure. "You're right," he said. "There's something evil going on. Well, the first thing to do is to find out if Wyeth really did get taken to a hospital. There's a soda fountain in this block, I can telephone around. Georgine, can you keep watch up this street?... Good girl. If anyone comes out of that house, lean on the horn." He glanced up its narrow length. "There aren't any spaces between houses. I suppose they may have some kind of back exits, but we can't stop all the rat-holes... Have you cigarettes with you? Then lean back and smoke one, and see if you can relax. I'll be as quick as I can."

He vanished into the small store, and Georgine sat unmoving, her eyes fixed on the mirror. She was mortally tired, but the sickness was abating and her head no longer throbbed so badly. Todd was here, and whatever evil had been in the street she had traversed was melting away; actually, a small boy emerged from one of the street-level doors and sat down on its step, looking filthy but normal. It was just an odd street of old houses, that was all.

—No, not quite, she told herself. In that one house the unknown terror was still waiting.

CHAPTER EIGHT

THE SUN WHEELED slowly overhead and its light disappeared from all but the topmost windows of the little street. Georgine got up enough energy to smoke her cigarette and to feel the better for it, even to realize that she had had no lunch and needed it now. A woman came out of the corner house and gazed at her incuriously as she passed; except for her and the little boy there had been no one moving in the narrow lane. And at last, Todd came back.

He had a sandwich on a paper plate, and a carton of coffee. "I'll train as a car-hop if worse comes to worst," he said, giving her the food and getting in. "Well, nobody answering to Wyeth's description has been admitted to any hospital in the city today. What's more, the storekeeper says there's been no ambulance around. It couldn't turn in that street, it would have had either to come in or go out on this side." He watched her begin to eat, and said no more until she had finished. "I feel fairly sure that he's not in that house, too," he added.

"I think he never was," Georgine murmured.

"I think you're right." Todd waited a minute, and then took a short audible breath. "You've never been anything but honest with me. —If he did turn out to be alive, would you want to go back to him?"

"After *you?*" she cried out. "Oh, Todd, don't be an utter fool!"

"There was a chance that I had been, and a fatuous one at that. But thank you, dear Georgine. Dear Georgine," he repeated, and looked at her; and all at once she relaxed, and warmth went flowing gently through her for the first time since she had gone taut and frozen at the words of that telephone call.

She had tried not to think of the complications, during the past hours, but certain things had come inexorably, again and again, to batter at the door of her thoughts: the feeling that she always had with Todd, like coming home at the end of a long day; and his hands, and half-sentences spoken in darkness. She had known that it would be like giving up life, to give up those.

"Nobody could make trouble," she said, vaguely smiling at him. "He was declared dead—and even if he'd just disappeared, there's a statute of limitations or something, isn't there? I did worry a little about Barby. She's his child after all, and if he'd wanted to see her—but it couldn't have gone any farther than that, surely?" She frowned a little. "But, Todd—if the whole story were untrue, where on earth did anyone get the details? And is it—do you think it could be connected somehow with Mrs. Majendie and the Beyond-Truth? I couldn't help thinking of that; but I didn't tell her, I almost did but I swear I never said a word."

Or had she? Had she somehow conveyed the whole story, perhaps without opening her lips, as the Mother-Superior eyes had met hers in the mirror? Georgine was overtaken by another shiver.

"It's got to have something to do with this mix-up," said Todd slowly. "But I'm damned if I see what. And yet—I'd bet everything we've got that it was a trap of some kind; whoever thought this up imagined he'd found the one thing that would make you come alone. —If I'd been home, would you have told me?"

"I—I don't know. Maybe not." No, she thought, I wouldn't.

"It was a risk, of course. How'd they know I wouldn't be home?"

Georgine's lower lip went up. "I've just remembered something. Do you know anyone called Haynes? Of the firm of Haynes and Hunter? —Of course not. She checked, first."

"Well, I spoiled the plan by turning up."

"Todd," Georgine whispered, "what was the plan? What did they mean to do to me?"

"God knows," he said. His muscles tautened involuntarily.

"I've been thinking about it. If it was to murder me, it would be simpler somewhere else, wouldn't it? They might know I'd leave word of where I'd gone! And I'm hardly the type to appeal to a white-slaver."

"I might argue that point," said Todd, "but we'll se'le that some other time. When did you think of all these possibilities? Before you left the house? H'm. And you didn't feel any reluctance about coming?"

"Reluctance! I could hardly drag myself—and yet I had to do it. They picked the one thing that would make me come, trap or no trap. Don't be disgusted, Todd, I wasn't just walking into it unarmed. I've got your gun in my bag."

"You've got my gun," said Todd mildly, and covered his eyes with a hand. "Oh, God. You go to see your husband that was supposed to be dead, and you take a gun with you!"

"Good grief," said Georgine in a suddenly appalled voice. A moment of pregnant silence ensued.

Then she turned abruptly in her seat. "They couldn't have foreseen that, do you think? Could they have wanted me to do exactly that—and was I supposed to be found standing over the body of somebody? You know, so I could be blackmailed or made to keep still about something later on?"

"That's an idea. That's really an idea." Todd thought it over. "But what have you witnessed?"

"Not one thing," said Georgine firmly. "There isn't a detail of any meeting or conversation that I haven't described to you, and you haven't passed on to Nelse, *already*. Why, suppose the thing I was supposed to keep still about were something that Joan Godfrey might have told me yesterday afternoon. The time to shut my mouth would be last night, not today!"

"Well, hell," said McKinnon helplessly, "maybe it's something that hasn't happened yet; that's all I can think of."

Georgine stirred uneasily. "You mean something I was meant to witness inside that house?"

"I don't know. Damn it, Georgine, I don't know. And yet— this can't just have been an act of senseless cruelty. It has to tie up somehow."

She sighed. "Why are we sitting here? It must be almost an hour since that woman turned us away."

"Well, I'll tell you. While I was doing my telephoning, I called up Nelse, to find out if there were someone in the police over here whom we ought to notify about this. And what he said was, the police wouldn't touch it. You see, nothing happened."

"Nothing happened. Is that how they look at it?"

"That's how. If you'd gone in, and one of the occupants had snatched your purse or bopped you over the head, we could report it. If we could get in now, and discover anything wrong, they might condescend to come and inspect it. As matters stand, nobody's so much as committed a misdemeanor."

"Mrs. Trumbull—"

"Might have made a mistake. That's what she'd say. And so, since the Law won't do anything, I mean to do my li'le best and watch the rat-hole in the hope that somebody'll stick his nose out."

"Oh, Todd, can't we just let it go? Let's not get in any farther!"

"No, we won't let it go," said Todd in his gentlest voice. "I don't like what's been done to you today."

"But no one's come out of that place. You've scarcely taken your eyes off the mirror, and neither did I while you were in that store. If they've left, it was by a back door, and we—"

"Hold it," said Todd, sitting up straight. "I knew something would happen if we waited."

Georgine swung round hurriedly. No one was coming out of the house, it was true; but a car had driven into the narrow lane from its far end, and stopped. A man was getting out of it; he was crossing the street

"It's David Shere!" she cried out. "He's going in there!"

"Right you are. And so am I." Todd flung open the car door, and then turned a searching glance upon her. "Do you feel up to coming along?"

Georgine got out and hurried after him. As they came up to the door of 968, David Shere was fitting a latchkey into its keyhole.

"Wait a minute, Shere," said Todd mildly.

The young man turned, startled. "McKinnon! What the devil are you doing here?"

"What are *you* doing, if it comes to that?"

"I own this house, if you've got to know."

"I see. There's something you might want to know. Your Mrs. Trumbull has been up to some funny business—with us."

David Shere scowled at Todd and Georgine impartially. "*She* has? Well, if so, she's mighty candid about it. She called me up herself, over an hour ago, and said there was something going on that she couldn't handle, and I'd better come over. No, she didn't say what. Is it any of your business?"

"I rather think it is. D'you mind letting us look through the house?"

"Look here McKinnon, you annoy the hell out of me. What—"

"Shut up, and let us in," said Todd in a surprisingly good-natured tone. Only his face betrayed anything, and that to his wife alone. It looked as if it were carved out of hardwood, and bits of flint stuck in for eyes.

Perhaps David Shere felt it also, for he stepped back sullenly and admitted them to a hall scarcely wide enough for two persons. It led off into darkness at the rear of the house;

at its right, near the door, a steep and rickety staircase rose to the upper floor; and both stairs and hall smelled as if they had worn the same paint and carpets for sixty years of tenants' cooking.

"It's a dump," Shere said gruffly. "Ought to've been condemned, I suppose, but—Trumbull rents it from me and it's her funeral how it looks."

"We'd like to see Mrs. Trumbull," said Todd. "And don't start yelling until I've told you why."

He told him why. Shere's ruddy face lost several degrees of color as the story went on, and he glanced nervously at Georgine and away. "You see," Todd concluded smoothly, "it's just possible there's a dead body upstairs."

"Yes. Yes, you're right, we've got to see about it. But I don't understand—" The young man shook his head wildly, and then disappeared into the depths of the building.

The McKinnons stood waiting. A cool draught of air swept through the open door, but made no impression on the iron strength of the smell.

Shere came back, looking bewildered. "Trumbull's gone," he threw at them as he began to mount the stairs. Todd and Georgine followed wordlessly.

He knocked at door after door, and when no one answered, used a master key and marched unhesitatingly into the squalid rooms. They were in varying degrees of messiness, but almost all were untenanted. Todd peered over his shoulder when he entered the second-floor front, darkened by its tattered green window-blind, but withdrew without speaking, and as if he hadn't expected to see much. There was one answer to Shere's knocking, given in an ancient and feeble voice. A crone came inching to the door and looked out at them suspiciously, but she seemed almost blind and was certainly hard of hearing, and Shere gestured to indicate that it was nothing, they'd made a mistake...

There were three floors to the building, and on each one were three or four incredibly small and noisome rooms, their wallpaper peeling, their iron beds in a late stage of sagging dissolution. Georgine went unsteadily along the black passageways, her handkerchief pressed to her nose, her shoulders compressed so that she need not touch the walls. There had been something wrong in this house, she knew it with a certainty deeper than thought. Perhaps it had vanished, but it had left a sort of psychic trail behind: a clamminess, an odor that had nothing to do with the physical atmosphere. She knew that she might be needed—perhaps for identification. She would have given anything she owned to be out again.

The last room they came to was the third-floor rear. Shere gave his usual bang on the door, but this time a low grumbling sound came from within. "There *is* someone here," he said in surprise.

He fumbled at the doorknob; the door was unlocked, and he flung it open to release an overpowering stench of stale whisky. In a tangle of dirty covers a man was lying on the bed, his face turned away from them.

Georgine wheeled about as if she meant to run away, but her feet would not carry her more than two steps. She stood there gazing unseeingly at the grimy wall of the corridor, her handkerchief pressed so closely to her nose that it almost strangled her. —No, I can't, she was repeating helplessly to herself. —I can't take it, they mustn't ask me to look—

"Your pigeon, Shere," said Todd agreeably, stepping back beside her. She leaned against him, shaking uncontrollably.

"He's alive, all right," said David Shere from inside the room. There was a squawk from rusty bedsprings, and a querulous mutter from the man on the bed.

"And I know him," Shere added. "Been here for years—name's Burch. He works at night, and gets swacked every night after he's through, and sleeps it off all day. You want to look?"

From some deep source Georgine dragged up the strength to turn. The unshaven, unconscious object on the bed was a man about sixty years old, with hair which had once been flaming red and was now mostly gray. She had never seen him before.

She said so, in an almost inaudible croak. Todd nodded. "Now let's get out of here," he said, and propelled her down the perilous staircase as fast as he dared. Shere came at their heels, breathing heavily, and all three of them tumbled out the door, the house-owner barely waiting to close it before he pursued them down the lane.

Todd got Georgine to the car just before her knees gave out entirely. He said nothing, but put his hand on her shoulder for a quick hard pressure. David Shere clambered into the rear seat, and wiped sweat from a colorless face. "Man," he said plaintively, "I don't know why I got so scared all of a sudden; for a minute I really thought that bird was dead! And even when he wasn't, I couldn't get out of there fast enough."

"How do you suppose my wife felt?" Todd inquired.

"Worse, I guess. Hell, I'm sorry, but you know I didn't have anything to do with—what went on."

"Are you sorry enough to talk?" Todd said with a gimlet glance over his shoulder.

"Sure, but I don't know anything!"

"You know who the Trumbull woman is."

David Shere gave a sort of wriggle which made him look like an enormous schoolboy. "She turned up two or three years ago, I was just out of the Army and the old bag who used to run this place had died, and I needed somebody. It's worked all right. Trumbull's paid up on the nail every month—and a good thing, too, or I'd be sunk."

"She just turned up out of the blue? Where had she been before that?"

"I dunno. Somewhere down south, I guess." The young man seemed to feel that his business acumen was being questioned, for he added defiantly, "She posted a guarantee fund, and then—she always paid up."

"And that's all you know about her? How did she happen to come straight to you?" McKinnon prodded gently.

Shere said nothing for a moment. Georgine, by now somewhat revived, wondered what had happened to the waves of vitality that he usually sent out. Maybe she was too tired to feel them—or maybe he had withdrawn them like a snail's horns. He might not be feeling too well himself; he was certainly rather white.

"Look, Shere," said Todd in a tone of controlled exasperation, "if you go around with that hole in the head any longer, you'll catch cold. It's no use trying to keep secrets forever."

"I'm—trying to think," said Shere in a muffled voice. He waited for a moment, looking at the floor and grinding his big hands together. Then he glanced up, wet his lips and said, "I guess you're right. The—the Johnson girls heard I wanted to rent the place, and they said their aunt might know of somebody. And so—Mrs. Majendie sent her to me."

"Yes," Todd said. It was the merest exhalation of breath.

There was the tie-up, Georgine thought. There was the pattern: at first shaped to touch only the Beyond-Truth and its supporters, and now spreading to take in others, like Hugh Hartlein, and like herself. She could almost see the shape that had covered her. It would be like a great feline paw, with its raking claws unsheathed.

"All right, Shere," said Todd abruptly. "I may ask Nelsing to talk to you about this."

"Oh, God, not again!"

"There'd be one way to avoid interviews," Todd said, twisting around so that his eyes met the younger man's.

Shere looked at him for a long moment. "I know," he said, "but I can't take it. Good-by, Mrs. McKinnon, and—I'm awfully sorry for everything. I hope you'll be all right."

Georgine said she would. He got out, and Todd started the car and headed homeward at last. Not until they had turned down Fell Street, toward the Bay Bridge, did he speak, and then it was to say, "Georgine, when the Trumbull woman answered the door today, did she come from upstairs?"

"She was on the ground floor at first. Then for some reason she went upstairs before she let me in."

He nodded. "Getting instructions as to the change of plan, I'd bet you."

"Was—was Chloe Majendie up there?"

"No, I don't believe she was," said Todd, settling himself into a firmer position behind the wheel. "And I hadn't really thought it was Trumbull. You see, as I came down the street I glanced up at that second-floor window."

"You didn't see anyone? The shades were all down."

"No, but I saw a hand. It was holding the shade aside, so the person could see who I was; and it wasn't Mrs. Majendie's hand. It had long finely shaped nails with deep red polish on them."

❀ ❀ ❀

The family across the street from the McKinnons was mildly astonished that evening when Todd appeared and asked to hire the seventeen-year-old son as a wife-sitter. Georgine, it seemed, had taken a number of aspirins and gone to bed, and he didn't want her left alone in the house. Once this new category was defined, the youth was willing to oblige, and showed a commendable lack of curiosity as to why an able-bodied woman should need protection during the early evening hours.

Todd, with the firm planes of his face looking perceptibly harder than usual, drove himself up the switchback roads to Cuckoo Canyon. He had Miss Godfrey's alligator handbag as an excuse for his call, but the Majendie house, where it might most normally have been left, was dark. The absence of Chloe suited his purpose well enough.

He coasted down the street and put on his brakes opposite the garage of the Johnsons' cottage; then, walking silently on the grass, he approached.

There was a light on the small porch, but none in the upper part of the cottage. Around the corner, however, on the north side where the ground fell sharply away from the house, a flood of light poured out, reflected on low bushes and the tops of trees across the Canyon. Todd, who had said good-bye to scruples that afternoon, went as quietly as he could around the house and found a narrow foothold on the north corner close to the foundations.

He could not have got far enough to see in the window, but at the outset of his career as spy, beginners' luck was with him. One casement of the big window had been set open, and dimly mirrored in it he could see someone moving inside. It was one of the girls; she seemed to be alone, and presumably she thought herself unobserved, since she never looked toward the window.

She was sitting on a stool in the middle of a studio room. There was a table in front of her, and several square flat objects which looked like canvases were stacked against the table leg. The girl—whichever it was—seemed to be doing something to one after another; each canvas was lifted to the table, one point on it was scrubbed with something—probably an artgum, for there was that motion as of brushing away crumbs—and then a label was licked and affixed to the same spot. It looked like an innocent employment, certainly, and yet her body—if it were not a trick of the oblique reflection—seemed to be hunched over the table with unnatural tenseness. Todd told himself that you could imagine a counterfeiter working in that pose, with the constant possibility of the tap on the door...

After a time the girl set the last canvas on the floor beside her. He could make out a blob of black on a lighter background, but that was all the window reflected. She rested her head on her hands for a moment, in a gesture of utter weariness that was almost like despair; and then she pushed off the turbanlike covering so that her hair fell long and sleek over her shoulders, and pressed her hands here and there along her scalp. He could make out, now, that it was Ryn Johnson who sat there.

Todd began to inch back along the wall. He couldn't make much out of what he had seen, and the evening was getting along. He reached the front of the house safely, and without noticeable noise, brushed the leaves and twigs meticulously off his suit, and rang the bell.

It was several minutes before he heard any answering stir in the cottage. In the interval he kept his eyes fixed on the flaming scarlet of the door. Presently, however, the tiny Judas window framed a pair of eyes, and the door opened. "Oh, Todd, it's you," said Ryn in a somewhat bewildered tone. "Come in, won't you?"

Todd stepped inside, proffering Miss Godfrey's handbag, which he had previously removed from inside his coat. "Your aunt isn't at home, I'm afraid," he said easily. "I wonder if you'd return this to her companion? It was left at our house."

Ryn glanced at the bag, and her olive-leaf eyes widened. "Return it—to Joan?" she said, and moistened her lips. "But— she isn't at the big house either. She—Aunt Chloe doesn't know quite when to expect her."

"Oh?" Todd said, moving a few steps into the room. "Then perhaps I may leave it here for safekeeping." She made no move to take it, and he laid it down on a bookcase. "I've never seen your house before. Charming room."

The living-room had, indeed, given him a slight shock. It was not what one expected of a painter, somehow; there was a medium-sized Persian rug, there were woven draperies across the western window, there were some handsome pieces of furniture which might be either genuine or good reproductions, there was a record player. It all struck a curiously reminiscent note, of a personality that was housed in an older body than either of the sisters', and that had come to its full flower in the redwood house on the hill. "Charming," he repeated. "Who is the decorator in your family?"

"Oh, we both did it, Cass and I."

"That looks like you," said Todd appreciatively, looking toward the one original note in the room: an abstraction in deep jewel-like colors above a low gray sofa.

"Yes," Ryn said. "I did that last year. Won't you sit down? I—I was just going to have some coffee, may I pour you a cup?"

"Only if you'll let me carry in the tray," said Todd agreeably. "I'm a domesticated man, you know." She turned toward a half-open door and he followed her, commenting vaguely on the size of the place, these small houses were so deceptively

roomy... There was the kitchen, brilliant with deep red lino-
leum surfaces, and there on the wall at an angle to the window
was a cupboard with its doors painted in a design of comic and
impossible vegetables. Todd looked at it steadily while Ryn
Johnson heated coffee in a glass pot. He let her open the gay
doors and get down the cube sugar before he informed her that
he took nothing in coffee, and thereby saw a bright tin labeled
"Cornstarch" on an upper shelf. He moved to examine the
cupboard as she closed it, and said, "I imagine there's nothing
else quite like this in Berkeley. Your aunt, now—I can't see her
with anything but plain enamel in her kitchen."

Ryn said, rather absently, that he was right. She gave him
a nervous look as they went back into the living-room, but he
had begun to talk about her painting. "Last year you did that
one over the sofa? Yes, that must have been before that green
period of yours set in. About how long do you find yourself, uh,
impelled to use one color like that?"

Ryn said that it varied, and stirred her coffee round and
round and round. "I should very much like to see some of your
recent work," Todd pursued smoothly. Almost without volition,
he found himself adding, "I know a great deal about Art, but
I'm never sure what I like."

Ryn smiled faintly. "Then it would be a pleasure to show
them to you—if they were ready to show. I never do let anyone
see them, you know, for months after they're done."

"So your sister said. But there was one she spoke of, with
a good deal of black in it—"

Ryn's coffee cup went down with a crash into its saucer.
"Cass hasn't seen them!" she said loudly, almost with a questioning inflection at the end.

"Oh, you don't show them even to her? But I had an
impression—never mind, it may have been something entirely
different she mentioned," said Todd, watching her intently.

"When did you meet her—without me?"

"Oh, the other day. It just happened. Don't tell me you two
go everywhere together."

"No, of course not. Only—"

"You are devoted, indeed. No one could help realizing that. This afternoon, for example, I suppose you were in each other's company?"

"This afternoon? Today?" Ryn set down the cup and saucer which she had just lifted again from the table. A little coffee was spilled, but she did not take her eyes off his. "What—what happened this afternoon?"

"Nothing," said Todd. "Nothing at all—or so I'm told. You and Cass were together?"

"We—why, no, we weren't. Is that so remarkable? I—I was over at the Legion of Honor, to see the new exhibit. And Cass was—I don't know exactly where she was—she got up this morning before I did and went out, and I haven't seen her since." Her beautiful hands gripped each other in her lap, their nails a burnished red against the muted plaid of her wool skirt. She said, "What difference does it make to you? Why are you asking?"

"To frighten you, Ryn," said Todd pleasantly.

"*Me?*"

"You, or somebody. Perhaps you'll be good enough to pass on what I have to say to your family—and Miss Godfrey."

Ryn's clear pallor had gone almost gray. She wet her lips. "But—what about?"

"That's what I don't quite know," said Todd in his lightest and most casual voice. "I'm shooting in the dark, I'll admit, but I'm shooting into a very small room with five persons in it. A bullet's bound to hit somebody." He chuckled, all but inaudibly. "Metaphorical bullets, of course. I shouldn't want to use physical violence—unless I had to."

"I don't know what you mean."

"Some one of you does, and the rest probably have a fairly good idea. You're all in a conspiracy of lies, that's been evident from the beginning."

"What beginning?"

Todd shrugged. "No telling how far back it really started. Maybe with your Uncle Nikko's death, maybe with your sister

Sibella's." He saw her eyelids stretch and her look grow vacant. "Maybe just with Hugh Hartlein's."

"You—you've got some kind of obsession, it's all wrong. Even the talk about Hugh has died down. Nobody's been near us for days about that. It's all over."

"It's not over. It's set up a sort of slow chain reaction, things blowing up all over the place, things that don't seem to make sense at the time; but they will, Ryn, they will." He waited a minute and then went on. "His death, and those others, could have stayed unsolved till Doomsday for all of me—until today. I'm not a detective nor a judge, but I'm a man with a family of whom I'm rather fond; and when Georgine and I get roped into—into the enclosure where things are blowing up, I do care."

He sat immobile, facing her across the coffee table near the hearth. His head was at its usual angle and his face expressionless, but his voice had taken on a metallic twang which his wife would have recognized with respect and a little foreboding. Ryn said nothing, but her eyes still looked into a void.

"You've been using us, of course," he went on. "Every li'le act that you put on, any of you, was rehearsed for us first: trying it on the dog, I imagine, so you could see how it might go over with the police. But that's all right, I've been using you too. We were fairly even—until this afternoon."

"*What happened* this afternoon?" Ryn burst out.

"We met your friend Mrs. Trumbull."

Something happened to her face. A faint shade of color stole back into it, its taut muscles relaxed a trifle. She met his eyes at last, with every sign of complete bewilderment. "Who?" said Ryn Johnson, blinking.

"You know who. The woman who rents David Shere's property in the City."

"Oh, that woman. Mrs.—oh, yes, of course. But what would she have to do with us, now?"

"She had something to do with you a while back. You got her that place, you recommended her to Shere—someone in this family did, at any rate. I shouldn't be surprised if one of you put up the money for her deposit."

This was another shot in the dark, but he saw it register in the flutter of Ryn's eyelashes. She said, composedly enough, "Well, what did she do to you?"

"She told us a number of unpleasant lies," said Todd. His voice was twanging now, like a deliberately plucked wire. "And the basis for those lies came from somewhere in this family. On the day that you and Cass had lunch with us, our daughter Barby took you to her room to freshen up, didn't she? She talked to you for some time. There's a picture of her father in that room. She told you his story, didn't she?"

"I—I don't remember." Ryn's face was enclosed and wary.

"Mrs. Trumbull used that story today, but not on her own. She had someone in that place directing her, telling her how to change plans on the spur of the moment when I turned up unexpectedly. She changed them, not very skilfully, and then—she disappeared, clean off the map, and I'd guess she did her disappearing out the back door with the person who was directing things. Now, where do you suppose she went? I'd like to renew my acquaintance with Mrs. Trumbull. I'd like it very much."

"I scarcely know the woman," said Ryn coolly, "and I wouldn't have the faintest idea where she went. What were the plans?"

"That's another thing I don't know." Todd had not taken his eyes from hers. "I only know that it felt *bad*, like the concentrated solution of evil, and that one of you had a part in it. That was a blunder, you see. The police can't do anything, because the plan failed, but I can do something. That's what I wanted you to realize."

He got up. He told himself that he wished to heaven he knew what it was that he could do, but no hint of this uncertainty had sounded in his voice. There was a good chance that he'd stirred something up, and that someone would really be frightened.

Ryn rose with him. "I suppose," she said, "you wouldn't believe me if I said there was no—what did you call it, conspiracy? That you are just suffering from an obsession?"

"No, I wouldn't believe you." Todd picked up his hat from the bookcase near the door, where he had laid it beside the alligator purse. "You'll see that Miss Godfrey gets her handbag?"

Ryn looked away from him. "Yes," she said tonelessly. "I—I'll care of it."

"And, if you really don't know what's going on, how about taking care of yourself?"

The gray-green eyes flashed up to his. "*Will* you go home?" she said, wrenching the door open.

Todd drove home thoughtfully, and still thoughtfully mounted the steps to his own front door. The wife-sitter was at the telephone in the lower hall, giving a strong impression that he had gone to it immediately after Todd left and hadn't moved since. This, however, was not quite the case; the youth reported that everything had been quiet except for once when the back door had blown open. "I went out to look," he said responsibly. "I kind of figured you wanted a man in the house just for that sort of thing. Nobody was there, though, I guess it was the wind."

When the sitter had been paid and dismissed, Todd also went out to look. The yard was serene and domestic under a flood of moonlight that artistically touched up the whirligig and the big empty clothes-basket propped at the corner. The next-door windows were dark, but on the hill above, houses were close-set along the irregular streets, against the contour, and their white stucco and wood caught the moonlight almost dazzlingly among the black shapes of trees. Though it was not very late, even as he watched some of the gold squares of their windows blinked out.

Todd went upstairs. His wife was still asleep and safe, and he went to bed himself, wearier with bafflement than with exertion.

It was much later when he awoke to find Georgine standing with chattering teeth beside his bed, and urging him to move over. "I'm scared again, Todd," she said apologetically, sliding under the covers and pressing her head against his shoulder.

"Bad dream?" he said.

"No. I hate to be so traditional, but I'm sure I heard noises downstairs."

"Want me to go down?"

"Yes—no—I don't know. I have visions of you getting shot…"

"I won't get shot. I'll leave my own gun up here, that's safest."

"I'd go with you," said Georgine faintly, "so we could die together, only my knees won't hold up."

Todd went down, soundlessly. There was no one in the house, and nothing but deep shadow in the yard; only the kitchen door had once more slipped its latch and was banging in the fitful wind. He put a chair against it; if he couldn't fix it himself tomorrow, they'd have to call a locksmith.

Georgine was still in his bed, with her head frankly buried under the covers; she emerged with relief when he reported. He said, "Stay here for a while, till you get calmed down," and laid his arm lightly over her. The heartbeats that had shaken her whole body gradually diminished, and one by one her tense muscles softened.

"Funny, the little extra things you love people for," she murmured after a time.

"I'm waiting," Todd mentioned.

"You always know when not to laugh."

"Well, that's good as far as it goes."

There was another, longer silence. Presently she said in a drowsy monotone, "I guess I'd better go back to my own bed so we can get some sleep."

"You don't mind if I laugh at that one?" Todd inquired.

CHAPTER NINE

LOCKSMITHS, IT APPEARED on investigation the next morning, were so far participating in the current prosperity that they could be high-handed about employment. The kindest of them was willing to rearrange his schedule so that he could repair the McKinnons' back door a week from the next Monday. When advised of their needs he merely said, "Whyn'tcha put a chair under the knob and go out the front?" and hung up.

"And the chair," Todd observed, "I'd already thought of." He bent once more to fiddle with the lock, whose repair was beyond his powers. When he straightened up, it was to glance around the kitchen as if trying to capture an elusive memory. "I keep thinking that there was something different here when I came down the second time last night," he said slowly. "The first time, just after young Al left, I didn't look around inside as carefully as I might; but there was some li'le thing that photographed itself on my mind, and I can't get it now."

"Well, nothing's missing," Georgine said, hanging up the last cup and flinging her dishtowel over a rack. "All the pots and pans are here, and the remains of the cake, and the knives—now, if our steak knife had gone, we could really get worried."

"No, it was something on a wall. As you say, though, there's nothing missing now." He sat down beside the table and began absently to run a scale or two on his mouth-organ.

Georgine waited. In a minute or two he would work up to the Running Jump Symphony, and when—yes, there it came. "Look, chum," she said ominously, "you can't do that there 'ere. I'm going mad hearing that theme. Can't we talk it out?"

"What? Oh. Yes, I suppose so. Georgine, if you wanted to lose a horse, where would you take it?"

"Haven't you got that wrong?" Georgine said. "I thought it was, 'I thought where I'd go if I was a horse and I went there'—"

"No, I meant what I said."

"I see." She thought for a moment. "Well, I suppose in a field with a lot of other horses."

"Yes." He tapped the mouth-organ on his palm, his agate eyes narrowed and hard. "I wonder if there are any landladies' conventions, or clubs, or hideouts."

"Are you still thinking about that woman?"

"Still thinking. Does it bother you?"

"No, I've recovered pretty well." Georgine polished the drainboard. "It—the thing that bothers me most is the uncertainty, not knowing what would have happened to me; it would be easier somehow if I knew they'd meant to kill me."

Todd looked at her soberly for an appreciable time. Then he said, "You've never been to the Colony. Want to drive out there with me?"

Georgine's heart seemed to leap sideways like a skittish colt. Mentally she spoke soothing words to it, telling herself that Todd had been safe on that other occasion, that she'd be with him, that she needn't even get out of the car unless she chose...

"All right," she said finally. "I suppose there's some definite reason?"

"Not definite. Just a long chance." He got up and went into the hall. "While you're getting dressed I want to make a telephone call."

From upstairs she could hear him, not all the words, but enough to make out that he was talking to Mrs. Majendie. One sentence rose clearly. "Not yet? You haven't looked for her?" Then the softer murmur again.

He explained, as they got into the car. "I wondered if Miss Godfrey might have gone back to the Colony the other night. Mrs. Majendie says no, that it would be unlikely, and that she hasn't seen her since the big scene on Tuesday, but that she'd evidently been home—which we knew already—and had cleaned up the house in a frenzy of leave-taking and done a few things about the garden that she'd been putting off."

"Why do you want Miss Godfrey?" Georgine said. "No, you drive, I don't want to be entertained with mouth-organ solos all the way out there."

Todd started the car. "I don't want her. I most particularly don't want her at the Colony. She's probably got some other place she goes to when the Cosmos won't vibrate right."

They were through the tunnel and running smoothly along through the milder air of the Orinda section before Georgine said, "Todd, do you think this whole thing began at the Colony?"

"It depends," he said thoughtfully, "on which theory and which motive I'm on at the moment. If Chloe Majendie's been directing the Hand of God, it started when Nikko Majendie was caught getting out of that warm bed, but if she didn't take revenge on his partner in sin, that theory falls through. I sure hate to give it up—I've never bagged a Ritual Repeater."

Georgine gave a spurt of unsympathetic laughter. "I doubt if anyone ever has. But what about it if Nikko died naturally?"

"Then it might still have started out here, with the one who had the forbidden baby—and was probably nursed by Joan, too. The old girl has her uses; you could forgive quite a lot of oddities if you had a good chauffeur and gardener and nurse rolled into one. —Joan was around, no doubt, when Bell Johnson started off on her wedding trip," said Todd meditatively, "and she was certainly there when Hartlein paid his evening call and laid the inhaler on the table, and had to be reminded of it."

They drove for a mile or so in silence. Then Georgine said, "Todd, I don't see how a person could follow two or three patterns at once."

"How's that again?"

"Look; you've got Joan being a Ritual Repeater, and a Maniac, and a Perfect Murderer—trying to implicate someone else—and even, partly, the Policeman's Little Helper. It's too much."

He thought it over, slowing the car to watch the road signs. "You've got a point there. Of course, I don't confine myself to that one theory. What if the murders didn't start at the Colony, but with the death of Bell and her husband? They might be caused by simple greed. We've got Cass and Ryn both inheriting from Bell; we've got Cass collecting some of Hartlein's insurance, and technically both of those murders are of the Perfect type... Or suppose that old debbil Sex is at the bottom of all this, you could see David Shere bumping off his lost love and the successful rival, all in one, and then going on to the just impediment in the person of Hartlein, and removing that, and even taking a few swipes at a sister who might be some other kind of impediment."

"No, I couldn't. The methods are too indirect."

Todd slowed for a turn, and glanced sideways at her. "Ah, my dear stooge, but have you considered that that furious manner Shere affects may be put on just so that we'll consider him a big straightforward bumbling schoolboy? 'Not in character,' we say, and dismiss him. If you could really work a personality disguise, it'd beat all the false beards and plastic surgery that ever turned up in the history of crime."

"Okay, but I'll stick to my own character reading. And not one of these patterns takes in that business with the Trumbull, yesterday."

"No," Todd said, "but if we could get to the bottom of that, maybe we could work it in. You know what it fits? The pattern of the Nervous Murderer, and we haven't got one of those yet."

"Well, dear, by all means have one. Let's get in the whole collection, even if we have to kill me off to make it plausible."

Todd laughed callously and swung the car into the gateway of the Beyond-Truth Colony.

The grass circle was as smooth and verdant as ever, the walks and shrubbery as neat, but today the Sabbath hush was absent. There were sounds of activity, of lawn-mowers and clippers and voices calling; in fact, the first person the McKinnons met was Mr. Alvah Burke, clad in overalls, standing on a ladder and clipping away at the top of a hedge near the circle. He turned and saw them and descended with a look of ingenuous pleasure on his sprightly old face. "Well, well," he said. "Back again, eh? And with a lady, too. There's lots of our visitors that get interested and come back."

Todd introduced him to Georgine, and added, "I'm afraid we're still in no state to be converted, Mr. Burke. We came to call on one of your other visitors."

"Yes? Who would it be?"

"She calls herself Mrs. Trumbull, but that may not be the name she'd give you. She would have come here last night, and I think that one of Mrs. Majendie's nieces would have brought her out and arranged for her stay."

"A stranger, you mean? There's not a soul here that we don't know," said Mr. Burke, and shook his head for added emphasis, his candid old eyes on Todd's. "I guess you made a mistake, Mr. McKinnon. Nobody's here but our own members."

Todd grinned at him. "Honest, Mr. Burke? We just want to talk to the guest, that's all. You mean nobody came here last night?"

"No one but members." The old gentleman smiled back at him. "That's World Truth, sir."

"Nobody could have come without your knowing?"

"Well, now, that's possible. You might ask the ladies, I reckon. There's a lot of them over there turning out the guest cottage."

Todd thanked Mr. Burke, and directed Georgine across the circle toward the guest cottage. "Hell," he said in a low voice as they walked, "I think he is telling World Truth, too. Most transparent old codger I ever met. We might as well look around, though."

As they neared the guest cottage, it was evident that the ladies who "took pride," in Mr. Burke's earlier phrase, were doing it today in the most strenuous fashion. Cheerful elderly voices were exchanging directions and comment from every point in the cottage's vicinity; a corps of four were washing windows, several more were attacking wicker furniture with a paint-spray gun, and a plump gentleman was pruning vines under the instruction, given in no uncertain terms, of another. The ladies had all protected their hair with bandannas, and their wash dresses and aprons might have been photographed on the spot for a soap advertisement.

"Oh, dear," Georgine murmured. "I ought to wash our upstairs windows this week."

"Easy," Todd said. "I didn't bring you out here to get those ideas in your head." He tipped his hat back to look up at a window whence one of the ladies had just hailed him by name.

"Good morning," she was saying briskly. "We were sorry you and your friend couldn't stay for the meeting on Tuesday." He had to gaze at her for an appreciable moment before he recognized the Miss Cortelyou who had guided him, today wearing her nice old face completely unadorned.

He repeated his request, while Georgine stood mutely trying to look as if she had left her own house in irreproachable order: a difficult feat at any time.

"Why, no," said Miss Cortelyou after a minute's pause, "I haven't seen anyone who isn't a member. All the ladies are here this morning, anyway. You can look around and see for yourself."

"When I made that remark about the field of horses," said Georgine, sotto voce, "I should have added that the horses ought to be all alike." A shapeless gray-faced woman working with a spray gun, who might have been near enough to hear a word or two, glanced up at her and looked faintly surprised; and then wiped her forehead with a short sleeve and returned to work.

"Well, Holmes," Georgine added, "it was a wonderful idea, only it didn't work."

Todd shook his head. He had completed a survey of all the visible ladies, and now was leading his wife slowly around to the back of the cottage where one or two other workers were hanging blankets on a line. Georgine could sense the rising of those invisible antennae of his; he let go her arm and walked quickly around to confront a woman whose face had been hidden.

"Oh, how do you do," the woman's voice said pleasantly. "I hope Mr. Burke told you all you wanted to know, the other day?" Todd's voice, politely answering, sounded deflated.

"'A blank, my lord,'" said Georgine softly as they retraced their steps.

"You're right, damn it. I expect we'd better go back to the City and look for that landladies' convention." He took off his hat in farewell to Miss Cortelyou and started back across the lawns. "And I can tell you that, from the landladies I've known, I'd just as soon jump into a den of lions."

"How *do* they keep their grass like this?" Georgine inquired inattentively. "It's almost like a putting green."

They reached the car. Todd held open the door for her, and she got in, smiling. "I've just reacted to the landladies' convention. It's one of those pictures that kind of builds up in your mind, all of the brass-haired and high-busted ones in a solid phalanx, with those distrustful eyes on you and their eyebrows... *Todd!*"

"What's the matter?"

"We're a pair of perfect fools! Didn't you rather expect to find Mrs. Trumbull with all her make-up on?"

Todd paused in the act of inserting his ignition key. "You think one of those women was the Trumbull after all?"

"You don't know what a difference it makes if you take off everything."

"That I would have noticed, like the witches' sabbath."

"Lunkhead," said Georgine without rancor. "I mean the eyebrows, the mascara, the corsets—*and* the henna. Yes, I looked too, for an edge of red hair to show under one of those kerchiefs, and they were all gray except for the one with the spray gun. Hers was still pinkish, Todd. She couldn't wash out all the henna overnight."

"Nobody but members," he said slowly, thoughtfully. "I believed that story. I still believe it. But if those old innocents were telling the truth both ways—Georgine; wait here for a minute."

It was not much more than the actual sixty seconds before he came back through the screen of trees that masked the guest cottage. Ahead of him walked the woman who had been using the spray gun. She walked hurriedly, unsteadily, with her head bent, like the pictures of an accused person coming out of court and ducking the photographers.

Todd herded her almost to the car; he sat her down on a stone bench on the edge of the grass circle, and beckoned Georgine to join him. The woman looked up defiantly, and it was easy enough now to paint, in imagination, the black eyebrows and the dark lipstick on her colorless face, and to recognize her.

"Georgine," said Todd softly, "this is Mrs. Trumbull, of course, but it's also Frances Sagers."

Georgine's eyes began to spark a vivid and ominous blue. They met Todd's, hard as a whetstone, and the woman's, sullen and fearful. Slowly she got out of the car, closed the door and leaned against it.

"So they were telling the truth," she said. "Once a member, always a member; and the old people took you in because they thought you'd returned to the fold. It might have worked except that my husband spotted the connection between you and the Beyond-Truth." She waited a minute, remembering the cruelty of the lies that had been told her yesterday. "Todd, do the people out here know what kind of member she was—what she did to Dr. Majendie?"

"Not yet," said Todd. He glanced at Mrs. Trumbull, who had shut her mouth in an ugly stubborn line. Georgine guessed what kind of pressure he had exerted to get the woman to come with him.

"They couldn't do anything," said Mrs. Trumbull roughly. "They wouldn't—the old softies. Wouldn't even believe you."

"They'd believe Mrs. Majendie," Todd pointed out. "She'd be interested personally, too. You got off too easily that other time. She was sorry for you—and she went farther yet, she recommended you for the job at the lodging-house."

"I didn't do anything."

"Perhaps not, but what was done couldn't have been fixed up without your connivance." Todd looked at her implacably, and his eyes narrowed. "Where were you, all those years between the early Thirties and the middle Forties?"

"None of your business."

"We can find out from Mrs. Majendie. She'll tell us when she knows it's important. But in the meantime, I can make a guess. Shere said you'd come 'from the South,' but I'd bet that it wasn't any farther south than the Tehachapi Mountains. You were in the women's prison, weren't you?"

The woman said nothing, but a muscle twitched in her face.

"What you pulled on Dr. Majendie," Todd added, "was the old hotel-room con game. You probably tried it again, and one of the times you got caught."

Georgine watched the colorless face. Trumbull wasn't the smartest deceiver in the world; her eyes jerked nervously sideways and her lips tightened. Georgine nodded as she met Todd's look.

"And after you got out, you came crawling back to Mrs. Majendie, and said you were sorry, you meant to go straight now, she'd been kind to you before and maybe she'd help you again. That was the set-up, wasn't it? But," said Todd softly, "You weren't going straight yesterday. She'll have to know that, and so will the police. You know about terms for multiple offenses."

"I didn't do anything," Mrs. Trumbull burst out again, a frightened tremor in her voice. "She came over there and made me do it—threatened me, same as you're doing now, only she was going to tell Mr. Shere all about me, he didn't know before."

"*Who* came over there?"

"That girl, that girl! And it didn't sound like any great harm, she knew a woman in Berkeley who'd been telling lies about her, and she wanted to give her a scare. That's what she said."

"What girl?" Todd repeated patiently.

The Trumbull's voice was sullen. "The Johnson girl."

"Which one?" said Georgine with emphasis.

"I don't know. I can't hardly tell 'em apart, I never saw much of either of 'em, only that time they took me to see Mr. Shere. She just said she was Miss Johnson."

"What did she look like?"

"Well, kind of middle-sized, pretty, with dark hair. She had on one of those camel-hair coats that cost a mint."

"They both have them. How about her eyes, and her hair, and the shape of her face?"

"I don't know, I tell you. She had on dark glasses, those slantwise ones, kind of like a mask—and her eyes looking through—" She paused, swallowed and added, "But you couldn't see the color."

"Mrs. Trumbull," said Todd with quiet concentration, "that sounds as if you'd felt something wrong about her too. She frightened you, didn't she? Aside from the threats, I mean?"

"Yes, she did. I don't know why. I didn't want to—so help me, I did go straight after I got out, and I got a man friend that's—well, she did scare me into it. And she said there wasn't any harm in what was going to happen."

"But what was planned?"

"I don't know." The rough voice was desperate. "I was just to do the telephoning, and meeting at the door, and then show you—" she looked at Georgine, with a sort of miserable appeal in her eyes—"to the stairs. I don't know what else."

"And then the plan was changed, because my wife didn't, after all, come alone. The Johnson girl rushed you out the back door, isn't that so?"

"That's right. Said there was going to be trouble, and I better get out. And she drove me to the bus station and left me. I was to stay out here until she 'phoned me to come back."

"There was going to be trouble," said Todd thoughtfully. "There still could be, you know, unless we find out which of the Johnson girls worked out that plan."

"What was her hair like?" Georgine said.

The woman shrugged. "I told you. Black. Done up in a kind of thick roll at the back of her neck, coming up to cover her ears."

"Could have been either of them," Todd said. His eyelids contracted, and he met Georgine's look. She shook her head. She said, "That hair-do would disguise the shape of her cheeks, and so would the glasses. She didn't mean Mrs. Trumbull to know which one she was."

Todd stood up. "Perhaps we'd better take you in to talk to the police—and Mrs. Majendie."

"No, for God's sake," the woman said with sudden desperation. "I couldn't tell you any more, I swear it. And you know nothin' happened, you can't pin that business on me! Just lemme stay here, I won't move from the place. You tell the old people I've got to."

"That might do," said Todd deliberately. He looked at Georgine again and gave an infinitesimal shrug. She knew what he meant; there was, after all, nothing of which to accuse Mrs. Trumbull, and there was also the strong impression that she had told all—or nearly all—she knew. She would be safe here.

And yet—there was the uncertainty, still unresolved, and the added fact that this woman also had felt the sense of something wrong. Eyes, looking at her through dark tilted glasses: that had been enough.

"Let's drop it," said Georgine abruptly. "For now, anyway."

Todd nodded. In silence he gestured to Mrs. Trumbull, so that she rose and started back, walking behind him, across the green circle. Georgine sat waiting for him, feeling that if she moved too suddenly her nerves would give out an audible twang. Something wrong was abroad, something evil, but nothing that you could grasp; an evil so nebulous that for the police and the law it would not exist; a crime as yet invisible, related to life only as the Beyond-Truth was to ordinary fact, a kind of vibration of wrong-doing which only the initiate could see.

Todd came back. Watching his approach, she thought, —We'll drive home, we'll be in time for a late lunch, and afterward I am really going to wash the upstairs windows; I might even—yes, I will, I'll put the bedroom rugs through the washer.—

The lunch part of this program went off as planned, but the rest of it fell far short of Georgine's ideal. She had seen herself being the conscientious housewife while Todd was at home, scrubbing away to the accompaniment of cheerful sounds from the typewriter. It developed, however, that Todd meant to drive

up to Cuckoo Canyon and gently sound out Mrs. Majendie on
the subject of Frances Sagers' relations with her nieces.

"Oh, Todd, *no!*" she said violently. "You're just sticking
your neck out!"

"Dear Georgine, I've got to stick it out. I've got to get
those damned stories of mine into workable shape. Do you
know how many I've managed to finish so far? Two; and not
masterpieces, either. It's not enough."

She answered his inquiring look. "Of course I'm scared.
Nobody seems to have a sense of danger except me. Hugh
Hartlein did, of course; and look what happened to him!"

"As a matter of fact," said Todd rather sheepishly, "the
police say that he was a suicide."

Georgine looked at him. "*Now* he tells me! How did they
finally decide on that?"

"Three days before he died he'd sent an old suit up to
his mother's home. They found aluminum filings embedded
in the material, and traces of crystalline cyanide in a pocket.
He made that inhaler himself. They think he stole the cyanide
from the Majendie greenhouse, and of course he planted the
experimental inhalers in the compost heap."

"You sound," Georgine said, "as if that doesn't satisfy you."

"It's hard to go against that kind of evidence," said Todd
slowly. "Maybe I'd be like Nelse and say that the case is closed,
except for those goings-on yesterday. They might have fitted
into a murder pattern, but they certainly don't into a suicide.
And maybe the police can afford to ignore the Trumbull business; I can't."

"Oh, dear me. I see. If there's no mystery about Hartlein,
that other thing is just—the result of dislike."

"Yes, and who hates you that much?"

"I thought nobody did," said Georgine plaintively. "I've
done nothing but ply them with creamed shrimps and coffee
and Coca-Cola, and I wish to heaven they'd feed *me* some
time! The only one—"

"Yes?"

"I can't make anything of this either, but every time David Shere and I have met we've ended up fighting—or at least, he's been mad at me."

"And that doesn't fit any of the patterns either," said Todd, unhappily running a palm across his hair, "unless he got the idea that you'd done him out of the money. I admit I wouldn't mind finding out that it was Shere. I want very much to poke somebody in the nose over that business yesterday. You're sure you won't put the Curse of Rome on me if I go now?"

"No, I think you have to be at least a Cardinal to do that. But I will assert myself somehow; wear a sweater under your coat!"

"I'll wear five sweaters if you like," said Todd, springing up. "Batten down the hatches, Georgine, and don't speak to any strange men. I shouldn't be gone more than an hour."

He drove slowly up to Cuckoo Canyon under a sky which today was veiled by a thin, mean-looking haze behind which the sun and all warmth had retired. The wind had blown itself nearly out. Gardeners who would not have dared to light a trash fire in the dry northern gale of the past few days were now busily raking up leaves and cramming them into incinerators, or watching over smoldering piles in the gutters, hurrying to get their yards cleaned up before the winter rains began in earnest. Todd sniffed the pleasant smoke soberly. His mind was busy with the proper opening for the afternoon's business: —Mrs. Majendie, we've found Frances Sagers, but I assure you it was quite by accident; —Mrs. Majendie, just how much do your nieces know about Frances Sagers' past history? — Mrs. Majendie...

He hadn't yet found the really tactful approach when the low redwood house came in sight over the top of the cliff. He parked his car beside the Majendie driveway and strolled into the garden, where a shapeless felt hat was moving deliberately along behind a tall row of chrysanthemum bushes.

Chloe Majendie reached the end of the row and saw him. She said, "Good afternoon, Mr. McKinnon," in her beautiful deep voice, and came into the open with her eyes fixed on his. "How may I help you this time?"

"By letting bygones be bygones, for one thing," Todd replied. "When this is all over, Georgine and I would very much like to call on you as friends."

"And I should like to have you. But surely 'this' is all over now?"

"Not quite, I think. I was a li'le worried over Miss Godfrey, Mrs. Majendie."

"I doubt that you need to be," said the old lady kindly.

"Has she come home, may I ask?"

"No, not yet. I never have known where she's gone on her other—let us call them, leaves of absence." Mrs. Majendie's eyes twinkled faintly. "Nor have I known when to expect her, but I think she'll be home soon." She looked at him curiously. "Was it she who inspired this call?"

"As it happens, no," said Todd, smiling. "I was just leading up to my other subject in what I hoped was a graceful way. Easing into it, you know. Start with Joan, ask if her handbag had been returned safely, work round to your nieces—seemed less abrupt, I thought."

Mrs. Majendie's attention had been caught earlier in his remarks. "Her handbag?" she said. "Joan's?"

"Yes. It was left at our place, and I returned it to Ryn last night."

"Was her money in it, Mr. McKinnon?"

"Yes. Rather a large amount, I believe." He debated a moment and added, "Georgine said that Miss Godfrey was a bit upset, still, and indicated she didn't want to take along anything you'd given her."

"That would scarcely include money. She earned her salary." Chloe's lips pressed together briefly. "Will you come in, Mr. McKinnon?"

Todd followed her into the house, and sat down on the chair she indicated. From another room her voice sounded intermittently, the words inaudible. It was evident that she was telephoning. —So much for tact, he told himself resignedly. — The old lady's got off on another subject and I'll never get her back to Frances Sagers until she's exhausted it.—

It was perhaps ten minutes before Mrs. Majendie reappeared, and when she did her craggy old face looked flushed and anxious. "I called Ryn," she said. "The child's been asleep all morning after a bad night, and hadn't had a chance to bring the bag up. And I called the bank. Joan hasn't cashed any checks, Mr. McKinnon. She would need money; she's not as unworldly as that." She paused a moment, and her keen eyes seemed to glaze over. "I believe I will sit down. —This is Thursday afternoon, and I haven't seen Joan since she left us at the Colony on Tuesday. She was gone when I got home that night."

"We saw her here at about six o'clock. She was sweeping the porch," said Todd.

"Yes, I noticed. Coals of fire on my head, was how I interpreted it. She did a number of odd jobs that we usually finished together: swept every ash out of the fireplace, tied up the old newspapers, fumigated the—"

Her voice broke off as if something had clutched her windpipe. She had been gazing past Todd; now she looked at him squarely, and her weathered face turned ashen gray. "She fumigated the greenhouse," she said on the merest thread of sound. "I saw the sign on the door, 'Danger, cyanide fumes, do not open for forty-eight hours.'—That last is to make sure that the fumigation is thorough. But—I didn't go in."

Todd said nothing. The little core of concentration was drawing together in his mind.

Old Chloe's voice and vigor had returned. "There's only one thing to do, of course," she said, rising. "That's to go and investigate. Will you be so kind as to come with me?"

"Of course," Todd murmured. After the comfortable warmth of the house, the cold November air hit him with a physical shock as he followed her across the porch, but it did not dissipate his almost hypnotized attention. —Mrs. Majendie had not thought of the greenhouse until now—until she had an impartial witness.—

The dowdy, impressive old figure moved deliberately across the garden to the edge of the cliff, the first point at which both the greenhouse and the Johnsons' cottage, far below, were visible. The greenhouse stood on a natural shelf at the second turn of the path. Mrs. Majendie looked down at it, paused only briefly, and began to round the hairpin curve.

At the same moment something moved in the Johnsons' garden. Someone had come quickly out of the house and was running through the gate, up the road to the place where the cliff path began. A long, full, gray-green coat swung out behind the figure as in desperate-seeming haste it began to climb...

Mrs. Majendie had reached the door of the greenhouse. Her big hand reached out and unhooked the hand-lettered sign from the doorknob, opened the door and motioned Todd back.

"We'll wait for just a minute," she said quietly. "Let the place air before we go in."

Through a clear space scratched in the thin whitewash that covered the glass Todd could see the wooden tables inside, covered with flats of earth in which small leaves showed green. He glanced downward at the plank walk between the tables. A short cylindrical glass jar was visible there, partly filled with a colorless liquid. Through the open door he glimpsed two more. The warm, steamy, earthy smell of all greenhouses drifted out and blew softly away on the wind.

"Now," said Mrs. Majendie, and walked in with a firm step. She looked up and down along the ground. Complete stillness came over her, and at the same moment Todd saw what she had seen. From under one of the tables protruded a thin brown hand, curled like a bird's claw.

Without moving, old Chloe said, "My poor Joan. My poor, poor Joan." Then she bent with surprising ease and swiftness, going on her knees beside the thin body that the table all but concealed. She touched the hand briefly. "She's dead, I'm afraid. She must have died a good many hours ago."

"Please," said Todd sharply, "I needn't remind you not to move anything, I suppose?" He in turn glanced around. The plank walk was clean and dry. There was nothing on it but the three jars.

Mrs. Majendie shook her head. "I gave way to an impulse, last Tuesday," she said as if to herself. "It was a terrible mistake for me to tell you about my husband. This is what I have done."

Todd, now squatting beside her, remarked, "You will forgive me for doubting that?"

"Why else should the poor soul kill herself?"

"You think that is what she did?"

Mrs. Majendie got to her feet, more stiffly than she had gone down. "I am afraid so." She took a container from a high shelf and glanced into it. "We were low on the cyanide eggs. There were only three left. Joan knew where they were, she used them all in these three jars of acid to—to make sure. And then she lay down, I think, and closed her eyes."

"Yes. They're closed. I have never heard how the gas chamber—" Todd broke off and stretched to look around past the top of the still head. "There's something—the pieces of a heavy flowerpot, I should think, and the earth that may have spilled out of it. Did you leave broken pots under these benches as a rule?"

The old lady looked at him keenly. "Never to my knowledge."

"And—I can't see very well without moving her, but there's something like a bruise on the far side of her head."

"There is? Could Joan have been bending over, and tipped the pot off the table so that it stunned her?"

"And put the eggs into the acid afterward, Mrs. Majendie?"

"Mr. McKinnon, what do you want me to tell the police?"

Todd looked up at her. Presently he got to his feet and brushed the knees of his trousers. "I should tell them that you have found Miss Godfrey dead, and that's all," he said.

"I'm grateful for your advice. You will stay until they come? Yes, of course, you would have to." She turned her head. "Very well, Ryn, come in if you want to, but I see no need for it."

For the past few minutes Todd had forgotten about the figure that had been climbing the cliff path. He glanced outside at Ryn Johnson, who was standing motionless on the gravel, her green coat tightly wrapped around her, her eyes dark and ringed with what seemed like fatigue. "Joan?" she said unsteadily.

He turned back and stooped once more. Yes, he was right. The loose earth from the pot had been pushed into a ridge on the far side of Joan Godfrey's head. It looked very much as if she had been pushed under that bench after she was unconscious.

He went out, shutting the door behind him. He'd done the best he could for Nelse, but he hadn't been quick enough to keep Mrs. Majendie from picking up that can that had held the cyanide eggs. He had, however, noted just where she'd taken hold of it.

"—see her Tuesday night?" Mrs. Majendie was finishing a sentence to her niece.

Ryn shook her head dumbly, her eyes fixed on Chloe's. With a sudden unaccountable feeling that was like a crackling of the nerves, Todd realized that he had never before seen either of the Johnson girls with their aunt. Perhaps this was hardly the right time for evaluating an attitude, but something about Ryn's tucked-in chin and the way her eyes were lifted gave the impression that she loved and admired her Aunt Chloe and went in terror of her.

"It's a shock, I know," said the old lady with great kindness, "but you must get yourself in hand, my dear. What time did you get home on Tuesday night?"

Ryn Johnson forced out a few hoarse words. "Not late. About—eleven."

"I was home by then, myself. Joan was already gone. When did Cass come in?"

Again Ryn shook her head. With what seemed like a great effort she unclasped one hand from the front of her coat, and moved it shakily in the direction of the greenhouse. "Is there—" she said in a painful whisper, "is—is it only Joan—in there?"

Todd looked at her narrowly, turned and stepped back into the greenhouse. There was another bench at the far end, on which some sacks had been spread out to dry, their hanging ends shadowing the space underneath. He bent swiftly and looked.

There was a large basket there. He took a plant stake from the table near him and carefully lifted the basket's lid. For a long minute he gazed at what was inside it.

From the open air came that almost unrecognizable voice. "Cass—Cass hasn't been home since yesterday morning. She was asleep when I got in Tuesday, she left Wednesday before I got up—I didn't know where she was going, she didn't come home at all last night, I sat up waiting for her—this morning I called David Shere, but he hadn't seen her—"

Todd stepped out again. "She's not in there, Ryn. We'd better tell the police that she's disappeared, at the same time we—"

Ryn's shadowed eyes turned to his. "But you did see something. I heard you suck your breath in."

"Yes. There's a wicker carrying basket, and Joan's Siamese cat is inside it."

"I thought she had taken Dian with her," said Mrs. Majendie gravely. "Evidently she did—but farther than I knew. Isn't that a point in favor of suicide, Mr. McKinnon?"

"That's hardly for me to say. It isn't just—" Todd hesitated—"that the cat has been gassed. Its head was crushed, Mrs. Majendie. It looked almost as if someone had—swung it against a rock wall."

"Joan—" said Mrs. Majendie in a low voice, "Joan would never have done that to her cat."

Todd, his attention caught by a stifled sound from Ryn, looked around quickly. She was gazing at her aunt, and this time the meaning of the look was plain; she was in mortal terror.

"We—we must get the police. I'll call them, I'll call Howard, you stay here, I'll do it," she cried out through chattering teeth; and then she had wheeled and was off up the slope toward the redwood house.

Her eyes, her voice, every movement of her body while she stood there had told a story of cruel strain; Todd had stood near her, expecting that at any minute she might crumple up in a faint; but her feet were swift and steady on the cliff path, her speed did not slacken as she rounded the turn, the green coat flying out behind her, and disappeared beyond the lip of the cliff.

CHAPTER TEN

GEORGINE MCKINNON, having set her hand to the plough—or, in this case, the bottle of Windex—was not going to turn back, but she was performing with a very ill grace. The bedroom rugs had gone into the washer immediately after Todd's departure, so that part of her resolution had been fulfilled. Of course, getting them to dry flat was something else, but they were now hung up to get the first moisture out, and maybe tomorrow they could be laid on the Manfreds' basement floor. She told herself, however, that no part of the window-washing could be postponed. She would tackle the big bedroom at the front of the house first, and a dismal job it was, too, what with her having to work in a heavy sweater... The bathroom window was of nubbled glass, and the opaquer it was the better. She needn't bother with that. Todd might be at home any minute, wanting to work in his study, so perhaps it might be better not to go in there and get the air as chill as the grave... As for Barby's room, that had been done fairly recently—well, only a few weeks ago...

The house seemed very still. She longed for the sound of the typewriter; she would even have welcomed the First Symphony. On a gloomy sort of day like this one ought to have company, providing, of course, that the company was the right sort.

This bedroom looked out both on Cragmont Avenue and the cross-street. Georgine polished soberly, watching the autumn look of sky and trees, smelling the bonfire smoke, seeing the small children coming home from school, each with the day's achievement of crayoning or finger-painting in a proud grasp. —It must be at least half-past three, she thought. —Todd's late, I wish he'd come back.—

A sedan full of young women in smart fall suits went past. All the women were laughing and talking and lighting cigarettes, and Georgine looked at them with ignoble envy. She had had this feeling before, of being set apart, the world moving on normally about her, and herself the only person who was beset by fear.

"But then," said Georgine half-aloud, "I feel that way when I'm going to have a tooth out, too. All those happy people who aren't going to the dentist... Oh, dear, and I have an appointment tomorrow morning—only to have the inlay put in, of course."

She dropped her work and went downstairs, somewhat defiantly, to telephone the hairdresser. It would make her feel better if she could get her hair shaped and washed tomorrow, too, and nuts to the expense—she'd save it somehow.

Deeper and louder voices could be heard from the sidewalk now, and she could easily identify the high-school crowd, who began to straggle homeward not earlier than four. She looked at the telephone dubiously, and then picked it up and called Mrs. Majendie's number. Probably it wouldn't be answered, or at best the old lady would be there, and would tell her that Todd had left two hours ago. But it wasn't like him not to let her know—

The bell at the other end burred twice, and was answered; briskly, efficiently answered, by a deep bass voice. Georgine recognized it at once. "Allen Slater, what are you doing at Mrs. Majendie's *again?*"

"Oh, it's you, Mrs. McKinnon. —Yes, he's here. I'll see if he can come to the telephone."

There were faint sounds of altercation in the background, and then Todd's voice, nearer the instrument: "Like hell I won't tell my wife!"

He told her.

When he had finished— "Todd McKinnon," said Georgine, "did you suspect something like this? Was that why you went to the Canyon this afternoon?"

"Word of honor, no, Georgine. I'm not happy about it."

"Oh, no? I'll bet Nelse made some crack about the vultures gathering... A tiger smelling blood? Is that any better?... Well, wasn't everybody rather relieved that there had been an undoubted murder? I'm sorry for the poor old creature, too, but I can't regret the cat much... And you had to help discover them!"

"I have a feeling," said Todd in a cautious low voice, "that anyone else might have done as well. And I don't feel at all relieved. It's the wrong thing to have happened, Georgine; it's all wrong."

"What do you mean by that?"

"I'll explain later. Slater's making faces at me from the door, I've got to get off the 'phone. Oh, by the way, you're still alone, aren't you?"

"Certainly I am, and not liking it much."

"I'll be home soon, with luck." His voice dropped again. "I think Nelse may take Mrs. Majendie and Ryn down to the Hall of Justice after a while... Yes, Allen, coming!"

Georgine hung up, put a hand to her head and groaned aloud. After a time she remembered her unfinished job and dragged herself upstairs. It had seemed that the depth of depression had been reached, but she had sunk to a new low at this moment. So there had been a real murder; better fifty alarums and excursions into the Beyond-Truth than this evidence that someone would really kill. What was it that Todd had said? "A clumsy attempt to make it look like suicide or accident; possibly a li'le too clumsy." Lucky that she'd saved some face; her fear had come out as flippancy over the telephone, but she was afraid now.

There was the homely task to be finished, there was the placid suburban street outside, and the high-school students still strolling home by ones and twos, the girls' soft mouths bright with newly applied lipstick, their burnished hair blowing in the chilly wind. There was nothing to be afraid of here, but she was afraid.

Twenty minutes later, when she was nearly done, a car stopped at the foot of the steps. *Todd,* she thought on a wave of relief; leaned out perilously to call a greeting, and then swallowed the welcoming words. The man who was charging up the stone stairs as if he meant to take the house by storm turned out to be David Shere.

He saw her, stood still with his head tipped up, and shouted, "Is Cass here?"

"Cass Johnson? No, of course not," Georgine called back.

"Do you know where she is? She didn't call you or anything?"

"Now, why should I, or should she?"

"Oh, God." David Shere deflated suddenly. "I've got to find her. She's been missing since yesterday."

"I know," said Georgine coldly, "and I also know what's been happening up at the Canyon. If you think I—"

Shere wasn't listening. "Look here," he said desperately, "I've been looking for her all day, ever since Ryn called me this morning to find out if I'd seen her. And I hadn't, not since we were here Monday. She goes to the Day Nursery on Tuesday, and she never lets me take her to lunch or dinner that day, so I didn't set eyes on her. And I wasn't home all Wednesday. There was that business with you people, in San Francisco, and I stayed over there till pretty late that night looking for Mrs. Trumbull. So when could I have seen Cass? And that was three disappearances!"

"If you're worried about your landlady," said Georgine, "we found her. Never mind where. That just leaves Cass."

"Yes, and you know what it might mean! The Godfrey woman was found dead, and—maybe Cass is somewhere else, dead too."

"She isn't dead here," Georgine informed him. "Hadn't it occurred to you that the police might have thought of this place? They asked Todd if she was here this noon, when he talked to Nelse." (He hadn't thought to tell her about it until half an hour ago, but that was unimportant.)

"Nor—alive?" Shere asked huskily.

"Are you crazy? D'you think we have her hidden in the priest's hole, to deceive Nelsing?"

"No. No, I guess not. Maybe I am sort of crazy." David Shere swayed a little, as if from overwhelming fatigue. "I—when I heard about Miss Godfrey—"

"How did you hear?" Georgine looked down at him in sudden suspicion.

"I called up Mrs. Majendie," he said. "—Look, couldn't I come in and tell you about it? I'm just about all in."

"I'm not letting anyone in. Sit on the steps if you want to."

He did so, after a pleading upward look. "You see, Mrs. McKinnon, I'd had a note from Miss Godfrey...Yes, the police know about it, I've just come from talking to 'em... She must have mailed it Tuesday night, they figured, but it wasn't picked up from that box near Mrs. Majendie's until Wednesday morning. It was under my door when I got home late that night. She'd meant to come and see me that evening, that Wednesday, for some crazy reason. I wasn't sorry to have missed her—if I had missed her; my landlady on Grove Street said she'd been in the lower hall all evening, and nobody'd been there. Just the same, I thought I'd better call up, the note said it was about something that—" His voice went into quotation tone—"'concerned me closely, both here and Beyond.'"

"And now you'll never find out," said Georgine slowly. He shook his head and then lowered it wearily.

She looked down at him. Something that concerned him—it couldn't by any chance have been some knowledge that Joan had of *his* commission of a crime? And could he have met her by chance, that evening as she was going to his room and he was returning from the City—met her, heard what she had to say, and killed her? He knew the set-up at Cuckoo Canyon. He could have driven Joan Godfrey up there and placed her body in the greenhouse without too much danger of being observed. Todd had said they thought she'd been dead since Tuesday night, but—there had been no time yet for an autopsy, and the passing off of rigor mortis wasn't an infallible test.

She thought, I'm safe enough here, surely; he can't get at me; but if he suddenly decided to shoot—

Shere looked up at her again. "They've got Ryn down at the police station now," he said. "I don't know what they're doing to her. If they think she had any hand in Cass's disappearance—"

Something about his attitude caught Georgine's attention. It was almost as if this were the only thing that really worried him; as if he wanted to find Cass only for Ryn's sake. She said, "Mr. Shere, which of the Johnsons are you really in love with?"

"*What?*"

"I said, which of them are you in love with?" Georgine shouted.

"What business is that of yours?" he shouted back, leaping to his feet.

"Sit down and keep your temper. If anyone around here gets mad, it's going to be me. You owe me something, David Shere—plenty, in fact. Now just answer that one question."

He sat down, and once more lifted his face, with a look on it that was almost piteous. "I don't know. Honestly, I don't know. Oh, Lord, I wish I had a drink."

Georgine's compassion, always getting the better of her at the unhandiest times, did so now. "You do look as if you needed one," she admitted. "I—if you'd stay right there, I'd get it for you."

She ran downstairs, found the meager remains of Nelsing's gift Bourbon, and after a little thought emptied it into a screw-top jar. If anyone happened to be passing the steps while he was drinking, it might look a bit better. She then put the jar into a large paper bag with twine handles, attached a length of string, went upstairs again and lowered the bag from the window.

It was almost down when without warning she was overtaken by laughter. "Catch it, quick," said Georgine in a muffled voice, and ducked behind the window-sill. After a minute she looked down again. Her demoralization was completed by the sight of Mr. Shere solemnly rooting in the depths of the bag like an out-sized child with a Christmas stocking.

She did not dare to come up again until she heard the involuntary whoosh given out by someone who has just taken a healthy slug of straight whisky. Shere was setting down the empty jar. "I'll feel better in a minute," he called up to her. "Thank you. And would you mind telling me why you asked that question?"

"About the Johnsons?" Georgine was luckily able to speak with fair composure. "Why, it might make things clearer if we were sure for whose sake you've been keeping still so long, and probably telling a lot of lies into the bargain." He opened his mouth. "No, don't bother to tell another. You know there's some kind of conspiracy, and you're in it up to the ears. It isn't Mrs. Majendie you're protecting, I'd be willing to bet. Come on, now."

There was more color in his face now. It looked bewildered and somehow penitent. "I'll tell you what I told the police," he said. "I have no definite knowledge whatsoever about any crime that's been committed. I'm not protecting anyone in the way you mean."

"And I'll bet you are," said Georgine firmly. "I'd simply like to know if it's Ryn or Cass." —Or, she thought—yourself, my boy; but I'm not going to put that in. —"Didn't anyone ever tell you that the police have a right to your suspicions as well as your direct knowledge?"

"No, they haven't. I don't know what my suspicions are, myself. I don't even know who I'm in love with, or which of 'em I *ought* to be in love with! That'd make it easier, y'see? I don't know whish—"

His voice had grown louder and louder, and Georgine was struck with a new suspicion. "Did you have any lunch?" she called down in the middle of his sentence.

"Lunch?" He considered gravely. "No, I guess so, but that musta been yesterday. Coupla drinks this noon. Maybe three. Now, about love."

"Be quiet, for goodness' sake!"

"About love," David Shere repeated in a cheerful bellow. The Bourbon was evidently having a field day with its brothers in his foodless stomach. "If it was you, now, I'd be sure right away. No wonnerin' if you're bad and don' look it or act it, or if you're good and somebody else makin' you *look* bad, see what I mean? I wish it was you, honest, Georgie. Be sim—simpler."

"No, it wouldn't," said Todd's voice from around the bend of the path. He came into sight, his face completely wooden and his step purposeful.

David Shere cast a wild look upward at Georgine, another downward at Georgine's husband. "Oh, gosh, I gotta fin' Cass, haven' I?" he blurted out, and plunged past Todd and down the stairs.

Todd looked at the shopping bag and the empty jar. Then he, too, gazed upward at Georgine. "What did I tell you," he remarked, "about not speaking to any strange men?"

❀ ❀ ❀

Half an hour later, in the living-room, she was still suffering from recurrent giggles which made it hard to attend to what Todd was saying. His arguments were all sensible and seriously conceived, too: David Shere could not have had anything to do with Joan Godfrey's death, because she had certainly died on Tuesday night, and he had been with friends until very late that night; motive, also, was lacking—anything that the poor Godfrey had dredged up, or thought she'd discovered, about previous crimes would have been discounted by investigators; "Who'd believe her, especially a year or so after the event?" Todd demanded. "And besides, according to the police there haven't been any previous crimes."

"Couldn't he just have disliked her for herself?" Georgine inquired.

"She's been like that for years. Why should he pick this time?"

"*I* don't know. That would be up to him. But he talked too much, Todd." Georgine gave another little spurt of laughter. "No, not just at that glorious moment; before. He gave me a play-by-play description of how he hadn't seen Cass. If we find that he boiled her up in his laboratory, leaving only a few fragments of bone here and there, I shan't be surprised."

"As a fiction writer," said Todd regretfully, "I couldn't use that. It's been done too often—and too well... What I have to do is somehow to fit in Joan's death with the rest of the business, and I can't. It's all wrong," he complained for at least the third time. "She shouldn't have been murdered, she ought to have committed suicide."

"Todd, you kill me. Here you work like a dog to make a lot of natural-seeming deaths into murders, and here's an undoubted murder and you want it to be accident or suicide! Couldn't you just relax and look at it the other way 'round?"

"You mean that Joan's was the first murder? Then why did she have to be killed? If none of the others was a crime, she couldn't have known anything to reveal. She sure as hell wasn't murdered for her money, it—what there is of it—goes to the Colony; and she wasn't struck down by the Beyond-Truth because she was the one who kept on believing in it after the old lady proved to be a renegade. She won't fit into any pattern."

"There has to be one, I suppose?"

"There always is, after a crime," said Todd.

"Well, pooh on it. I've got to find us something to eat." Georgine got up and moved toward the kitchen, pausing at the archway to remark, "Why don't you just drop the whole thing and tell yourself that nothing's happened? You know, like the news item about old Mr. and Mrs. Borden, thirteen years afterward."

"What? Oh, yes; a fine sardonic one saying that they'd both died of excessive heat."

"There you are. Just convince yourself that nobody's been murdered yet, sell the stories you've already written and call it a day. —It'll have to be scrambled eggs, I can't keep my mind on anything fancier. —Todd, what is it now? What are you kissing me for? I know I'm almost irresistible at any time, but—"

"Georgine, do you know what you just said? 'There haven't been any murders *yet!*'"

"Oh, did I? What did I mean?"

"The real murder, the planned one, hasn't come off. We haven't seen anything *after* the crime, because Joan got in its way, and had to be killed before the original victim was. By God, everything fits with that. Everything!"

"But who's the original victim?"

Todd let her go, slowly, and slowly thrust his hands into his pockets.

"That," he said, "I don't know."

Todd finished his cake and handed over his cup for a refill of coffee. "The only flaw is," he said, "that it won't make more than one story. I have to decide some time which way it's going to end!"

Georgine sat across the table from him, smoking a cigarette and gazing at him thoughtfully. "You had me scared for a while there," she remarked. "I thought you were being the brilliant amateur after all. May I say that I much prefer the fiction writer? Not," she added, "that you haven't come to the same conclusion as the police, more than once."

"About a week after they reached it, and in company with half a million other citizens. No," Todd said. "All for Art and the hell with evidence, that's me as a usual thing. And life's so annoyingly unlike art, I suppose you've noticed? But this shapes up. It's good for a novelette at least."

"Go over it again. I can see you're planning to, but it looks well for me to ask, don't you think?"

"All right. It begins with Hartlein, handily enough, because that's where we came in. He's at the Johnsons' cottage half the time, pestering Cass to recognize their marriage, and he's in a position to see what goes on there. Last May he must have suspected that Ryn's attack of mild arsenic poisoning was more severe than could be accounted for by her licking her brush. Somebody's slipping a li'le extra arsenic into her food, he tells himself; and he thinks at once of the old lady, because his own mother is a matriarchal type too, and he's willing to believe the worst of anybody who resembles her.

"So, feeling no need for discretion, he kindly warns the girls that Aunt Chloe is putting the finger on Ryn for accepting David Shere's attentions. They both threaten him with excommunication if he ever mentions such a thing to the police, it's nonsense, there's nothing in it. Hartlein waits, he broods, he sees Ryn getting sicker and sicker; and then Shere transfers his attention to Cass, and Ryn begins to get better. Cass won't say yes or no to Shere; she's afraid of the vengeance of the Beyond-Truth, and Ryn's already had her lesson. But what's that going to do to Hartlein's prospects? As long as that finger's hanging over the Johnsons, he can't hope to get Cass back.

"And after a couple of months he can't stand it any longer. He comes around to us with the story, complying with the letter of the girls' law but doing his best to save them from the old lady. How does he work it? By giving me a lot of cases that he himself doesn't believe were murders, mixed in with those fiction names *because they weren't true either;* and at the last he slips in the real reason for telling the tale—the suspicion that Mrs. Majendie is poisoning her niece.

"It scared the hell out of somebody, because somebody *had* been putting that arsenic into Ryn's food, and that person didn't want to be detected. That person was still planning a murder. Maybe that slip-up scared her out of using arsenic anymore, but she'd have to make some other plan. And perhaps one necessary preliminary would be to get Hartlein—too suspicious and alert—out of the way so he wouldn't spot that one too. No, not murder him; just make sure that he won't come around any more. So one of the Johnsons goes down to his rooms and tells him that Cass is really through with him, she can't stand him, they never want to see his face again—something like that. And Hartlein, really broken up over the thing, decides to commit suicide. But he's not going out peacefully, not he; he'll pull the temple down with him if he goes. And, working it both ways, he tries to frame the old lady for *his* murder so that she'll be apprehended for that if for nothing else; and that if the police have to investigate, they'll uncover the other shenanigans; and that he'll have fulfilled his duty to his mother in the same gesture, leaving her his insurance. He fixes up that inhaler so that his death will look like a murder, and goes out on a blaze of glory, self-sacrifice and revenge all wrapped into one. D'you know," Todd ended, draining his coffee cup, "if the old lady had been the murderer, I think he'd have been successful. But he made the mistake of lots of, uh, brilliant amateurs; he picked the wrong suspect."

"Give me another cigarette, please," said Georgine weakly. She passed a hand across her brow. "I hope you'll simplify this in your story?"

"It will be as clear," said Todd with a spacious gesture, "as a bo'le of the best gin... Hartlein hasn't died entirely in vain, though, because his death sets off all sorts of things. It makes everybody nervous, the whole lot of 'em begin to act oddly when they're questioned. It sends Nelse and me snooping out to the Colony on a wild goose chase. We happen to catch a wild owl instead and it flies in our faces and goes flapping off to catch more trouble."

"That's a sweet metaphor, but I advise you to drop it now. Joan decides to forget personal loyalties and tell the truth, is that it?"

"I think she'd been telling it all along," said Todd. "She was the Marvelous Female Witness, all right, but now and then those miraculously observant women turn out to have been accurate in every detail. I heard about a case—no, never mind, you don't have to take that too. Very well, Joan decides to tell the truth about something she saw in the past, which probably wouldn't be believed. It isn't enough to motivate her murder, probably. But remember—she wasn't supposed to be at home that evening. Every Tuesday she drove the old lady out to the Colony and both of them stayed there till after ten o'clock. I think someone counted on that, someone from the cottage who couldn't see that Joan was at home on top of the cliff. What if that person were laying the groundwork for the real, the planned, the main murder— and Joan caught her at it?"

Georgine shivered. "In the greenhouse?"

"It's not impossible. The Hand of God may have been reaching out for one of those cyanide eggs—no, that sounds blasphemous. The hand of the murderer, trying to fix up something that would look natural."

"I never heard of anything that sounded less natural than cyanide poisoning."

"Now, I don't know. A li'le more luck, and Joan's death might have been made to look like accident. Suppose one were starting to fumigate a greenhouse, and had dropped the cyanide eggs into the jars of acid, and started to skip out? Suppose one tripped and fell and hit one's head—and the door slammed shut in the wind?"

"Oh, dear *me!*" said Georgine prayerfully. "You think your murderer planned that for the real victim, and had to—use it up on Joan?"

"Draw a distinction there, dear heart. That's what I'm going to use in my story. McKinnon, no matter what you may think, is not omniscient."

"Honest?" Georgine said.

"But I can guess, can't I? It's going to work like a charm," said Todd dreamily. "Joan points the accusing finger at the murderer. 'Up to your tricks again,' says she. 'I saw you once before, and today I told Mrs. McKinnon all about it.' She neglects to mention, of course, that the tale was so wrapped up in cosmic revelations that she didn't identify the murderer. Murderer thinks, 'I can keep Joan from telling about this episode,' and lets fly with the flowerpot. And then—having hastily fixed up the gas chamber and hung the sign on the door to delay discovery—she gets to thinking about Mrs. McKinnon. She may not know anything definite, but suppose she does? Better fix it so she can be silenced—not murdered, because that would really cause too much trouble—"

"That's the one cheerful remark you've made for five minutes."

"—But put in line for blackmail, or her word discredited in advance somehow. Joan died Tuesday night. The lodging-house business came off as soon as the murderer had had time to think it out, the next morning. She's the Nervous Murderer—before the fact."

"Todd, is this your story plan or what you really think? You mix me up, using people's real names, and I start getting scared."

"I don't know, Georgine," said Todd soberly. "I'd like to think of it as pure fiction. It's easy enough—except when it touches us; and then I start trying to figure out *who*."

"Oh, dear. I suppose it has to be one of the girls?"

"For my purposes it does. I don't believe in these willing tools; I think if Mrs. Majendie or David Shere had fixed up the business with the Trumbull woman, he or she would have done it himself, not asked one of the girls to arrange it. And the arsenic racket was worked from the cottage, there isn't much doubt of that."

"And Cass Johnson slept at home the night after Joan died—and hasn't been seen since."

"There," said Todd, "we get to our li'le problem. Ryn Johnson got the arsenic in the soup, but in non-fatal doses. Did Cass give it to her—or did she give it to herself?"

"Oh, Todd. Don't tell me about the Styrians who used to eat the stuff, or Mr. Maybrick, or Mithridates."

"No, the Styrians can stay out of this. Suppose Cass had died suddenly? Ryn could come up with the tale of the long-term poisoning, and say that Cass had got by mistake the fatal dose she'd meant for Ryn. There'd be witnesses to prove she was being mysteriously poisoned. *You* could be one."

Georgine, about to rise and clear the table, sat down again. "How on earth—oh, you mean the day I saw her pouring out the milk shake for the cat?"

"Yes. She looked up at the path, where you were, before she disposed of it."

"That doesn't mean she saw me."

"So it doesn't. In that case, Ryn really suspected that Cass was making food with the arsenic. She probably ate as li'le as she could of anything that dear sister had cooked."

"Oh, yes. That would explain the long fasts that Cass told me about—and Ryn's having such a good appetite when she went out for lunch. But Todd, what motive? For heaven's sake, did you ever see sisters who seemed more genuinely close to each other? They even explain what's in the other's mind, it's like twins. Why on earth should one want to kill the other?"

"I can explain that," said Todd grandly, "on paper, in about three different ways. Money: sister Bell died and left 'em a pile, and one of 'em got the idea that that was easier than working for it. Then, there's this highly charged young man who can't make up his mind between them—maybe one sister would like the other out of the way."

"Or maybe *he* would," Georgine put in. "If t'other dear charmer won't go away of her own accord, poison her."

Todd was struck with this idea. "I wonder if I could do anything with that? He'd have to out-vacillate Hamlet, of course, but—" He broke off and cocked his head. "That's the telephone."

Georgine opened her mouth to beg him not to answer, and then shut it again. No mother whose child isn't right under her eye can ever ignore the thing.

It was Nelsing, she inferred. She hustled the dishes into the pan and began to run the water on them, irritated again at the constant invasions of murder and its by-products. Why couldn't Todd start writing love stories instead? —Well, no, perhaps that would be worse yet, young lovers all over the place and calling up even more frequently to weep on someone's shoulder—

The door to the hall opened a crack, and Todd's eye appeared, gazing warily through. "Are you in a good temper?" he inquired.

"Pretty good. What gives?"

"Nelse wants to know if we'll have Ryn here for the night."

"Ryn *Johnson*?" Georgine shrieked. "Certainly not! When there's a fifty-fifty chance that she's a criminal?"

"Seems she's begging for your company."

"Who does she think I am, her loving mother? Nelse must be crazy."

"You come and talk to him," Todd said.

She picked up the telephone, and immediately Nelsing's voice said, "All right, Georgine, I could hear you refusing. Now listen. Ryn's in a bad state. The matron's trying to cope with her, but there's no use our letting her work herself into a collapse. She hasn't slept for a couple of nights, her sister's missing, and what she needs is just one night in an ordinary home."

"One night of having her go to pieces all over *us*?" Georgine broke in. "No, thank you!"

"She'll have a sedative. All you have to do is give her something to eat and turn down the bed covers."

"And then lie awake all night myself wondering if she's going to creep in and knife me?"

"What's the matter?" said Nelsing elaborately. "You and Mac got separate bedrooms now?"

"Certainly not. She'd knife him first."

"She won't with a police officer on guard. We've got to hold her, Georgine, and make sure she's safe. So far as I can find out, she's not a material witness to anything—and she won't go home."

"Absolutely not, Nelse. If you feel I owe you favors, I'll come down and scrub floors at the Hall of Justice, but—"

He was murmuring to someone else, at the other end of the line. The next voice that spoke was Ryn Johnson's, heavy with strain and fatigue, but holding by a thin thread to control. "Georgine," Ryn said. "Please let me come, just for one night. I need it so."

"If you're afraid to stay alone, why don't you for heaven's sake go to your aunt's?"

"*No.*" The low-voiced monosyllable seemed to brim over with repugnance and terror. "No. I can't, Georgine. I'm afraid."

"Then I think you'd better stay right with the police."

"Oh, please." The voice shook with entreaty. "Look, wasn't there ever someone who helped you when *you* were in trouble? And didn't you feel that that help couldn't ever be repaid? Please, Georgine, pass it on to me, and I'll help someone else some day."

Georgine's lower lip folded over the upper, and her eyes sought Todd's. He was leaning against the kitchen door; now he bent forward and whispered, "It'll be safe. I promise."

"Well," said Georgine into the telephone, "I don't see what good I'd be to you. I have to leave the house at nine-thirty tomorrow morning, and I won't be back till early afternoon. It's going to be a terrible rush—"

"Oh, that would be enough, just tonight. You will let me come! I won't ever forget it, I'll be so grateful—"

"All right, come along," said Georgine crossly, hanging up the telephone. "Darn the woman," she added to Todd, "she would use the one argument that would have any force with me. But that won't make me glad to see her!"

Todd patted her shoulder and laughed. "Maybe not, but I know you. You'll be taking care of her as if you *were* her loving mother."

❀ ❀ ❀

It was certainly a pitiable young woman who arrived twenty minutes later, in company with an extremely personable officer. She was paying no attention to his good looks and manners; her eyes looked straight ahead at nothing, with that look of trying to evaluate pain that Georgine had noticed once before, and her hair was uncombed and seemed actually to have lost its sheen. She was trying to retain a grip on her own manners; she murmured a few words about gratitude, and then sank limply into a chair and sat there with her head bowed into her hands.

"We'd better get you to bed," said Georgine briskly. "What's Nelse running down at the Hall, a sort of Gestapo?"

"No," said Ryn drearily, "he's awfully polite, you know. But I—I want my sister. I want to find my sister."

"Tomorrow, honey. Come along upstairs now. Did they give you some pills or something to take?"

"I thought I'd go home and get my own. We should have gone up on the way here, I guess, but all I wanted was—just to get to you. If I could just rest a few minutes—"

"I'll go and get anything you want," Todd said, "if you'll tell me where to find it."

"You're so kind." Ryn raised shadowed eyes. "There isn't much: a robe out of the closet—my room's just next to the stair that goes down to the studio—and a nightgown out of the second drawer. The capsules are on my bed-table."

"All right," said Todd. "You left the house locked, I suppose?"

She rubbed a hand across her forehead. "Did I? Yes, I remember snapping the lock and taking the keys when I ran out to—to the greenhouse. I haven't been back there since, have I?"

"Give me your keys, then."

There was just a second's hesitation. She wet her lips and looked away from him. "Give me your keys, Ryn," Todd repeated. Georgine thought she detected a curious urgency about his manner.

Ryn put her hand in the pocket of the green coat, and brought out a bunch of keys. Looking dubiously at Todd, she laid them in his hand.

"I'll just pick up the things and be right back," said Todd cheerfully.

"That," muttered Georgine for his ear alone, "was what you said the last time."

"Oh," Ryn added suddenly, "would you mind turning off the floor furnace? I'm quite sure I left it going."

"I'll attend to everything. Didn't I tell you I was a domesticated man?"

Todd left, with Georgine gazing suspiciously at him from the doorway. The personable officer was standing calmly behind her, every line of his face and body proclaiming competence. The situation was well in hand.

Todd drove the now-familiar streets to Cuckoo Canyon rapidly. He didn't want to be away any longer than would seem normal for his errand, but there was one more thing he meant to do in the Johnsons' cottage. He wondered if Ryn had suspected he meant to do it.

The robe, a handsome one of Chinese brocade, was easy enough to find in Ryn's exquisitely ordered bedroom. He took a satin nightgown from the bureau drawer, dropped the prescription box from the bed-table into his pocket—after a quick glance at the red capsules inside—and then laid robe and gown on a bench at the head of the stairs and conscientiously turned the key of the floor furnace. "Business before spying," he remarked to himself, and ran downstairs to the studio. One couldn't call it breaking and entering, when one had the owner's keys.

The studio was warm, redolent of turps, and—when he had flicked the light switch—uncompromisingly lit with white fluorescent lamps. There was no work in progress visible; the few canvases stacked against the wall proved to be blank. Todd looked around speculatively. There were one or two other doors which might lead to closets; another two in the wall which might be cupboards.

He stepped over to open a section of the big window, and cold night air flowed gratefully in. Then he began methodically with the cupboard nearest the window; it held nothing but artists' supplies, neatly ranged. The next was a closet in which hung cotton slack suits with paint stains on them. There was one more big cupboard on this east side, and he unlocked it in its turn.

There was what he had been looking for: Ryn Johnson's paintings. The wooden racks held perhaps a dozen of them, and with no pangs of conscience at all he lifted them out and stood them along the window-ledge, first looking at the back of each. It was on these that Ryn had been pasting the labels, the night he had seen her through the window. *That was last night,* he thought with a little shock of surprise. It seemed a full week ago.

Sure enough, Ryn had had a "green period." Six or seven of the paintings showed portrait subjects withering away in a jungle gloom, and abstractions which seemed to have sprouted fresh moss, and there was indeed something haunting about them. The other four pictures, however, were what interested Todd.

One was a curious and pleasing angled pattern in dull red-brown, ochre and white; another a formalized picture of a black cat sitting upright and somehow menacing against a gray wall, a bowl of lemons beside it, and the cat's eyes repeating the exact tone and shape of the lemons. There was, amazingly enough, a representational painting of the Bay on a steel-gray afternoon, with the Marin hills a deep violet shadow on the far side. The last was what Todd always thought of as a nightmare picture, of a forest of leafless trees against a lowering sky, brown trunks reaching away into a sullen distance, and two or three unhealthy-looking fungi of a vivid orange in the foreground.

He admired them sincerely, especially the cat and the nightmare, but that wasn't what he had come for. Breathing in the night air, thinking abstractedly that one of those autumn-leaf bonfires must still be smoking away in a near-by garden, he turned the pictures over. The cat was labeled, "Vassily, September 1948." Todd slid his penknife blade under the paper label and began working it gently off. On the canvas underneath had been penciled some other letters. Ryn had tried to erase them, but there was enough pencil left to be legible. They read, "Vassily, June 8."

He had not the slightest doubt that the brown, the gray and the violet pictures would tell the same story, but he meant to check on it. The date had been changed, he found, on one of the green ones at least; he attacked the label of the nightmare trees, paused, listened, and sniffed the air. Surely that bonfire was very close to this house—*and very hot?*

He had been standing facing the window, with his back to the stairs. Now he turned quickly. The second closet door, the one he had not opened, was next to the stair-well. The cracks around it were glowing a red-gold color that was discernible even in the hard white light of the fluorescent bulbs, and as he stood momentarily paralyzed a long tongue of flame came waving through the side crack.

In the next moment there was a dull explosion behind the wall, the cupboard door burst from its latches and swung open to reveal a raging mass of flame, and the whole opposite wall of the studio snapped into a blaze that went roaring up the open staircase.

The heat had barely struck across the room when Todd, by pure reflex action, had flung himself over the window-sill. Below it was a sharp declivity of earth and rocks and bushes;

he scrambled wildly for a foothold, lost balance and went half sliding, half falling down into the Canyon. At some point in his descent he found that he was still clutching the canvas of the nightmare wood, and flung it heedlessly away from him. He was still on his feet, to all practical purposes, but he could not check himself, it was only by some sort of miracle that he kept his footing, and if he went head-first down here there were ugly outcroppings of rock that could crush one's ribs or one's skull. His foot skidded on a patch of gravel, he shot sideways, he was falling in the darkness—

A large manzanita bush received him like springs. Its stiff twigs crackled, but the bush held. Todd lay in its knobby embrace thankfully and lovingly, and when he recovered breath enough, said "Jesus Christ!" in all reverence.

His descent, at avalanche speed, could not have taken more than thirty seconds, and it was not much longer before he found that he was completely uninjured; yet when he extricated himself and turned to look up the slope, the Johnsons' cottage was ablaze from cellar to roof. He had come to rest not far from a curve in the road. As he struggled through bushes onto the pavement, a car hummed by going upward. "Turn in the alarm!" Todd yelled to its unfamiliar driver, and then, his wind regained, sprinted up the road to get his own car away from the Johnson gate. Before he reached it sirens were screaming below, and the darkness had melted before the rush of flames.

Todd McKinnon had had enough of being detained on the scene of a disaster. They could bring him back later if necessary, but he meant to go home and telephone Nelsing from there. As yet no one had arrived to see him leaving; he started his car and gunned it up the hill.

CHAPTER ELEVEN

GEORGINE HAD PUT her guest to bed in Barby's room, washed the dinner dishes with the courteous assistance of Officer Wilmoth (who had left the door to the hall open and kept a vigilant eye and ear on the staircase) and was seated on the sofa listening to his able analysis of the recent election, when the front door opened to admit her husband. "I suppose your friend finished the whisky this afternoon?" was his greeting.

"Yes, he—*Todd!* What happened to you?" Her sewing shot from her lap and she was across the room, holding onto him.

"Kind of a narrow escape," said Todd mildly; but his eyes and the set of his facial muscles belied the casual tone. "The police will probably want to know about it, Wilmoth, but before I tell you what I have to report, I want to see Ryn Johnson."

"She's just got to sleep, I think," Georgine began.

"Wake her up, Georgine, and bring her down here. It's possible she's awake and listening anyway."

After one more look at him, Georgine complied. He was right, she discovered as she entered the small bedroom and found Ryn sitting up in bed in her slip and her hostess's bed-jacket. She said, "I guess it's no use trying to get any rest, Ryn, until later in the evening. Will you get your dress on again?"

Ryn complied in absolute silence, her eyes on Georgine's. They seemed to grow more enormous, and her face whiter, with every second of the two minutes it took her to slide the checked wool dress over her head and fumble the buttons into place. From below came the cautious murmur of male voices. "—to se'le a personal score," Todd was saying as the women reached the foot of the stairs; Georgine cleared her throat and he stopped.

"Sit down, Ryn," he said pleasantly, and Ryn let herself down slowly into the blue chair. "You scare me, Todd," she said with an attempt at a laugh, "sitting there like a trial judge." He did look rather formidable, Georgine recognized with a sinking of the heart, upright in a straight-backed chair with his hands on the arms. "Is that what this is for," Ryn added, "to frighten me again?"

"Not necessarily." His voice was normally light, but there was a queer sort of purr in it. "Just a few questions I want to ask. I suppose you guessed that I'd go down to your studio and look at your pictures?"

"Yes. I—thought perhaps it was time," said Ryn oddly.

"I had a li'le difficulty in finding them. That's the neatest studio I was ever in. No brush-cleaning cans in evidence, no bo'les of turpentine or fixative—where on earth do you put those things away?"

"In a cupboard." A puzzled frown creased her forehead.

"Which one?"

"The one nearest the window, where the paints live."

"What lives in the one near the stairs?"

"Easels, a few oddments like tin carrying-cases for paints—what is all this about, Todd?"

"Never the cans of turps?"

"No, indeed. It's too near the floor furnace. Of course, that's on the floor above, but I don't want any inflammable stuff right below it."

"Very prudent," said Todd genially. "Well, I'm glad to have seen your pictures, they seemed very fine to me. Here are your sedative capsules—" He took the box from his pocket and held it out to her, "—and I did all my errands, I believe. I turned off the floor furnace as you asked me. I'm sorry, though, that I couldn't bring the robe and nightgown. I'm afraid they're gone—along with the house."

"What?" Georgine and Ryn exclaimed together.

"Yes. You didn't hear the fire-engines? The place must be pretty much of a ruin by now. I got out in a hurry, luckily for me." He was speaking more rapidly now, in clipped, clanging syllables. "Odd coincidence, wasn't it, that your studio burst into flames about ten minutes after I turned off the floor furnace? Just time for the blaze to get started in the cupboard near the stairs, and work down to some open containers of turps; nothing but highly inflammable liquid could have gone off with such an explosion. It blew the cupboard door out, and for one second I saw what looked like a long iron rod that went up to the ceiling of the cupboard. If I'd just turned that handle up above and gone away, the fire would have seemed spontaneous—wouldn't it? Almost like the Hand of God. And if I'd been in the studio and hadn't had the window open, *I*'d have been part of that bonfire— wouldn't I?"

Ryn had sunk down in her chair, looking almost boneless. Her face was plaster-white. She whispered, "I don't know what you're talking about. Our cottage burned up? *All my pictures are gone?*"

"Not quite. I saved one of them—or at least, I think so. It's somewhere in the Canyon bushes. It was the brown forest—the one you painted in July, while you were supposed to be getting poison off brushes with green paint on them."

"But—the floor furnace? I don't know what you—I haven't touched it, the thing's been on—why, I haven't had it off since yesterday morning, I was up all night, it was so cold—"

"So I turned it off at your request. There's no doubt in my mind that that fire was set, down below. What was it meant to burn?"

"I don't know. But they're gone, my—my pictures—oh, God, a whole year's work, and some of the best things I've ever done. I was planning on showing them next—" Her eyes suddenly became even larger. "Todd," she breathed hoarsely, "what was that you said—that fire was *set?*"

"That's my guess." His voice still purred.

"But who—why—that doesn't make sense! Why, it would be savage cruelty—for anyone to burn my pictures—"

Georgine, who had been struggling for breath, collected enough for a shriek. "Your pictures, you cold-blooded harpy! What about Todd? He might have been burned to death!"

Ryn looked at her as if with blind eyes. "Burned to death," she said in a shred of voice. Then, slowly, her beautiful face went slack, her mouth dropped a little open. "Yes. But it—it wasn't meant for him. Not for him."

"He would have been just as dead!"

"You don't see." Ryn began to pull herself forward painfully in her chair. "It couldn't be—no one could—" She was on her feet now, swaying. "My bedroom—it's right above the studio."

"I'd noticed that," said Todd. "But you weren't in it."

"I might have been, last night." Ryn's head swung from side to side as if she were in dreadful pain. "And we always— if I hadn't sat up—" Her voice rose to a shrill cry. "I never believed it, I never would—oh, no, no, I can't—" She put both hands suddenly to her face and ran from the room. Her feet thudded on the stairs.

Officer Wilmoth came in from the hall, where he had just finished a rapid and low-toned conversation on the telephone.

Todd looked at him inquiringly. "We can't very well begin an investigation before tomorrow," said Wilmoth serenely, "but if there's any evidence, it'll be found. The laboratory does very precise work."

"Evidence?" Georgine said hoarsely. "Of what, arson?"

Todd looked at her and smiled. "That, of course; but there's the possibility of a body as well."

"*Cass?*" She gulped. "Could they—Officer Wilmoth, if that were possible, how did Nelse *dare* send that girl here to us?"

"I couldn't say, Mrs. McKinnon," said Wilmoth.

"But I thought she—Ryn believed it was a trap for *her!*"

"She certainly gave that impression," Todd remarked. "But reactions can be prepared in advance—can't they, Wilmoth?"

"I couldn't say that either, Mr. McKinnon."

❉ ❉ ❉

The army of invasion had come, billeted itself in Georgine's house for most of the evening, and departed. Nelsing had been there; the fire chief had been there, along with a special investigator; the telephone had rung and an assistant Inspector or two whom the McKinnons knew only by sight had arrived for brief murmured colloquies with Nelsing. When they left, the personnel of the house was the same, but considerably shaken—with the exception of Officer Wilmoth, who quietly emptied all the ashtrays and washed the coffee cups, and then stationed himself at the foot of the stairs, holding—but not detectably reading—a copy of the *Readers' Digest.*

"I don't *want* to go to sleep," Georgine muttered fiercely into the darkness, at some unnoted hour of the morning. "If I don't have nightmares about your being burned alive, I'll sleep too hard and anything might happen."

"Relax, dear heart," Todd's soothing murmur replied. "It's all over now. You're still unstrung, that's all."

"You're the one who ought to be unstrung."

"No, I feel fine. Nasty trick that was, springing the news on Ryn the way I did, but I hoped for—something more definite than I got, and Wilmoth was there to make it official."

"She probably deserved it. I hope she's having nightmares, seconal or no seconal. I keep thinking I hear her stirring around."

"Maybe she is," said Todd placidly. "If so, the handsome watchdog will know about it."

In spite of herself, Georgine began to sink deeper and deeper into drowsiness. The familiar night sounds came comfortingly to her ears: a soft scrape of vines against the house wall; farther away, clear down at the edge of the Bay, the rapid trundling sound of freight trains picking up speed on their northward journey, and the sweet minor chords of their whistles; farther still, a mysterious hooting from ships miles across the water. She lifted her head as Todd, after a long silence, slipped out of bed and through the bedroom door, and then she lay down again, resigned to sleep.

He was gone for some minutes, but came back before she had quite lost consciousness. "Just our guest," he said softly. "Wandering. She'd got into the den by mistake for the bathroom. I locked her in this time, and Wilmoth's got the key."

"Aha," said Georgine sleepily, "chasing brunettes up and down the hall."

"She doesn't run very fast, either."

"Is no woman safe from you?"

"'I wish it was you, Georgie,'" replied Todd.

She gave a faint chuckle, and suddenly slept, to wake again as suddenly to Friday morning and a clock whose hands pointed to 8:20. Oh, heavens! Breakfast for everyone, and a whole morning of appointments to be kept, and her shopping list for the week-end mislaid somewhere—

But Ryn Johnson would be out of the house when she came home.

Todd had been up since half-past seven. He had fortified himself with a cup of coffee, taken in the company of Officer Wilmoth—who after a night of watching still looked well-groomed, clear of eye and entirely capable—and had gone at once to his workroom. By the time Georgine called him to breakfast he had achieved several pages of typescript, a detailed outline of his story about the devoted sister, complete with psychological and material clues. It was headed "Perfect Murder," although this was naturally not its title, but referred to the behavior pattern by which Todd set such store. He stood looking down at it thoughtfully, stubbing out a cigarette. Everything was in line for the framing of the innocent sister by the devious one. He couldn't at the minute figure out how Harrington Harte, his despised fictional detective, was going to trap the criminal, but that was a minor matter.

He left it and ran downstairs just as Ryn emerged from her room, hollow-eyed and walking slowly. She had answered every question put to her by Nelsing and the fire chief, the night before, with the vague expression of a person suffering from shock, who does not know what she is saying, and her answers had contributed exactly nothing to the sum of general information. She was now moving past the head of the stairs as if she hadn't seen him, as if the sedative were still fogging her brain.

She ate a little breakfast in the same manner. At the end of this extremely silent and hurried meal, Todd saw Georgine out the front door, promising to wash the dishes, to get Ryn into someone else's hands, to do everything. In the kitchen, Ryn still huddled over her coffee cup. In the hall, Officer Wilmoth was conducting a low-toned telephone conference.

The door had barely closed behind Georgine when he called Todd to the telephone. "Listen, Mac," said Nelsing's voice, "there wasn't any body in the Johnson cottage. We're taking the guard off Ryn, she can go anywhere she likes."

"Oh, you are?" said Todd skeptically.

"Yes," said Nelsing with peculiar dryness, "we are. I've told Wilmoth he can go. You want to give Ryn a lift up to the Canyon?"

"Certainly," Todd replied. Nelse wouldn't say it, but it stuck out a mile; they were letting Ryn free in the hope that Cass Johnson would try to get in touch with her. "I'll dump her. From then on it's your show."

Ryn came with him like a sleep-walker. He watched her go toward the ruins of her home, where two or three men were standing looking over the destruction; then he turned his car around and headed for the Tunnel Road.

It took him half an hour to get to the Valley Ranch School, and to get his stepdaughter out of classes on the plea that he needed her help for an hour. Barby came leaping out, alight with joy. "Toddy, you angel!" she screamed. "You came just at the right time to get me out of that droopy old History class, did you know it? Where's Mamma? Are you just taking a drive, or do you really want me for something?"

"I didn't know, she's at the dentist's, and I do want you," Todd replied. He gave her a conspiratorial glance as the car swung out onto the highway. "I didn't want to tell the Head why, it might have seemed a li'le too frivolous, but I need you to do a couple of imitations for a woman I know."

"Oh, I'd love to! I'd just adore it! Toddy, did you see where they're going to put our swimming pool if we ever get the money to build it? Gosh, I wonder if we ever will, it'd be simply super to have it there all the time."

"Cricket, on a cold day like this the very thought of a swimming pool makes me shudder."

"Why, the sun's shining," said Barby, surprised. "And I'm missing History," she added, to herself, and relapsed into a contented silence.

Within twenty minutes they had turned in at the gate of the Colony, which Barby surveyed with a complete lack of curiosity, and had parked at the point nearest the guest cottage.

"You wait here, if you don't mind, until I call," Todd said. "I'm sorry I didn't tell you beforehand, you might have brought along your History text to study."

Barby turned an appalled look on him, and then burst into giggles. "Silly man," she said maturely. He grinned back at her, waved as he neared the screen of trees, and then quickened his steps toward the white cottage.

Mrs. Trumbull was there. She had the look of someone who had accepted confinement, but was growing restive under the necessity; her magazine lay unread in her lap, and there was a large pile of cigarette stubs in the tray beside her. She got up when she saw him, and opened her mouth as if to begin a complaint, but Todd cut in: "Mrs. Trumbull, do the people out here know that Mrs. Majendie's companion has been murdered?"

"I guess they do, but they don't talk about it. I heard it on the radio." The woman sat down again, eyeing him curiously.

"Didn't you begin to feel a li'le queer when you heard it? The Johnson girl who was in your house on Wednesday is more than likely the murderer."

"Huh?" Mrs. Trumbull said blankly. "I figured it was the old lady."

"There's very li'le evidence against her. There's a pile of it against either Ryn or Cass Johnson. I want to know which."

"I told you I didn't know."

"There's a way you might be helped to identify her. It'd be to your interest to find out."

"How's that?"

"Suppose," Todd said, "the sister who's a murderer came out here to see you. Suppose she offered to take you somewhere else, to lie low for a few days. Would you want to get in the car and drive off with her? You know, you're a witness to some phase of this business—just as Joan Godfrey was."

Mrs. Trumbull looked back at him shrewdly. Her hair had not been retouched, but she had put on her make-up again; the hard eyes under the thread of penciled brow considered and accepted the argument. "I get you. I'd figure it out if I could. There's been—something I didn't like about this, specially after I saw what kind of woman your wife is."

"That's a nice mild way to put it," Todd observed. "You were holding out on something the other day, weren't you, because my wife was here? I think you knew what the Johnson girl meant to do to her."

The woman stirred, and gave an embarrassed half-laugh. "I wouldn't have stood for no killing, I can tell you that. But the girl made it seem like it wasn't going to be much, it was to get even with her for something she did—I was going to take her up to that room where the old drunk was, and the Johnson girl was going to dope her somehow, chloroform maybe, and then put her in bed with him. Then Mr. Shere was supposed to come and—"

Todd would have sworn that not a muscle of his body or face had moved; but the woman, looking at him, suddenly sprang to her feet, and backed off across the room, her face gray under the paint, her hands outstretched as if to ward him off. "Don't you do it, don't you touch me!" she whispered. "I didn't think it up, maybe I wouldn't 'a'—"

"It wasn't going to be much!" He heard his own voice savagely ripping out the words. "You god-damn filthy hag, telling me you didn't think it up—when you were jailed not long ago for just that sort of game! You'd have been party to that, you thought it was *funny*. I could—"

"Don't you dare touch me," the woman whimpered. "It wasn't me that wanted to do it, I tell you she threatened me—"

Todd took in a rasping breath and drew a hand across his mouth. His control was coming back slowly, and for a moment more he stood looking at her. "All right," he said at last. "She'll be dealt with first. You stay here."

He went out and called Barby. In the minute it took her to run across from the car he schooled his features and voice to blankness. "In here, cricket," he said. "You don't need to be polite to this woman, nor—nor even go near her. Just stay near the door." They went into the small living-room, immaculate in its paint and fresh chintzes. The woman was still in its farthest corner, backed up against the wall as if she were trying to push through it.

"Now," Todd said, "one of the Johnson girls went upstairs in Mrs. Trumbull's house. Barby, will you walk the way Cass does?"

"What—" Barby said. "Oh, yes, I know what you mean!"

She turned her back and with remarkable fidelity imitated the rabbit-like wiggle of Cass's hips. Todd looked at Mrs. Trumbull, whose face expressed nothing but the aftermath of terror. "Now," Todd said, "do Ryn's walk."

After a moment of the slow gliding movement, again repro-duced faithfully by Barby, there was a croaking sound from the corner. "I don't rightly know," Mrs. Trumbull muttered through dry lips. "I watched her go up, all right, and it—it seems as if she started up like that one, like the kid just showed, and—and at the top she kind of swung her hips like the first one. Honest, Mister, before God I'd tell you if I knew. I want to know, too, like you said."

Todd believed her. He looked at her in weary defeat. This was a washout again, and he'd counted on it—more heavily than ever since the Trumbull's revelation. If Ryn had been the woman, she might have remembered Cass's characteristic walk and superimposed it on her own. If Cass were imitating Ryn, her own unconscious habit might have asserted itself as she reached the top of the stairs. He shrugged, and said in a tired voice, "Okay, cricket, let's get out of here." They left the woman still pressed into the corner; her hard frightened eyes watched them go.

On the way back to the school, Barby said little, but looked curiously at Todd more than once. "You look awful queer, Toddy," she ventured at last.

"I feel rather queer, cricket. Never mind, it'll pass."

"Why did you want that woman to tell you if she'd seen Ryn or Cass?"

"It's rather complicated," he told her, "but one of the Johnson girls did something very unkind to your mother."

"She did?" said Barby, up in arms at once. "I didn't like those girls much."

"You entertained them nicely the day they had lunch with you, Georgine said. I guess you told them about your father."

"Yes. Wasn't it all right? Mamma never told me not to mention it."

"Perfectly all right. One has to make conversation somehow. What else did they want you to talk about?"

"Oh, about school—oh, that reminds me, what time is it? Nearly half-past eleven? Oh, for Pete's sake step on it, Toddy, I can't miss riding class!—School, and what kind of neighbors we had on Cragmont, and how we got on with 'em. I told 'em about the Manfreds' being away and how we kind of looked after their house, but we had to lock it up every time we'd used the mangle or aired out, and then they'd do the same for us. And they wanted to know about your writing and if you'd ever solved a real case."

"Did you give me a good reputation?"

"Well," said Barby candidly, "you always say yourself that you guess the answer after the police've announced it, so that's what I told 'em. —Oh, good, we're in time, nobody's mounted yet! Lookit, there's my horse. I'm coming, Goldie!" she yelled at the top of her lungs, presumably to the horse, and flung herself out of the car before Todd had brought it to a complete halt. "Hey, wait, kids! Wait'll I get my jeans on!" The sweater and skirt and the blonde mop vanished through the door of the school.

Todd drove away, unconsciously scowling at the road so that an innocent hitch-hiker, catching sight of his face, almost dove into a ditch with his thumb gesture half completed. He had gone only about three miles on his homeward way when an ominous unsteadiness of the wheel, coupled with a bumping sound, told him that his rear tire had decided to join the day's list of failures.

"Fooled you one way, though," he snarled at the tire. "We're in sight of a service station."

The station looked more like a one-car garage, set on the edge of the road with no other building in sight, but its sign announced that its Prop. also had tires and accessories for sale… "And lucky for you I've got 'em," the morose Prop. assured Todd ten minutes later. "That spare of yours 'ud blow out before you got to the Tunnel. Wouldn't dare put it on. Now this one you come in on, I could fix you up with a noo toob an' vulcanize the tire, but it'd take an hour, maybe, an' I wouldn't answer for it even then. Wore right down to the fabric, that is. You need a *noo* one, Mister."

"All right," Todd said impatiently. "Put on a new one. I guess I've got money enough."

He had, but barely. The tire took all of his emergency ten dollars, and a bit more. Well, he didn't need money to drive the few miles back to Berkeley; forty cents would be enough margin… He helped the Prop. to change the tire; a growing sense of uneasiness was nagging at him even during this brief delay. There was something that Barby had said, about the Manfreds' house—no, that wouldn't work, of course; Georgine was careful about locking it every time she left, and the police would have noticed an open window or a forced door. And yet, there was something—

He paid, got in his car, and turned the ignition key, and was some distance up the road before his subconscious memory became conscious thought. Key—the key of the Manfreds' house, hanging up inside his own kitchen door. That was what had been missing when he inspected the kitchen on Wednesday night; and later that same night, when the door had blown open—as he'd thought—the key had been returned. Both the Johnsons had heard Barby telling about the house—and Ryn had insisted on staying with the McKinnons the night before.

Todd swore, scanned the side of the road for signs of habitation, and braked to a grinding halt in front of a minute crossroads grocery. He had come by back roads, a short cut from Barby's school which would bring him out nearly at the mouth of the Tunnel; but in the occasional way of short cuts, it was proving far less practicable than the highway route. He demanded of the storekeeper, "Got a 'phone here?"

The man shrugged and pointed to a pay instrument at the rear of his tiny store. "May I have nickels, please?" Todd snapped, grabbed up the slowly given change and plunged at the telephone.

"Yes, she was here, Br. BcKiddod," said the voice of Georgine's hairdresser, "but I've got ad awful code in the head, ad she was afraid of catching it, I cad't blabe her. I'd tried to get her earlier to cadcel... I thigk she said she'd go right hobe, there wasd't adother operator free, ad she was cobig back this afterdood."

Three nickels jingled down into the maw of the telephone. Todd got the operator again and asked for his own number. He didn't know quite whom he expected to find there, or what would be going on, but after several rings the voice of Georgine herself answered, sounding placid and cheerful. Yes, she had got in about ten minutes before, she hadn't wanted to stay in the hairdressing shop; look at all the trouble they'd got into the last time one of them caught a cold! Why, certainly everything was quiet. And where might *he* be?

Todd told her. "I thought you were safely downtown for at least three hours, or I wouldn't have come out here. Look, Georgine, I have a fairly shrewd idea that Cass has been hiding in the Manfreds' house." He went on talking through her exclamations. "She may still be there, for that matter. You get out of our place, will you? Go across the street and telephone to Nelse, and then stay there."

"All right," said Georgine, "but there's nobody here. I've been upstairs, and the study door and Barby's were both open, not a soul inside. I'll do it, though."

"That's the girl. I'll be home inside of half an hour."

He put the receiver back on the hook. In the split second before the connection was broken, he heard Georgine's voice once more; far-off, but quick and urgent. *"Todd—"* it said.

He snatched the receiver up again, but the line had already gone dead. She'd thought of something—of course, it might have been only to tell him that his suit was ready at the cleaners' and he should stop for it on the way home; but one couldn't be sure. She'd thought of something, or she'd heard or seen something... The toll call to Berkeley was fifteen cents, and he had only two nickels left.

"Will you cash a check? A small one?" he called to the storekeeper. The storekeeper said *"No,"* explosively.

Todd swore again, silently, and clawed through his pockets. He had a few pennies—four—no, there was one more. "Well," he said testily, "will you accept legal tender and gimme a nickel for these?" Reluctantly, the storekeeper counted the pennies and pushed the nickel across the counter. The McKinnons' home telephone gave back the busy signal: brr, brr, brr, over and over. Todd, listening, looked around him with unseeing eyes; weeks later he could remember every detail of the store's meager stock even down to the stain on the label of a can of tomatoes.

His home line was still busy. He hesitated, seeing the bright autumn day outside the door, thinking that Nelsing had never failed to be one jump ahead of him and probably had been through the Manfred house long before this... You called, you said "I think my wife's in danger," and—assuming that they believed you on such slender evidence as one word spoken in an odd voice, you sent the police up to your house only to have them find that your wife wanted a loaf of bread.

He lifted the telephone and called one more number.

CHAPTER TWELVE

GEORGINE MCKINNON had reached home about a quarter of twelve, having been offered a ride by a neighbor whom she had luckily met downtown. She came toward her house from the rear, down the cross-street where the friend had dropped her, feeling at peace with the world.

This neighborhood seemed almost deserted, too, at this time of day, but it was a different sort of quiet from that of the evil alley in San Francisco. These windows gave back the sun as blankly, though from cleaner panes; but you knew that in one house a woman might be fixing the sandwiches for a tea party that afternoon, and in another a new baby was perhaps getting its first home bath from a mother divided between ecstasy and mortal terror. A nice, middle-class neighborhood; she would not ask for anything better as long as she lived. Even the man fixing the engine of his delivery truck, at the corner of Cragmont, looked pleasant. He glanced up at her with a cheerful grin, as she went down the narrow path to her own kitchen door.

She had forgotten her keys in the morning's wild rush. It had seemed to her that she'd put them in her purse the last time she used them, but the way her brain was working these days, she might have moved them a dozen times since. Now, if only Todd had forgotten to put that chair under the knob— oh, good luck, he had. A slight jiggle and heave got the door open and she walked in and threw her hat on a chair with a sigh of relief.

It was wonderful to be in her own house, alone, in the full knowledge that the police were taking care of any disturbing matters. Georgine found a piece of stale gingerbread in the cake box and ate it, trying out her new inlay, which performed its duties admirably. She glanced idly around her, noting that Todd had done a nice job on the breakfast dishes—even to emptying the sugar bowl and washing it; she had observed some crystals stuck on its rim that morning, but it was shining and empty now. The left-over coffee in the Silex was gone. No matter, she'd make some more when she came downstairs... He'd even drawn the shade at the south window, against the blinding sunlight.

She strolled up to the bathroom for a better look at the inlay, and did a little work with toothbrush and dental floss. The cabinet needed to be straightened up, but that too could wait. There were Todd's vitamin capsules far up on the top shelf, violently red in their glass jar. Better put them down lower where he'd be sure to remember to take them. They looked smaller than she'd remembered, somehow; a funny effect for glass to make...

The bathroom was built out on a little jog over the kitchen, with a window in the jog. She looked out and saw something that caught her attention: the clothesline whirligig cast a shadow on the hedge, and that shadow showed that there were clothes hanging on it. Had the Manfreds come home, then, without notice? And was their post-vacation wash of such magnitude that they'd had to borrow her lines? She craned out a little farther. Her own big clothes-basket was there on the grass, with a few white pieces still in it.

She'd run over and see, she thought, as soon as she'd changed her shoes. She was going down the hall to the closed door of her own room, when the telephone rang downstairs.

What Todd had to say was just a little unnerving, she thought, talking to him with her eyes on the dim upper hall. Just how did that theory about Cass tie in with the wash on the line? Yes, she'd get out—

"Good-by, Georgine," said Todd at the other end of the line. As the words struck her ear she saw the light in the upper hall gradually change, brightening as if a door had silently swung open: a door that gave on a southern room—*her bedroom.* "Todd!—There's someone here!" She called into the transmitter, and in the middle of the sentence heard the click of his receiver going down.

Georgine kept the telephone off and wildly jiggled the bar. If the operator would only answer, she could yell "Police!" and the law would be notified—but it took them long seconds to realize you were trying to get them again—

A flying figure swept round the head of the stairs, and down them. Georgine gave one muffled scream, backed away still holding the telephone, and found herself facing Cass Johnson.

"Don't, don't scream, please," Cass was saying in a hoarse voice of entreaty. "*I* won't hurt you, you ought to know that, and she—she can't hurt anyone now."

Georgine was dumb and motionless from sheer surprise; only for the space of a few seconds, during which someone quacked from the telephone, "Operator. May I help you?—Operator." Cass put a quick hand on the bar, breaking the connection. "No, don't! Please, wait just a minute, let me tell you—why, Georgine, you look scared to death! Oh—you didn't think it was me, did you—that's been doing all this? I didn't believe she could fool you, too!" She reached over and took the handset from Georgine's almost unresisting grasp. "It's all right. Ryn's upstairs in your room. She's killed herself."

"She—what?"

Cass nodded. Her gray eyes were swollen from crying, but their gaze was steady. "She took all those seconal capsules of hers, about an hour ago."

"She can't have died right away!" Georgine found herself stammering. "It—it would take—"

"No, she's not dead yet, but she's going to be left to die in peace, do you hear me?"

"Get away from that telephone," said Georgine, suddenly angry. "This is a police matter, and the police are looking all over hell's half-acre for *you*, don't you realize that?"

"I won't get away," said Cass. She saw Georgine starting to move toward her; she grabbed up the telephone and banged the transmitter hard on the corner of the table. Something made a crushing sound, and a fragment of vulcanite bounced on the floor. "There, you can't talk through it now. I won't let anyone interfere with this!"

The door was three long strides away from the telephone table. Georgine's hand was on the knob when she felt Cass close behind her, pressing something cold and hard behind her ear. She jerked her head around; it was Todd's gun.

"I don't want to shoot you," Cass was saying, breathing hard, "but I'll have to if you try to get help. Can't you see? She's my sister, I don't care what she's done, they're not going to take her to—I guess it would be the—the asylum. She's chosen her own way out and I'm going to see that she succeeds."

"You!" said Georgine furiously, "forcing your way in here and breaking our telephone, and stealing Todd's gun to threaten me with! He'll be here in twenty minutes, himself; he knows you're around here, and you can't get away with any lies. Ryn upstairs—I don't even believe that!"

"You can come up and see," said Cass in a weary voice. She motioned Georgine ahead of her to the stairs. "I'm sorry, it makes me sick to have to do it this way, but—I can't do anything else. If Todd comes I think he'll see I'm right. I'll stall him, anyway."

Georgine, torn by doubt, an uneasy feeling that Cass might be telling the truth and be justified, and a frank terror that the gun would go off, was mounting step by step with her head over her shoulder. She saw the face that had once been roundly pretty, now ravaged by emotion, the dark hair loose and disheveled, the smart dress crumpled as if it had not been changed in several days. "I was a fool to run away," Cass was continuing drearily, "but I—I didn't expect her to do anything like what she did to Joan, and when I found out I lost my head. Oh, Georgine, I hope it's over soon for her."

They turned the corner. A flood of sunlight came through the door of the big bedroom, spilling out from the cube of light in the room itself. It seemed as if the very brightness should wake the still, colorless figure on the bed, the warmth revive the body whose hand, when Georgine touched it, was so softly cold; but Ryn Johnson lay there unmoving, her long lashes black against bluishly transparent cheeks.

"Cass," Georgine cried out, "I can't just stand by and let your sister die!" She felt for Ryn's heart, and discerned a slow throb under her fingers. "Why!" She turned about, aghast— "How do I know she really—"

"You see?" Cass said. "I was foolish enough to run, I thought everything would tell against me, and now—I suppose I won't even be believed about this. But it's true, Georgine."

"But when did you run?"

"Wednesday morning. Ryn had—had come in late the night before, when she thought I was asleep. I heard her sort of muttering to herself, but she'd got so she resented my trying to take care of her, so I didn't go in. I knew something had happened at the greenhouse, and the next morning I got up as soon as it was light and—and went up and looked through the peep-hole. And then I knew, surely, that she'd meant to—to lay it onto me, and I was scared." She looked down at the still figure. "—I can't stay here and tell you, not over *her*. Couldn't we go into the next room or somewhere?"

Georgine assented, in a sort of daze. She looked from Ryn, who was dying, to Cass, who still held the revolver. Who could tell the right thing to do? If she screamed and got shot for her pains, would there be anyone near to hear her? And Todd was on the way...

Cass locked the door of the big bedroom behind her, and left the key outside. The key to Barby's room was still in the lock as it had been when Ryn had been released that morning, but she made no move to shut herself and Georgine in, which was something of a reassurance. She sat down on the bed and raised her shadowed gray eyes again. "I just—wandered around all that day, I didn't know where to go."

"*Why* didn't you go to your aunt, at once?"

Cass's eyes glowed suddenly. "I'd never let her know what had been happening to me. I would have been tortured rather than tell her! I love her, can't you see that? And you know how she is, she would have got it out of me, and—never mind. I couldn't go to her. When it got dark I realized I had to have some place to sleep. I'd seen where you left the key to that house next door, it was easy enough to steal it and then put it back when I'd got the place open—and when you were all asleep. But Ryn knew where I'd be likely to come. This morning she came back here, she'd stolen *your* house keys out of your bag so it would look all right if anyone was following her—you know, not having to break in or anything—and—and she thought someone *was* watching, there was a man—well, it doesn't matter, but she hung out the clothes in your yard so it would seem natural for her to be going back and forth. And she came and called me."

Georgine, still in a daze of doubt and indecision, was about two sentences behind Cass. A man, she thought, watching—oh, heavens, it must have been the one who was fixing the truck! The thought seemed to raise her bodily off the slipper chair and launch her toward the window—

"Sit down!" Cass snapped, and the gun was pointed.

Georgine obeyed slowly, her skin prickling with the realization that Cass really would shoot to protect her sister. Or was it protection? Was the victim of a murder gradually dying in the next room, while she sat here?

"And I ducked over here," Cass went on with a choking sigh. "She said she—she knew it wasn't any use, but she didn't want to be alone when she died, she wanted me with her. And she emptied the powder out of all those capsules—looking at me—and put it in some coffee with lots of sugar so she could get it down, and—drank it."

"You let her—you knew what she was doing?"

"Of course I knew! I thought of the same thing she did, of a trial, and a commitment—that would be the best thing she could hope for, wouldn't it? I thought of Aunt Chloe, and of myself. Of course I knew. We sat and talked while the stuff took effect, and then she came up here and lay down on your bed. She's been asleep for two hours, and in another hour they won't be able to save her, I should think. There must have been twenty grains of that seconal. Think, Georgine—she's just sleeping slowly into death. If it were Todd, or your Barby, wouldn't you do anything to let her go that way?"

"Three hours—" Georgine heard herself murmuring aloud.

"She hasn't an idiosyncrasy like mine," said Cass matter-of-factly. "If I'd taken all that I'd be dead by now. Until I heard her telling, calling to me from downstairs in the next-door house, what she meant to do, I was afraid to answer, to admit I was there; I wondered if she meant to try killing *me* with it. But I believed her when she said she'd given up, she'd tried too many ways, and then Joan got in the way and she knew they would get her for that one. She thought Todd suspected. And this was the only way. —Oh, *Ryn!*" she said suddenly, on a cry of desolation.

"Cass, you can't do this." Georgine tried once more, desperately. "It's like an execution. You don't know what you're doing!"

"Oh, yes I do!" The gray eyes filled with light, and Cass's head went high. "And nobody's going to stop me!"

From the lower floor of the house came the sound of a door opening, of firm steps on the floor. A beautiful clear penetrating voice called, "Casilda! Dorinda! Where are you?"

Cass Johnson's face had changed at the first syllable, and her head swung quickly from side to side. The revolver was hanging at the end of an arm suddenly gone limp. Georgine pulled herself together and leaped for it, but Cass retained just enough of a grip so that it could not be immediately wrested from her—and in the doorway Mrs. Majendie said, "Just what are you doing? Cass, behave yourself. Give that gun to me."

Georgine saw it relinquished with a sense of relief that was near to collapse. Her knees gave way and she sat down abruptly on the slipper chair.

"Where is your sister?" said Mrs. Majendie.

Cass put both hands over her face and turned away, stumbling against the bed.

"She's in the next room, Mrs. Majendie," said Georgine thickly. "Cass says she's dying of an overdose of seconal. I—I'll get help now; she wouldn't let me, before."

Chloe gave her a long penetrating look. "No, Mrs. McKinnon," she said, "don't call anyone. There are a few things I must know first."

"What—how did you happen to come?"

"Your husband telephoned me to say that I should probably find both my nieces here, and that one of them was a murderer. He didn't say which one. I am going to find out."

Her big hand, holding the weapon, was at her side. She reached out the other one and shook Cass gently by the shoulder. "Look at me, my child."

As if against her will Cass turned. Her hands came down from her pallid face and her eyes met Chloe Majendie's. "She took the seconal herself, Aunt Chloe," she whispered.

"You were with her? You might have called me, Cass."

"I—I didn't want you—to know."

Chloe looked at her for a silent moment. Then she said with infinite gentleness, "Why should Ryn want to die?"

Cass's breath caught in a sob, but her eyes were unwavering. "Aunt Chloe, you mustn't ask that."

"Yes. I must."

"It's the Beyond-Truth," Cass whispered. "About—about marrying."

"What do you mean, my dear? Not that she wanted to marry, and was afraid to?"

"No. No, don't you see? It forbids world marriage, doesn't it? And neither of us ever met a man who'd agree to that, so when a—a courtship began to look serious it meant—oh, Aunt Chloe, that poisoning, Ryn's illness during the summer—that was when Hugh was still after me, and I couldn't make up my mind—and then David began—"

"Cass, you must speak more plainly. Are you telling me that your sister was jealous of you and tried to kill herself then?"

"Not—not quite. She meant it to look as if I had been poisoning her; and then—if I accepted David—I'd die, and it would look as if I'd been caught in my own trap, and no one would ever suspect her."

The grizzled brows drew together. "This—in order that she might have David Shere herself?"

Georgine had begun to inch unobtrusively toward the door. They were both absorbed, she thought. She could get out and yell from the bathroom window—

"Stay where you are, Mrs. McKinnon," said Chloe Majendie, with a slight gesture of the hand holding the gun. Georgine stopped as if she had actually been shot at.

"*She* didn't want him. Oh, no, Aunt Chloe. She was sure that neither of us should ever make a world marriage, she wanted us to keep on being together always; but if I—showed signs of breaking away, it was better for me to die."

"My dear Cass, don't tell me that Ryn was still living up to everything that the—original rules of the Beyond-Truth taught or forbade."

Cass nodded vehemently. She had not once taken her heavy eyes from her aunt's, but now it seemed as if they were not focused. "Yes, everything, the fasts and the forbidden foods, and the marriage laws."

Georgine drew a quick breath and was on the verge of speaking, but the old lady broke in. "But it forbids the taking of human life!"

"Not if it could be construed as the Hand of God. It would be, if it even *looked* as if she were innocent. And then, how else could she get the money?"

"What money?" The beautiful old voice was harsher now than Georgine had ever heard it.

"My share of the estate. We'd already had Bell's, of course, but it wasn't enough."

"Enough for what, my dear child?"

"Why, to live the way you do, to have everything you have," said Cass simply.

Mrs. Majendie let go of her shoulder and stepped back a pace. Her weather-beaten face seemed all at once to develop new lines, as if the flesh beneath it had fallen away, and her eyelids drooped. "God forgive me," she said in a very low tone. "So Joan had to die—I should have listened to her when she told me that one of you was going the wrong way. And you tell me now that Ryn is dying because her plans failed?"

"Yes, Aunt Chloe," Cass said. "You wouldn't try to stop her from that, would you?"

Chloe Majendie opened her eyes full, and bent their piercing gaze on her niece. "No, not for a moment," she said ringingly, "if I were sure that she *was* the one whose plans failed. Cass, do you realize that everything you've told me about her motive might apply to *you?*"

Cass fell back a step, a hand over her mouth, her gray eyes glinting wildly. "*Me?* No!" she said explosively from behind the hand. "You can't think that!"

"I'm not sure of it. How can I be? But I must be sure, before any more time is lost." The old lady's head bent a little. "Your story sounds like the truth. God help me, I can believe it. But—"

"Mrs. Majendie," said Georgine urgently, "it's the Beyond-Truth! It's the kind of truth that they tell at the Colony, that isn't quite a lie, but is twisted to suit them—the kind Miss Godfrey used to tell when she got that queer shine in her eyes. Haven't you watched Cass's eyes?"

"You're not against me too?" Cass cried out. "No, Georgine, not after your husband nearly got caught in that last trap she set!"

"The fire? She couldn't have meant that for you, you were already gone!"

"And so was she! It was meant to look like a gadget that was supposed to kill her, only she would have escaped. It was something I could have set before I went away—only I didn't set it."

Georgine opened her mouth and shut it again. It could have been that way; she had thought of it as something Ryn did—but to catch Todd, not to go off when the house was empty.

"You see?" Cass had detected the return of her doubt. She came across the space between them, catching at Georgine's hands. "And when you asked her about it, didn't she look terribly frightened, and refuse to say anything, as if she were shielding me?"

"Yes," said Georgine slowly, "she did. And I'll admit it made me think afterward that she was—suspecting you, but not able to put it into words. She loves you."

"We love each other, why, we're *sisters*. But there was one thing more important, and that was the Beyond-Truth... I don't know if she could have—just stood up to me and shot me, if she'd found that gun. I don't think so. But if it could happen quietly—"

Cass paused, and a new sort of terror came into her eyes, as if a black shape had appeared in a room that was not yet totally dark. "Oh, my God. I hadn't thought of it before. It—this suicide of hers—you're thinking about it, you and Aunt Chloe, just what she wanted you to: that it's my doing! Why didn't I see that? She *is* killing me, she's taking me down with her. How am I ever going to—"

She stopped; her head turned sharply, and so did Mrs. Majendie's, as a voice sounded from below. It was Todd's.

"Everything under control?" he called cheerfully.

"No!" Georgine shrieked. They wouldn't dare shoot her with Todd coming up the stairs. "Get the ambulance, Ryn's dying of an overdose of seconal, the telephone's broken—"

Todd's footsteps had paused only for a moment, midway up the staircase, and then continued upward. "Don't come up, you lunkhead!" she cried out despairingly. "Do something!"

In the next second Todd appeared in the doorway. He looked at Cass, who was still clutching Georgine, and at Georgine who was vainly trying to break away. Lastly, he turned and gazed gravely at Mrs. Majendie and his own pistol.

"So you didn't notify the police, as I asked you?" he inquired of her interestedly.

"Indeed I did not, Mr. McKinnon. This is going to be settled within the family before anything is done," said the old lady levelly.

"Thank you for including us in your family. And I suppose you'll shoot me if I don't do what you say?"

"I will shoot your wife, Mr. McKinnon; not fatally, but painfully."

"Damned if I don't believe you would," said Todd, grinning at her. "There sits Nelsing's man outside, told to close in if anyone tries to escape; and nothing's happened but two or three innocent persons walking in and never coming out. Reminds me of that story, you know; The Three Big Sillies, all lined up in the cellar, doing nothing but talk things over and cry until the sensible man came down to see what gave. How about my calling the sensible man?"

"No," said Mrs. Majendie.

"Todd McKinnon," said Georgine furiously, "didn't you hear what I shouted at you? Why did you have to walk in here too?"

"It's our house," said Todd mildly. "I thought I'd see what was going on in it."

"But we don't know whether Ryn killed herself or Cass did it for her! —You let me go, Cass Johnson, I haven't made up my mind and I don't believe your aunt has either. —Do you know, Todd?"

"Kind of a toss-up, isn't it?" Todd said. He surveyed the three women with a faint smile. "Do you mind letting me hear the story?"

Georgine was almost beside herself. "Don't ask that! I keep telling you Ryn's dying in the next room, and you want to talk some more!"

Todd said, "She took all the capsules, did she, Cass?" Cass nodded, her eyes hopefully on his face. "Where'd she get them?"

"Why, from that box on her bedside table. We came up here together, and I saw her slip it into her coat pocket."

"That's all right, then," said Todd in his most casual voice. "She's getting a good rest, and she ought to wake up feeling wonderful. Only two of those capsules had seconal in 'em, and the others are my vitamin prescription. I changed them last night."

"You didn't," Cass moaned. She sat down limply on the bed. The gray eyes seemed to hold no terror now, only despairing grief. "Oh, you couldn't have been so cruel—to let her think she'd found the way out, and have it all for nothing!"

"Seemed best at the time," Todd observed. "And was it all for nothing? She confessed to you, I suppose, Cass?"

"Yes."

"But she mustn't be made to answer for it?"

"I thought it was all over for her. You—Todd, you have that look—if I were guilty, I suppose you'd expect me to be in a panic when you told me that? You're testing me, isn't that it? Because I don't believe you did change them!"

"Yes, he did," said Georgine. "I saw the others in the bathroom cab—" She caught her breath as Todd cut in on her deliberately and loudly. "If I can test anyone, I will," he said.

"There's plenty of time for Ryn to be questioned again. Oddly enough, what interests me is a li'le plan that someone dreamed up to compromise my wife. Did Ryn tell you about that?"

Cass nodded slowly. "She told me everything. She was afraid that Joan Godfrey really had put Georgine on the right track, and she had to be sure that nobody would believe the story."

"That was done," said Todd, "by someone who combined the discrediting of Georgine's word with—something else. That person has a pathological hatred of sex," his words clanged out with a savagely sardonic quotation, "of 'marriage in the world sense'—Something that Georgine, I'm glad to say, advocates."

Cass's unmoving gaze took on a tinge of bewilderment. "You—you aren't talking about that afternoon when David and I—but I told that to Ryn! I knew she liked Georgine, I thought—like a fool—that it might carry some weight with her! I'm sorry, I never thought that she might take it out on you, Georgine. Todd's right about one thing—" her voice grew husky—"that it was pathological. She was insane, you see. She thought everyone else was, that's a sure sign. She actually— went to Hugh Hartlein and told him that *I* was crazy, trying to kill her, and that neither of us could ever marry because there was insanity in the family. And so—he—you know what he did. He couldn't bear to live any more." She caught her breath on a sort of sob. "But you can't think of Ryn as a murderer! She was just—she was swallowed up by the Beyond-Truth."

A faint sound came from Mrs. Majendie, who had been standing silent and motionless, her tired eyes moving from one face to another. "I told myself it never did any harm," she said, very softly. Her face still hung in those deep furrows. She looked like an old proud Indian chief who sees the last of his tribe gone.

For a moment there was silence. For the first time since she had entered this small room, Georgine felt the quiet of the house: a deeper, more sinister quiet than if there had actually been death in the next room. The doubts came back, beating at her in strong waves. Supposing everything Cass had said were true? Todd had interfered with a suicide, and instead had let a murderer live to be tried, to drag her sister and her aunt through utter horror; to take the foundation of belief from a score of happy old people who had accepted it sanely and lived by its harmless-seeming principles.

"Todd," said Cass Johnson, with a beseeching gesture, "I can think of just one thing to do. Let me—let me get the real tablets and put them by Ryn where she is now. When she wakes up she'll know what's happened."

Todd's face was impassive and wood-hard. He looked at Mrs. Majendie. "Have I the right to pass judgment of that kind?"

"Perhaps you haven't," said old Chloe, "but I'm inclined to force it on you. Have you the right to do anything else? Can you go through the rest of your life, Mr. McKinnon, thinking that you denied a penitent the right to choose her own punishment?"

His face did not change. He said, "Georgine, you should have a voice in this."

Georgine waited. Again the silence came flooding at her; she remembered the still figure in the sunlit next room, and the range of expressions that she had seen for days past on that beautiful pale face. There was that look as if of one in mysterious pain...

"You're not sure?" she said faintly.

"How can any of us be sure?" Todd asked.

There was something struggling to be remembered, some detail about the rules of the Beyond-Truth. If the criminal had built everything on an obsession with the cult—

"Todd," she said suddenly, "the day the girls were here to lunch, I gave them shrimps. Cass said she wasn't hungry, but Ryn ate two helps. Isn't that against all the rules?"

"What?" Cass exclaimed. "Ryn did that?" She looked almost more horrified than at the thought of her sister's being a murderer. "She can't have known what they were!"

"They were whole. You can't disguise a whole shrimp."

"Or," said Mrs. Majendie wearily, "she may have realized that those minor rules were window-dressing. My husband was allergic to sea-food."

Georgine felt a wave of hysteria coming over her. "We're standing here like judges, saying whether someone shall live or die, and the talk keeps going off—Todd, did you really take away those capsules?"

"Maybe I didn't," he said. There was a curious expression in his eyes. "Maybe my instinct was right, that she was guilty and that—I'd let the law have its chance, and watch to see if it took advantage of that, and if not—" He drew an audible breath and shook his head sharply. "And yet, it shouldn't be in our hands, in any private person's hands. Joan Godfrey was struck down, perhaps in panic, but her death was ensured in the most cold-blooded way."

Cass shuddered once, strongly.

"You knew she was dead, Cass? Didn't you realize that you should have spoken then?"

"I wouldn't turn my sister in for a dozen Joan Godfreys," Cass said in a thick voice. "All I could do was to get away, to make sure I wouldn't be next. And even then Ryn was trying to put it on me! I knew I'd be suspected—there was that evidence, it would point directly to me—"

"You saw it," said Todd in a level voice, "when you discovered that Joan was dead in the greenhouse?"

"Yes. I couldn't see Joan through the peep-hole, but I could see the boardwalk, and the heel-tip of a shoe caught between the boards. I didn't dare go in to get it. The gas was still strong." She closed her eyes for a second. "There was a pair of my shoes gone from the closet, she said she was taking them to be repaired for me. I knew she'd pried off a heel-tip and kept it, they'd be sure to find out that it was from *my* shoe."

"Did she tell you that in her confession?" Todd said in a pained voice. "She might have spared herself that."

"Yes. She told me everything."

"Then," said Todd in a suddenly metallic voice, "she lied, or you are lying on the basis of having read my story outline. Except in my own imagination, there never was any heel-tip in the greenhouse!"

Cass's eyes flew open, wide and glittering. For half a second he was impaled on a gaze of murderous hatred; then she launched herself like a swimmer starting a race, straight across the room to the door, and in the same split second Chloe Majendie reached out an arm and jerked Todd aside. He fell sprawling at her feet, and the door slammed, and there was the click of a key turning.

The old lady stepped swiftly away and set her back against the door. "Now," she said, "not a sound from either of you, or I will shoot. You're going to give *her* a chance."

"A chance to kill her sister, really, and then escape?" Georgine gasped.

"She will not go near her sister again. Listen!"

Todd, picking himself up slowly, remained poised on one elbow, and Georgine held her breath. The room was full of soft light reflected from the hillside across the street, and the three figures were caught in it as if in a dim photograph, static, spellbound. Through the closed windows came faintly the sound of a car humming down the hill, and of someone whistling, very far off.

"You saw which way she turned, Mrs. McKinnon?" whispered Chloe Majendie. "Toward your bathroom."

Water was running at that end of the hall. It was shut off, and there was the rattling clink of a glass set down hastily, just anywhere. Then there were footsteps in the hall; they came slowly past the door of Barby's room, and its occupants lifted their heads a little, simultaneously. The steps did not continue down the hall to the big bedroom. They went down the stairs to the first floor, deliberately, step by step. At the bottom they died away.

"She has taken the sleeping powders herself," said Mrs. Majendie. "She must have her chance. An hour should be enough; we will stay here."

Todd got up without haste. He looked at the gun held steadily in the big hand; he glanced at the closed window as if calculating how far into the street his voice could be heard. His eyes met Georgine's.

He glanced again at Mrs. Majendie. "You are taking the decision out of our hands?"

"I am taking it out of your hands."

"Then," said Todd, "we may as well sit down. An hour is a long time to be on your feet."

The three of them sat down. There was a long pause.

It was absurd, it was embarrassing. Todd gazed at the foot of Barby's bed and the old lady looked straight ahead at nothing, while with infinite slowness the light changed in the still room. The silence had a curious quality. It was chilling, with the soft cold of snow-laden air, heavy and motionless. Once or twice Georgine tried to say something, anything, but her mouth was too dry.

Throughout those interminable sixty minutes no one spoke but Chloe Majendie. "I shall not go out to the Colony again," she said once. "I mustn't—help the pretence any longer." And, after another pause, "Let them finish their lives in peace."

The shadows wheeled, and Georgine found herself falling into a kind of stupor. Along the street outside the children were coming home from school, their voices twittering in the cold air; then again the silence, and again Mrs. Majendie's words abruptly breaking it.

"It's my burden," she said in a tired echo of her beautiful voice, "and nobody else's. I didn't believe in the rules myself, but I let the child learn them and counted on her finding out from ordinary people that it was all nonsense. When she grew up she began to laugh at it, and then—I thought she was safe."

She raised her eyes for a moment. They looked different, somehow, as if they might never be young again.

For the only time during the hour, Todd stirred and glanced at her. Then he went back into his motionless contemplation. The electric clock on Barby's bureau hummed faintly, and Georgine watched its thin second hand sweep round the dial. Another minute, and another; forty of them had gone past now. *She laughed at it,* Georgine thought, *and it swallowed her.* The smile on the face of the tiger...

Mrs. Majendie spoke only once more; not to her companions, not to herself, but to someone far off. "Nicholas," she murmured, as if she were saying good-by.

But she's old, thought Georgine, and was stabbed by an unbearable pang of compassion.

The hand swept around, and the hour was over. Mrs. Majendie laid the gun on the dresser and got slowly to her feet. As Todd raised a window to call the officer who waited innocently below, there were faint sounds from the next room.

The old lady waited with dignity while the officer unlocked the door. "I am going to my niece," she said with a level look at him, and walked steadily to the bedroom where Ryn Johnson was beginning to wake—while somewhere her sister was falling deeper and deeper into sleep.

She couldn't have gone far, the police said. She couldn't have got off the property on which the McKinnons' and Manfreds' houses stood, every side of it had been under observation. There was not a corner of either house which was not searched, when at last the alarm had been given.

The search took nearly half an hour. When one of the officers had finished beating the shrubbery and turned his attention to the high-piled basket of laundry, so domestically waiting under the whirligig, Cass Johnson was not yet dead; but she had death in her blood, and the hour and a half had indeed been enough.

"So it was the Maniac-Sane-on-the-Surface after all?" said Georgine wearily. She stood in the upstairs hall, unable to shake off the fatalistic lethargy of the past two hours.

"No, dear Georgine," said her husband from the door of his workroom. "Cass wasn't insane. She was just as illogical as any criminal who thinks he can't get caught, she was

obsessed by the desire to have as much money and power
as the aunt she admired, she had a deep-rooted aversion to
normal marriage—but in the end, after she'd given way to
violence, she followed a different pattern. She was the Damn
Fool. And," he ended on a sigh, "she very nearly fooled me."
He glanced down at the story outline in his hand, with the
penciled confession which Cass Johnson had scrawled across
one blank surface: "I killed Joan Godfrey, signed, Casilda
Johnson," he read, and shook his head. "The Damn Fool,
running away, panicking, making clumsy efforts to deny
her guilt—and nearly getting away with it because from the
fiction-writer's standpoint nobody could be as silly as that
unless she were innocent."

"How do you suppose she looked from the police's
standpoint?"

"I've no doubt," said Todd with resignation, "that Nelse
knew she was guilty. He probably had a nice li'le collection of
fingerprints or something to pin her down with; but nobody
tells me these things. Well—he'll want this confession, I
suppose. I can remember the outline without copying it."

"You're going to finish the story?"

"Sure; or one something like it. A story's—nothing but a
job of work."

❀ ❀ ❀

David Shere stood in the arched entrance of the McKinnons'
living-room, directing an unfriendly gaze at the big chair in
which Ryn Johnson was reclining, pale and drawn and yet still
lovely, like a ghost of the Princess Nefertiti.

"Well," he said gruffly, "I didn't help much—pretending
to drop you and run after Cass so we could see if the poisoning
would stop. How was I to know I'd halfway fall for her? She was
so damned plausible!"

Ryn, looking back at him out of shadowed eyes, murmured
some inaudible word.

"I'm sorry," said Shere, as if it had been forced from him. "I shouldn't have stopped believing in you. I wouldn't have," he added, his vitality blazing up in a crackle of anger, "if I'd ever been sure of you! —I suppose you thought the only way to bring things to a head was to let her kill you?" He took a step into the room, scowling, his hands in his pockets. "For God's sakes, what possessed you, letting her alone here long enough to put all the powders out of those capsules into the sugar bowl?"

Ryn stirred. She said, on a tone that was scarcely more than an exhalation, "I knew it was all right. I'd seen Todd change them."

Todd McKinnon, sitting across the room, emitted a faint groan and put his head in his hands.

"Well, it was a fool trick," said Mr. Shere, scarcely mollified. "Now that it's all over, do I try to get back into your good graces? I shouldn't think you'd want to see me again."

"Let's not talk about it yet, David. Not about anything."

David Shere removed his hands from his pockets, clenched them and raised them in the air. "Not yet, let's not talk about it yet!" he said savagely. "My God, that's all I've heard from you, from any of you, as long as I can remember. Can't I ever get anything *settled?* Seems to me I've spent my whole life dangling after Johnsons, one or another of 'em." He lowered his fists, and a look of surprise spread over his ruddy face. "I'm sick of it," he told her. "So help me, I am. Why don't I just quit, and get some of my own work done for a change?"

"Just as you like, David," Ryn murmured. A faint smile had appeared on her lips.

"Then good-bye," said the impassioned lover. "I won't be around for a good long time." He straightened, inflated his broad chest with a full breath of relief, and whizzed out the front door.

Ryn Johnson turned her head a little to watch him go past the window. The smile was still very faint, but it had spread to her eyes.

It was almost evening, and the McKinnons were alone in their house. The police had finished and gone. Ryn and Mrs. Majendie had gone away, too. Every time Georgine glanced at the window near the front steps she seemed to see, framed in its lower half, a craggy profile crowned with a bush of white hair, held stiffly erect as if braced against a burden.

Presently peace would begin to flow back into the household, but it was not yet there. In spite of her overwhelming fatigue she could not relax. "I keep asking myself," she said restlessly, "just how we got into this. It wasn't curiosity, it wasn't all our own need. From the very first it's seemed as if it had been laid on us."

"There was a li'le free will involved," said Todd mildly. He stood looking out at the cold sky.

"I suppose so; but I wish I needn't believe it. We set off so much trouble and tragedy..."

"It was happening in spite of us, Georgine; and we didn't get off scot-free ourselves. That was quite a reaming Nelse gave me," he said reminiscently.

Georgine's spirit began to revive. "I know, and how dared he? What else could we have done, with a gun pointed at us?"

"Well," said Todd, turning slowly to face her, "some time during that hour I could have jumped Mrs. Majendie. Nelse's man would have heard the shot and come running."

"Oh. Isn't that hindsight?"

"No. I thought of it then. But I thought, too, that if I handed Cass over to the police I could never be sure—"

He broke off. Georgine said, "Sure of what?"

He waited for a long minute before he answered, "—That I hadn't done it to se'le a personal grudge." His agate-hard eyes lifted, and he moved to stand close to her. "We aren't made to administer strict justice, people like you and me. Could you have handed her over deliberately?"

She tipped her head against the back of the chair to look at him. "I couldn't have, and I didn't," she said. "I—I knew how much laundry there was in the basket."

Todd laughed softly and sat down on the arm of the chair to hold her close. "We're well enough matched, dear Georgine," he said, resting his cheek on her hair. "Take it easy now," his casual voice went on. "We'll se'le down soon into our old ways. I can get on with my job now—"

"We've got that much out of it anyway."

"Bread as well as circuses," he said lightly; but after a moment, when she looked up at him, his eyes were still somber and far away.

"It's getting late," said Georgine after a moment. "Close the blinds, will you? I'd better start supper."

She went toward the kitchen, glancing over her shoulder at the empty lower half of the window. "Close them *tight*, Todd."